Set Me Free

Hina Belitz is a renowned employment lawyer who cares deeply about the issues raised in SET ME FREE. This is her first novel.

Set Me Free

Hina Belitz

headline
review

First published in paperback in Great Britain in 2016 by Headline Review
An imprint of HEADLINE PUBLISHING GROUP

1

Cataloguing in Publication Data is available from the British Library

ISBN 978 1 4722 3159 8

Typeset in Plantin Light by Avon DataSet Ltd,
Bidford-on-Avon, Warwickshire

Printed and bound by CPI Group (UK) Ltd, Croydon, CR0 4YY

Headline's policy is to use papers that are natural, renewable and recyclable
products and made from wood grown in well-managed forests and other
controlled sources. The logging and manufacturing processes are expected
to conform to the environmental regulations of the country of origin.

HEADLINE PUBLISHING GROUP
An Hachette UK Company
Carmelite House
50 Victoria Embankment
London EC4Y 0DZ

www.headline.co.uk
www.hachette.co.uk

For my beautiful mother, who so nearly got to see this.
I miss you so much.

We realise the importance of light when we see darkness. We realise the importance of our voice when we are silenced.

Malala Yousafzai, 2013

Part One

Part One

Chapter One

Clerkenwell, London

That day I heard a noise as I entered our home. It was unlike those of every day. A tremor hovered in my chest as I crept up our narrow steps to the sleeping rooms upstairs. My eyes fixed upon the rusty-coloured swirls of the dusty carpet. A banister support had fallen out a little while ago, fallen right away, and someone had with little skill tried to wedge it back in place. It leaned away from where it should have been, and for some reason on this day it troubled me. And then I heard my brother's voice from the bedroom at the top of the stairs. The door was closed. I looked around and saw the slatted airing cupboard door and the other painted white to Mama's room were just a little bit ajar. As if like me they sought to listen carefully.

'Papa, Papa, is that you?' Nu said. I paused not quite at the top. Was it true? Could it be that Papa was here?

'Nu, *beta*,* I was waiting for you. Your mother didn't say? She didn't tell you anything of why you left?'

I hadn't heard my papa's voice in years. I held my breath and took another step towards the bedroom door where

---

* Son.

voices spoke. Then I froze. I didn't want to see his face, wasn't eager for his embrace.

I heard a gasp and a shriek. 'Papa, Papa, why?' I heard Nu cry.

'You don't even know what you are? *Haramzada*!'*

Silence flooded in and deafened me. Something in me turned to electricity. A second sense, a knowing, punched the breath out from my chest. I panted, found I couldn't breathe.

'Well,' he said, 'it's time to put things right.' I heard the first crack and blow. And then a scream. A scream that carried on and on for years inside my head and took away the calmness in my soul.

'Mani! Mani!' my brother called to me. I ran to the door but stopped just as a thudding beat began. Something heavy drumming evenly in time.

'Ma . . . Ma . . . Maaa . . .'

The thudding carried on, Papa grunting harder with each strike. My hand was on the handle of the door, but trapped inside I felt a breathless, foolish anxiety. It stopped me in my tracks. I knew what I should do. I had to save my Nu. But I was scared, panic spinning in my head, and in that moment, in a flash, I hid behind the slatted door ahead. Curling like a sorry ball of cowardice, anti-hero, anti-me. I didn't want a bruise to land upon me too.

The beating slowed and morphed into a thrash, and now I couldn't hear the voice or breathing of our baby Nu. In my mind I saw him as a child again, playing with his stones the

* Bastard.

way he always did.

I listened hard to raspy breaths and heavy steps, but I didn't move. Silent tears damp upon my heated skin. But still I didn't move to save my Nu.

And then silence.

After a while I heard the cracking open of the door. Papa stepped out. I could only just make him out through the gaps in the airing cupboard door. His arms were red, with flecks of blood upon the shadowed darkness of his face. At the corner of his mouth the blood made smiley marks, the marks on children after berry drinks.

He stood so still. Then, without a glance to left or right, he turned to face the door where I was hiding. In a lengthy moment, through the angled slats, his eyes were on my eyes; he saw my soul. And then he smiled.

Not a smile that showers affection and connection. But one that lords its power over you. A smile that says: I have you. And he did. He had me then. He has me now.

He's had me ever since.

No hit, no pull, no scratch could ever hurt me more than that.

As he smiled, some blood spread on to his teeth. In that moment, with all his dark and ugly bloody looks, I despised myself much more than I did him. It was me that had let him hurt our baby Nu. He reached towards the handle of the airing cupboard door. I pushed back hard against cold wall, my feet slipping on the chipped floorboards underneath. As he touched the door, he pulled away, mesmerised by blood upon his arm. He rubbed his bloodied skin upon his shirt and turned to me again just as voices sang through the open window in the hall. Chat and laughter pierced by resonating heels walking on the street. He lurched away and ducked as if to hide, his sniping eyes shifting left and right. Then slowly he rose, still bending at the knees, pressed his palms upon his hair as if to tidy it and crept away. Down the steps, closing the front door carefully behind him, making sure the lock had latched.

I looked about the room. The bedding and some clothes were heaped along the wall, and further down and on the left, Nu lay curled up in a ball. Around him in a perfect swirl, a pool of his own blood. His right arm bent back, and cuts and gashes oozing blood on to his stripy shirt. White and blue and red. His jeans were slick against his legs, heavy with a liquid weight. And on the window pane above the bed, a firework of red. I fell to him and lifted him to me. His eyes flickered open, and he smiled a bit and said, 'I'm OK, Mani. Do you think that was our pa,' then faded out again.

I couldn't speak; I could hardly breathe. I just rocked him in my arms, deep and grainy sobs rising from the pit of me.

I stood to work out what to do. The floor beneath me seemed to move. 'Mama! Mama!' I screamed as I ran about the house. She was out. I ran back up the stairs and grabbed the bedding on the floor to cover up our Nu. And as I pulled it away, that was when I saw. Underneath the quilt was Ma. A mess of death all sprawled across the floor. I paced here and there, my arms held up, palms forward to push the scene away.

I screamed. Mad and rhythmic whooping screams rising

and falling with melody.

When the medics came, I showed them in, then hid in Mama's room. Placed a towel on the floor beside her bed. A makeshift prayer mat for my sins. I rubbed my forehead on the floor until it felt sore, and as I did, I begged, 'Dear God, please, please save my Nu and Ma. Forgive me for what I did.' I moaned and cried, the taste of salt and dried-up devastation on my tongue.

Quite quickly I was done. I folded up the towel and placed it on the bed. I knew that Mama would be mad at me if I left it on the floor. And then I swallowed all my grief within. I felt it moaning in my breast as medics swept away the death and took my brother's beaten body far away from me. Just where he deserved to be.

I feel the grief within me still.

I walked around our small square garden in the dark the night that Mama passed. The privet looked alarmed, all stalks of overgrowth, all ragged. I let its branches stroke my cheek and saw the smile upon my father's face again. The moon was moving out of sight behind a darkening sky, and I heard my brother's voice echo in my head from years ago. 'You are an and-gel' he'd say to me. I hid my face behind the privet bush, hiding like the moon. I knew that what I'd done would one day be found out. Just like the moon, it would eventually come out.

Chapter Two

You: bus route 12 to Big Ben

6 November

My dear,

I was thinking about you lots today. Your deep blue eyes and the way the lines around them smile deeper than your lips. I'm thinking of you reading this, your fingers stroking ink. Writing to you makes me feel I've lived. It's like a need, a gnawing deep inside that this alone can satisfy. And I will see to it that you get this letter, whatever it may take. I'll follow you. Make sure the moment's right. Make sure that I'm not seen . . .

I know it to be true now. That it isn't just memory that muscles have. They carry joy as well. Happy muscles are strong, sad muscles weak. Just days ago, right after the Day of the Frying Pan (light aluminium but still bruising), it wasn't with a confident, rounded hand that I wrote. No, my love. My helplessness bore down upon me like a weight and squeezed my muscles weak. The script of my secret letters to you all thin and stringy, like the cotton-thread legs of those unsteady spiders.

Today I feel as if I have swallowed a red-hot, pulsating thing. I am strong, blood-filled, throbbing. And my script is bold and curvaceous to prove the point. Grooves all nibbed across the sheet; the subtle bleed of ink. It's because of you.

People will say it's wrong, you and I. But they don't understand. They don't understand at all. I know you will, my love. When I tell you things I haven't said to anyone before.

You know how I feel. Loving you is real. The thing I was born to do. Look. The truth is, I'm all yours, not his. It's you I love, just him I'm sleeping with. And don't worry, I won't stop writing, whatever happens – even if it hurts. People hate bad things happening to them but they really shouldn't. I don't. We mustn't judge the forces that make us. And when I tell you all, you will know how I became the person that I am, and why I love you so. I wrote the story down, you see. I wrote it down for you. And I will tell you everything, a part each time we meet. Soon you'll come to know. The story of my love and how it came to you.

With all my love, until next time,

Mexx

I leave the house, banging the door too hard. You'd say I was happy if you saw me. Because for the first time in months, I am behaving like it. Firm stride, wide steps, arms swinging in a march. I love the feeling I have now. It swells so big, it's everywhere. Not just inside, but in the sky above and the floor beneath my feet. The rust-scabbed iron gate wolf-whistles as it swings me out, and every part of me is in step, in metronomic time. My letter to you is flapping and bending as I stride.

I wait for the bus. Ten uncomfortable minutes have passed. Uncomfortable because the letter pinched between my thumb and forefinger is electric, alive. Like a bird; some small sparrow or finch eager for release. Freedom. It sends currents to my stomach that tickle me on the inside. I feel it when I think of what I'm about to do. I feel it when I think of you.

The silence at the station breaks with a slap, flesh upon flesh. A young mother smacks her toddler's bare leg. I catch the hush before the ripping caw. Why do we hurt our own? I think.

The number 12 arrives. It's a red double-decker, and I take a window seat, not so much for the views, but to hide behind the veil of dirt smeared upon the outside of the window. The graffiti of London's grime. Modern art.

The faint smell of pummelled dust and dried urine rises as I throw myself down upon the bench. The bus swerves to the right as it begins to move. I hold the rail in front to steady myself as it makes its way through the streets of London. My sleeve falls back to reveal a dirty smudge of a bruise at the centre of my left forearm. I quickly cover it over. Do they ever clean these buses? I wonder. My eyes trail the theatrics of an abandoned beer can, rattling as it rolls, a curled trail of beer forming a near-perfect circle. I sit for quite a while watching tides of passengers wash in and out at each stop.

The excitement wears me down, but as Parliament with its many bays and towers comes into view, I spot you getting on. The bus idles at red traffic lights and judders as it stills. I feel comforted by it. You don't see me, do you? I get up, moving slowly, cautiously to you. You touch the back of your neck as if a part of me had touched your skin, my flesh upon your flesh.

We all do things we can't explain. I wonder if that's why I'm right behind you now. So close that I can touch the bare skin of your neck and breathe upon your hair. The pounding in my chest is spreading to my fingertips. I feel my cheeks rise. It's not a smile, but something promising to be. I hold my place, decide to wait a moment more . . .

Chapter Three

White boy in Lahore

Years earlier

I'm waiting and I'm watching by the door.

Chink, chink, chink. You always hear them first. Their ankle bells sounding with each footstep on the floor. And then the singing as the dancing begins. *Chink, chink-chink, chink.*

I'm seven and I'm watching from afar, crouching down like a little mouse hiding in our home. Commotion starts and I can see it clearly as our door is open wide. Neighbours coming out to see what's going on. Who's singing in the courtyard, dancing in our street. I've never heard or seen such things before.

'The *kusorey** are here,' I hear my papa say. I creep forward to the door. My face is hidden by the wall and only eyes and fingertips can peep. I see the three of them, two dressed in red saris, the other one in green. Each gently resting both their hands upon one swinging hip. Thrusting, lurching up. Their faces scare me: the way they force the feminine upon their strong square jaws; red lips, brown paint

---

* Transvestites.

to hide the stubble on their chins, something wrong about their wide clown-like smiles.

A few men from the local residences come out to chase the transvestites away. I see Sultan, who is my papa's friend. He runs to them with his finger wagging up and down. Sultan's son, Imran, is running with him, swinging round his thighs as if he's tethered by a leash.

'There is no wedding here,' I hear Sultan shout. 'You have the wrong address, now go!'

'But we heard about the birth and we came to celebrate with you.'

'*Chal chal*,* shoo, be gone.'

Pulsing jangles rise with a blur of dust as once again their stamping feet begin to thump.

'*Challo*, go! It was a girl.' Sultan shouts to stretch his voice above the noise.

The *kusorey* stop dancing all at once, and now only random chimes sound as they gather up their skirts and sari folds and start to leave.

'Commiserations, brother; we'll pray that next time it's a boy.' I hear their muted bells clatter as they step away, but then the one in green turns back and reaches out a palm. Vines of henna grow up his veined and sturdy arm.

'A few rupees for lunch? God bless you with good health and sons, brother.'

There's sadness in Sultan's eyes because the *kusorey* don't know that his wife, in giving birth, has died. He walks away. The transvestites leave and the chinking fades.

* Go, go.

I run back inside our home, and in the middle of an empty space I start to stamp my feet. I raise my arms up high and then I twist and spin inside our little room.

'What are you doing, Mani?' Mama says to me.

'I'm dancing, Mama, dancing for the baby girl.' Mama takes me in her arms and swings me round so fast her *dupatta** falls off her head. Then she sits me on her lap and feeds me dried *chapatis*** from the other night. I chew and chew until my teeth begin to hurt. Papa lays his hand upon my head the way elders do.

It was the first time I had ever seen the *kusorey*, and despite the strangeness of their looks and ways, it wasn't thoughts of she-men lingering in my mind; it was the silencing of bells because a baby girl had been born.

Lahore. That was where it started. Back when London was just a word. A word unknown to me, spoken to impress. That was how I learned that words could change a person's thoughts; make people like you more. In the courtyard fronting the single room in which we lived, you could hear people speak, and see them too; like a theatre stage, the homes curved and pointed in. I often saw my papa speak to guests and neighbours there. *London*. Each time he said that word out loud, they'd nod with eyebrows raised and downward smiles upon their face. And Papa would tell again how Mama's father, my *nana abu*,*** met the Queen of England

---

* Scarf women wear around their neck and upon their head.
** Flat bread.
*** Grandfather on the mother's side.

when she came to Gonda in a wide-brimmed summer hat. There was a picture he'd sometimes make me fetch. Proof that it was true. In its mock bamboo frame, Nana Abu sat beside this British lady amongst a group of men. We kept it on the high shelf in our home. He'd shine it up against his puffed-out chest, then hand it round the guests like the picture of a son who'd gone to study medicine. I think the lady in the hat wore pink, though I couldn't say for sure. Just like we didn't know whether this lady really was the Queen. We kept that to ourselves.

Papa was a short and sharp dark man. As if he'd caught upon his skin the darkness of night. If he loved at all, he kept it tight and closed within. He spoke in simple words, firing them at us like an insult or a nag.

'Hira, get!' and then he'd point and shake his wrist, eyes averted, knowing my ma would do just that. She would run across the tiny room in which we lived, past the cooking rings in the corner where she spent so much time crouching, feet flat upon the floor, knees around her ears, turning onions, lamb and *aloo** in heated earthen pots on top of massive flames. Then she would return and wait for what Papa would say next, always ready to obey.

I never saw Ma sitting still. She'd move around the room cleaning, cooking, tending to Nu. She never looked at me, just focused on Nu and the endless doing filling up her days. And when she stopped to think, her eyes upon some middle distance only she could see, she'd roll and turn the ring on her finger. Mama said it was real gold, so sometimes when

* Potato.

she cooked and cleaned, she took it off and put it high up on the shelf with Papa's watch and special things. That was where we kept the picture of Nana Abu with the English woman in the wide-brimmed hat. As a toddler, Nu merged the words into one. The new name stayed, and from that day we called our grandpa Naboo. Even Mama called him by that name. In the picture on the shelf, Naboo looked so different, young and fresh. The photo looked as if it had fallen into Mama's pot of spice. The black and white tinged with the colours of turmeric and cumin. We weren't allowed to touch those special things. But often Nu or I would climb up on a chair and stare at her. That British lady in a summer dress.

The air in Lahore was always loud. And where we lived, a place called Angel's Arc, the curve of single-storey homes seemed to funnel all the sounds to us. Thick with heat and the hum of activity: the faint whisper of moving traffic, the staccato squeal of a child, metal clanging against metal and a distant hissing like a thousand bees. The warmth oozed in through the windows and doors and squeezed little insects into the lattice mesh. The scent of jasmine. No breeze at all. And later in the night, the fizz of onions in a butter broth would push the other scents and sounds back out. The blur of sounds was only broken by the singing of *azaan*,* the call to prayer.

It was from here that Mama would soon run with us like animals being chased, casting backward glances all the way. Rain had started falling, fat, warm drops that mingled with our sweat. I didn't know where we were going or why we

* Call to prayer.

were running, I just followed on as any child would do. Mama held my brother Nu like some shoplifter's loot and left me clutching on behind, holding her sari as it billowed reds and yellows with each stride.

It was with the birth of Nu that things began to change. Nu arrived with skin as white as the sheet that he was swaddled in, despite the dark skin of our family. We all felt it. The mysteries that hid beneath his baby skin. Sultan brought sweet *mitai** to celebrate as Nu lay curled upon Mama's lap, eyes closed, a tree of veins, pink and blue, on his lids. And Papa sat in his corner on the floor, doubt and questions forming in his own eyes.

'Congratulations, Nafsi, Baji** Hira, now finally you have a son,' Sultan said. He didn't look at me, but I often noticed how his gaze would linger on my ma. He carried on. 'Someone to care for you in old age and help you with the burden of your daughter's dowry.'

Mama's eyes cut across the room to me, slim and stern and shadowed underneath, then flew back to Nu. I remember Mama's face. The way it changed when she looked at Nu. Her awe and admiration for the boy she had produced. Lips curling down a little as if to hide a smile, dark eyes holding their place just a while longer. Like a guilty secret.

When Nu threw his food on the floor, Mama never told him off. Often she would stroke his perfect chiselled face, stare into his eyes and run her fingers through his blood-red

* Asian sweets.
** Respectful term for a woman (literally: big sister).

hair. But most of all she'd marvel at the brightness of his skin, the flawless whiteness of the boy. And yes, I also knew that he was a thing of beauty, a rare and special child. Unlike me.

I was born a deep and dark and rounded brown. Much darker even than my ma. When I sat with Nu, we looked like night and day. To say I wasn't jealous would not be a whole truth, if a truth can be in parts. Because, you see, I also loved the boy. He was my little charm who sat beside me day and night. I smelled his milky skin when he ran into my arms. In bed he wouldn't sleep unless he felt me near, his hand moving loose skin at the bend of my elbow.

From the day Nu was born, I knew that Mama loved him more. I became a thought her mind had room for only after she was sure that Nu was safe and fed and warm. Then, and only sometimes, she would turn to check on me.

Chapter Four

Elders

Some days after Nu was born, the elders came to see his skin. Raising eyebrows, scratching heads. Trying to find an answer to this mystery. My ma and pa feared the council of these older men for the power they had. But Naboo came that day to set them straight.

'*La hawla wala quwwata illa billah*',* he said standing in the courtyard of the Arc, the elders in a huddle in front of Ma and Pa. He'd always speak those words when important things were to be said. He ran his fingers through his beard and pushed up his specs.

'Gentlemen,' he said, touching his embroidered cap, which matched the white hair of his head. 'We've seen things like this before. How the skin of babies doesn't always turn out as you'd think.' He looked like he was lecturing. 'Fairer, darker or sometimes with a hint of pink. They mostly change within days of being born.' Naboo himself had much more skin than he could ever need. A rich mahogany shroud. The flaps that hung down at his neck wobbled as he spoke. 'It's likely this child will go dark in days,' he said. 'And anyway, who are we

* All power and ability is with God alone.

19

to question this? Would you question God's work?' He paused. 'It's time for all of us to leave. *Challo*, now; bless the newborn boy and go.'

The elders nodded, said a prayer, then left.

But I knew that what Naboo said wasn't really true. Nu was like a creature from the moon, and it didn't stop at that. People whispered as we walked by. Pointing at him, sharing secret words behind cupped hands. Even Imran from our neighbourhood would tease.

'Is Nu really related to you?' he asked.

'He is my brother, as you know,' I replied.

'Half-brother, I'd say.' Imran laughed. 'Why don't you ask your ma?' he said, running off.

I knew that was what people were whispering as we passed. It was this way for months. But eventually they stopped and got on with their chores. Nu was just a quirk of nature they ignored.

When Nu was young, we played outside in the dusty courtyard with other kids, throwing sticks and stacking stones. With all his whiteness, Mama feared the whispers of djinn and man. So when she went out, it was only me that she took along with her.

Mostly Mama took me to Anarkali* to shop. I loved to watch the stallholders busy at their job. Feel the heat upon my cheek as I passed the *mitai* man frying sticky orange spirals in giant pans. And fabric traders whipping out measured cloth and drying dyed *dupattas* like how we made

---

* A large marketplace in central Lahore.

the sea in play, by throwing waves upon the long and gauzy cloth under the scalding midday sun. Most of all I liked to feel the *raunak*,* which happened when I blurred my eyes and took in everything at once, all busy, messy happenings in a single glance. The traders would smile at me as they bartered with my ma for cloth and string and lovely colourful sweet things.

When Nu turned eight, Mama said she now felt safe. She started taking Nu with us so he could see the marketplace and feel the *raunak* too. People on the streets asked us how we had a child who was so fair. Others just stared.

I never knew the reason Mama loved Nu more. On good days I decided it was fear. She'd often say: *we must protect Nu from the evil eye.* And anyway, I knew there was nothing I could do about it.

* Vibrant busy environment.

21

Chapter Five

Flute

Life was good. We lived in Shad Bagh on the outskirts of Lahore. I slept with Nu on the floor, and Ma and Pa occupied a little bed on the other side of the room. It was low, but if you lay flat on the floor, you could slide right underneath.

In each home around the courtyard of Angel's Arc lived a whole family. The Arc was curved like a jaw, the doors a set of mouldy teeth each day spitting people out. Dirt crying down in lines on once whitewashed walls.

Naboo came to visit us, as he did most days, bringing his *bansari** with him. I loved the earthy taste of the wooden flute upon my lips.

'Listen, Naboo, don't I sound divine?' I said as I played a nursery rhyme. I practised hard so that I could impress, but it was only Naboo who said it was great. I loved the sound the flute made: wood and wind through river reeds. It made me dream of things to come, forbidden things like love.

'*Vay-va.*** The angels in the Arc must have gathered round

* Flute.
** Wow.

to hear you play, *beta*,' said Naboo. I ran to him and squeezed my face into his fleshy waist. Then Nu started to sing, long-drawn-out notes to match my playing on the flute.

> *Lala lala lori*
> *Doodh ki katori*
> *Doodh meh batasha*
> *Jeevan ke tamaasha*

As he sang, he swung from side to side, lifting up his left foot, then his right.

'Stop that now, Mani. Come help me here,' Ma said with irritation in her voice. Her face was always tense when she spoke to me. She took the flute and threw it out the door. It landed with a dampened clattering upon dried earth. Naboo frowned at her, but she didn't seem to care.

I started doing chores and Naboo switched on his little radio, holding it up against his ear. I helped punch the *ata**
into dough, adding water as I did. And as Ma wheeled the rolling pin, I cooked the thin *chapatis* on a *tava*** that was curved and mounded up like the bald head of a man.

When the work was done and I was wiping flour off my hands, Nu sat down beside me on the floor. He pinched and stroked the skin of my arm in the way he always did. 'I told you not to pinch,' I said. 'Just call for me instead.' He looked at me, then winked so forcefully his whole face scrunched up and the brown-sugar freckles speckling his

---

* Flour.
** Hotplate for cooking *chapatis*.

23

nose all met. He pulled the flute out of his shorts and slid it secretly to me.

'Mani, I will always sing for you,' he said, checking that he wasn't seen. His tired eyes were drooping just a bit, lids half covering their green. I tapped him on the nose and pinched his cheek as I hid the flute inside my *kameez.**

Naboo had the softest flesh, which you could move around like baggy clothes upon his bones. We often did just that, both Nu and I. Every time he hugged us, he would press us into him, and we would sink into his belly and tap and wobble it. He always smelled of Surf and the cardamoms that he chewed. From the back you would think he was thin, but from the side, his belly rose steeply like a sideways hill, then disappeared as quickly where his legs began.

Many years ago, Naboo lost the hearing in one ear. Mostly that would be a tragedy, but not in Naboo's case. Because instead of two good ears, he had one secret gift. We weren't allowed to speak of it. But sometimes we sang loudly in the ear that couldn't hear, for fun. He never told us off for it.

He had no sense of sound within a space. When you called to him, he'd mostly turn the wrong way round.

'Naboo, tell us a story, plea-plea-please,' Nu and I said in unison. We wouldn't stop until he hushed us down, agreed to tell us another tale of mystery. His favourite story was the one about Layla and Majnun.

'She was a beauty, a heavenly sight,' he'd say. 'With hair as dark as a moonless night. They met at school and fell in love.' Then his voice would drop. 'But this was no earthly

---

* Shirt.

love. It was deep and pure and more real than the world about them. They loved each other totally.'

'What happened next, Naboo?' Nu said. By this time Nu and I would be huddled up beneath a *chadar*,* even in the warmth.

'When he couldn't be with her, he lost his mind and became a *majnun*,** a madman and a fool, doing anything to hear some news of her.' Naboo stopped right there. 'The rest, my *bachay*,*** is not for little ears,' he said. 'Not yet, in any case.'

Nu threw his hands up in the air, landing them dramatically on his head. 'Naboo, how can you stop there, in the middle of the tale?' Naboo smiled and nodded as he tucked us into bed.

He never told us what happened to the love they felt, or where the lost love went. Did it evaporate, or fade away? At that time, I didn't know the things I later came to learn. The hidden mysteries of love.

At night, as I closed my eyes to sleep, I thought of them, those lovers who could never be together in the end.

* Blanket or shawl.
** Madman.
*** Children.

Chapter Six

Respect

L ater on that night, when Nu was asleep and I was meant to be, Pa came home, his brow glossed with sweat shining brightly in the candlelight. I opened a single eye and watched him eat his *daal** *chapati*, sitting on the floor. Mama got into bed.

'Why do you come home so late?' she said. 'You don't have to drink *chai*** with friends when work is done each night.'

Papa didn't answer. He finished his food and wiped his steel plate clean of any trace of *daal* with the final sliver of *chapati*. Afterwards, he watched the candle flicker in the centre of the room, although I had the sense he wasn't seeing it. I slowly opened my other eye, certain he hadn't noticed me.

'Why aren't you asleep, Mani?' he said, without turning his face or his eyes to me. '*Sau jow*'.*** I squeezed my eyes so tightly closed that it hurt my face, then opened them again. I lifted Nu's arched arm gently off me and sat up, leaning on

---

* A lentil meal.
** Tea.
*** Go to sleep.

26

my elbows. Papa and I, we had a secret pact, although we never spoke of it. It meant that we shared things just between the two of us, like looks and sweets and sometimes things we spoke about.

'Papa,' I said. 'Can I ask you something?'

'It's late,' he fired back. 'Sleep.'

'But it's only very quick.' He didn't answer, so I carried on. He was putting things away and taking off his watch.

'Do you care that I'm not a boy?'

'No,' he said. 'Now go to sleep.' Papa didn't speak a lot and he wasn't like my ma and other people in Lahore. He loved me how I was, I knew he did, even though it mostly didn't show.

There was silence as he stood to change for bed. '*Isaat*,'* he said. 'Respect is all that matters in the end.'

Later on that night, when the light was out, I heard my ma and pa whispering, though I couldn't fully make out what they said.

'Nafsi,' Mama said. 'Children can look different from their family. Pay no heed to what Sultan says.' She released a frustrated huff. 'Don't let them drip poison in your ears. It's God's will that he's so fair. We are blessed. Remember that.'

Papa grunted out a sort of yes and seemed to ease down and agree. The speaking stopped, and soon the air inside the room was rocking back and forth with the rhythm of their sleep.

* Respect.

Chapter Seven

Praying mantis

How did it start?

It was a normal day in every way, except for whispers I'd heard when I awoke and the look in Papa's eyes on his early return from work. And it was extra hot. The kind of hot that makes you want to fall on cool sheets and go to sleep, but it was morning and we were late.

'*Sat sri akal*,* Mr Singh,' Nu said as we left our house for school. It was the Sikh greeting he spoke. He ran on over to the left and I called to him.

'Come on, Nu, let's go.'

'But I haven't finished my hellos.'

He stopped abruptly, placing his right hand upon his heart. '*Salamu alaykum*,** Ayesha' – the Muslim greeting, peace to you. Then in military style he spun a quarter-turn and raised a flat palm to his brow. 'And I haven't forgotten you, Prince Charles. Good morning, sir. Keep growing now, you're doing well.'

---

* A Sikh greeting meaning 'God is the ultimate truth'.
** Peace be upon you.

Nu was greeting trees, the banyan, peepal and shahtoot*
trees that triangled the courtyard of the Arc. *They keep us
company*, he had said one day, and so he gave them names
and always greeted them. Prince Charles was the smallest
of them, the young peepal. Nu stroked its trunk and Prince
Charles gave up a leaf; a broad green heart stretching down
and pinched into a tail beneath. Nu caught it in his hands.

'Mani, *baji*, look. Prince Charles heard me speak.' He held
the leaf up to me.

'Is that so?' I said. Just then, Imran ran up. He snatched
the leaf that Nu was holding and waggled it, inviting chase.
They ran around the courtyard in between the trees as I
walked on ahead.

'Come on, you two,' I shouted urgently, not slowing my
pace, 'or else we'll all be late for school.'

As I walked to school, I thought about the strange thing
that had happened that morning when I woke. Each day,
Mama would sweep and turn her long, straight dark hair
behind her ears and into plaited liquorice knots. That morning I was watching her. She coiled the plait round and round
and clasped the twisted braids into a ball, which rose upon
the nape of her neck. Taking up a shard of broken mirrored
glass, she checked her fresh and silky skin and bit some
redness into her lips, smoothing down her hair again and
again. The hoops that pierced her ears merged into the
golden colour of her skin and shouted out against the total
blackness of her hair. I always noticed the way they pulled an

* Mulberry.

29

oval hole in her childlike lobes.

When her beauty was complete, it would radiate like a source of heat. Dark slit eyes densely meshed with lashes, the endless curve of her lips, her shy nose pointing down, and chin and cheekbones rising and falling like a sculptor's work. She'd smile with satisfaction into the broken mirror shard. And then each day, in exactly the same way, she'd take the *dupatta* scarf looped across her breast, the one with purple spots on it, and place it carefully over her head. Her beauty hidden under cloth so no eyes could witness it. I was so in awe of Mama's face that sometimes when I looked at her I'd find my breath had held itself inside. I wondered why others didn't see it too; like a blindfold on the eyes of all around, they only saw her skin. Aunts and elders echoed, 'What a shame she's not fair.'

As Ma finished wrapping her plaited hair, there was a knock on the door. Nu was still asleep. I crept out of bed. Crouching down, I watched Mama as she raised her hands to catch the loose part of her scarf, which hung and swayed. She swept it right across her face and held it firmly in place by biting on it. Then she opened the door a tiny bit.

There was whispering; broken shards of voices.

'*Baji*,' the visitor said. I could hear it was a man.

'What?' Mama whispered back. 'What do you want?'

'Nafsi knows about Shamim,' he said. Mama didn't reply. 'Your cousin Shamim,' he said more forcefully. It was Sultan. Ma opened the door some more. 'They say she is a Hira Mundi girl.'

Mama said, 'Shamim,' lengthening the word as if she'd only just realised who Sultan was speaking of. 'I was a child . . .

we never met,' she added, as though to explain herself.

'*Baji*, there is more . . .'

'Speak!' my mama said, inching further out of the door.

'Dishonour flows inside . . . inside your blood. That is what they're telling everyone,' he stuttered, then added, 'And worse . . .'

Muffled words were spoken, whisperings and huffs I couldn't fully hear.

'They say that you're the same . . . and that this explains the fair skin of your boy . . .' A lengthy pause. 'That Nu is living proof of shameful deeds.'

Mama's breathing deepened.

'Hira,' Sultan said.

The door was forced, and Sultan stepped inside, his great form blocking out the light. Mama released a single breathy sob as I saw that he had pinned her up against the frame, his hands clasping her arms on either side.

'If what they say is true, why don't you come to me? Let me have a taste of you . . .' He breathed the words into Mama's ear. 'I promise you,' he said, 'Nafsi will never know. Just name your price.'

'No,' Mama said, a tremble breaking up the word. She muffled a cry. 'Shame on you,' she said. Her eyes were lowered. 'Now leave,' she whispered forcefully.

There was thick silence and nothing further said. Only the clattering of two coins that Sultan threw down upon the floor, and a grunt as he kicked the door and left.

Mama closed the door and fell against it hard.

'Nafsi,' she said, her hand shaking as she placed it on her mouth. Then she whispered, 'Shamim.' I don't think she knew she was speaking the words out loud. She swept away a tear from the outside corner of her eye. And from the downward turn of her lips, she looked as if she might be sick. I remembered that expression when Nu was growing inside Ma. Only then she'd lay her right hand gently on the bare skin at her waist, just above where silken sari folds poured out from petticoats.

She twisted the gold ring on her finger, then jolted as she saw me watching her. My jaw was hanging loose and I didn't know what to do. Quickly she moved from the door to start her daily chores. She threw the *jaroo** towards me and it hit me on the arm, its stiff bristles issuing a puff of dust as it landed by my side.

'Sweep the floor instead of sitting there listening to things you shouldn't hear.' She huffed under her breath, acting like it was just another day.

Mama was being bad to me, but I was used to it. I thought I might tell on her to Papa later on, and say how Sultan had come around saying things I didn't understand. I hated sweeping up. I picked up the *jaroo*, its stiff, straight twigs all longer than my arm and caught together with a binding of tight string. Below, they splayed out as if they were trying to escape. I hunched frog-like upon my thighs and walked the dust towards the entrance of the house. Then, in a single giant move to chase the dirt away, I smacked it hard and ordered it to leave. It rose up in a misty cloud like a djinn, defying me.

Mama went to Nu, worry showing on her face.

* Broom.

'Wake up, my *poother*,'* she said, one of the many terms of endearment she used for him. He was fast asleep on the bedding on the floor, a stone held loosely within his palm. He'd often hold a favourite stone, feeling its ridges as he turned it round and round. Sometimes he'd stare at a rock or pebble as if he saw within it something more than the rest of us could see.

'It's time for breakfast, come and eat,' Mama said, gently stroking him. 'Mani, you eat breakfast too. It's nearly time for school.'

When Nu awoke, he shouted for me straight away, as he always did. 'Mani, Mani!' He ran to me and pulled me by the arm. 'Let's go out to play.'

Outside, he showed me a dog he'd drawn with scratches in the dirt. Behind it were spiky mountains, and in the corner, far away, a tiny sun with lines to show the rays. Where the dog's eye was, he'd placed a smooth oval rock, and on the top, to shine the eye, a little sand. Underneath, in his childish hand, he'd scratched the words *dog* and *sun* all jagged in the dirt. There was an earthy smell thrown up by the artwork.

'That's beautiful, Nu, how clever are you.' I always said that for every silly thing he did.

He knelt and watched a leafy creature as it stopped and turned its heart-shaped head to the left, then stretched out its arms in supplication.

'Mani, what's that?' he said.

'It's a praying mantis.'

---

* Term of endearment for a son.

33

'Why's it praying?'

'Everything in this world prays, even sticks and stones.'

'Is that why I love my stones?'

'How do I know? Maybe.'

'What's it praying for?'

'That it doesn't get killed.'

'Then I will pray for that too.' And he sat down on the ground and raised his cupped hands, asking the Lord to take care of this 'funny stick-like thing'.

Then he smiled. His smiling face threw out such warmth that I would catch it on my face and find that I was smiling too. He'd scrunch his nose and pull his face up high, gums and teeth all visible to see. There was something different about that boy. I don't just mean his looks. He seemed to shift the feeling in the air about him wherever he went. Like the energy in the air before a storm.

I didn't know back then that one day soon it would be me raising cupped hands, praying, pleading desperately to save the ones I loved.

Chapter Eight

You: bus route 453 to Oxford Street

11 November

My dear,

Isn't it strange to know something you can't share? Like this secret love of ours.

I'm so happy we're in touch again. The way we should have been right from the start, when we first met. I was so excited then. It was a treat to see your eyes taking comfort, resting on me. Do you remember that? My skin became so sensitive, as if you blew some sort of lover's breeze on me.

Even then I knew I should contact you, but things got in the way. Things always do. Or rather someone did. It's funny, isn't it: we always know what we should do. But we do something else instead.

Last time we met, I promised to tell you all about my life. About the challenges I've had of late. It's hard, but let me start with this.

Someone's hurting me.

It's not just bruises, though I've plenty of those. I can cope with the odd graze here and there. A little time and rest and you wouldn't even know I'd been struck. The cuts and bruises go. It's the bruises on my heart that fill me up with fear. I fear I'll lose the love I have within. That I'll go cold and hard, as if a part of me has died. But you, my love, with you, no part of me can ossify.

A year ago, my life changed. Something happened, something terrible, and I was distraught. It's not easy to share the details, but, my love, in time you'll come to know. I will tell you everything.

A kind lady I know, someone much older than me, tried to help with the worst of it. She'd tell me to be strong, and as she did, she'd take my hands and squeeze them inside hers. Hers were fleshless hands that felt like bones clothed only in skin. It didn't work. I was a mess.

So, I'm in this dark and desperate place, and that's the moment *he* enters my life. Now, let me think – how to explain it so you'll understand. How did it start?

With love.

That's it. The agony and hurt and hate started with its opposite, with love. Isn't that the way it always is? It was a saving love, though. Rich and beautiful. The kind that lifts you from great tragedy. I was slipping off a precipice, hanging on with my fingertips – and he caught me as I fell.

A short while later, on a sunny day in spring, and in the midst of all this misery, he turns to me and says, 'Marry me, Mexx?' He sings it out, poised and confident.

'Well, I . . . umm . . . OK.'

That's right. Four stupid words in answer to his three-note melody.

And that was that.

I am stunned. Keep telling everyone. Next, those three words start changing me. I can no longer think, and everywhere I look, I see only references to him. When shopping (would he like this dress), an idyllic scene (will he ever take me there), at the supermarket (does he like fish, or is it meat that he prefers?). My world shines brighter than I've ever known, and every time I think of those words – 'Marry me, Mexx' – I feel the same crazy happiness.

But after a bit, I start feeling something else. A sort of dread. A subtle shudder in my gut. It must be nerves, I tell myself. You see, it's all so new. And he's gorgeous. (Did I say that yet?) Like a model from a TV ad for some overpriced perfume. I keep wondering: what's a good-looking man like him want with someone like me? Soon found out.

Happiness and dread. Those two emotions have no business being side by side. But thinking back, a part of me always knew what this was leading to. Eventually. There were signs. Wrapped within the little things he said and did. My grandad always used to say that inside most of us, there's a little bell which sits somewhere inside our gut. When it chimes, it makes the heart vibrate and every part of us becomes aware of something hidden, something we are meant to know. Perhaps that's what it was, the sense of dread I felt.

I'll tell you more, my dear, when we meet on the 453 where Oxford Street joins Regent Street. I love Oxford Street, with its endless people pouring from the underground, flowing through the streets. We've planned it so carefully. Our secret meetings here and there. There's a map of London in my bedside drawer, and every time we meet, I place a dot on it to chart our lovers' trysts.

Love you always,

Your Mexx

Chapter Nine

Djinn

After school, the day that Sultan came to Ma, I knew that something wasn't right. Papa was already back from work. Normally he'd come home late upon a breeze of spice and onion from the restaurant at which he worked.

Nu was sitting with his arms outstretched, talking to the Lord as the sun went down. Beyond his silhouette against a mango-coloured sun, I saw Papa watching us at play, partly hidden behind Ayesha the shahtoot tree. Something in his eyes had changed. The blackened centres, normally flat and dead, were trembling and darting in a pool of white. They ran all over Nu as if he'd never seen his son before. As if it was just now he noticed the fairness of his face and limbs, the dazzling redness of his hair. I walked up to Papa as Nu was supplicating to the Lord.

'Papa, Papa, is everything OK?'

He backed away, and stumbled as he did.

'You are a good girl, Mani,' he said. 'Nothing like your ma.'

I put my hands upon my hips and frowned. 'Is she being bad again?' I said. I knew that Mama could be naughty sometimes, like that time she threw the *bansari* outside. 'Was she mean to you?'

'Yes, bad, so bad,' he said. He gently touched his palm upon my head.

'What has she done this time?' I said in teacher tones, folding my arms and tipping my head a little to the left. Mama shouldn't be bad, especially to Pa. His eyes dashed around the dusty earth as if he was trying to catch a bouncing thought. 'You'd better tell her off, Papa,' I said, 'and tell her to be good.' I thought nothing of the words I spoke. I wish I'd seen it then, understood the gravity of what was happening.

'Go and play,' he said abruptly as he turned and walked towards the house.

I skipped to Nu and helped him dig up stones, my fingertips throbbing as dark muddy crescents gathered underneath my nails. I found myself wanting to spy on Ma and Pa and find out what was going on. It troubled me that even though the sun was almost down, Mama hadn't gathered us inside with tales of evil djinns who came to steal away good children at sunset every day. And anyway, why, I wondered, had Papa come home so early?

'You carry on, Nu. I'll be back soon,' I said.

'OK, *baji*,' Nu replied, examining a stone he'd found.

Sultan was sitting with another neighbour in the courtyard, drinking tea.

'Did you hear about Hira and her cousin, the working girl?' he said as they laughed softly. 'And to think she lives next door.'

They saw me walking past and stopped speaking at once. It made me chart a wider arc to our front door. When I got there, I crouched down and pressed my ear to the wood.

'It's not true.' Mama was crying softly. 'It's my cousin, who I've never met, not me.' Something metal tumbled across the floor. Then the door opened and Papa left, not noticing me balled up small beside the doorway.

I didn't dare do more than peek in case Mama spotted me. I waited until Papa faded in the distance. Then I ran to Nu and brought him home. Papa hadn't returned, and Mama hadn't moved. She sat still upon her knees, staring into space. She didn't even turn her ring.

I laid our bed on the floor and knew to get Nu ready for the night before he noticed something wasn't right. I helped him button up his sleeping *kameez* and laid him down beside me on our bed. He swung up to place a kiss on my cheek. 'Mani, *baji*,' he whispered. He didn't understand that something strange was happening. We both went to sleep.

Mama's greatest fear in life was the djinns that locals said lived in the nearby hills. I recall her words.

'It always starts with a feeling in your heart. You never know if they are nearby, except that children sometimes see their dark and smoky shadows.' She was good at telling stories. As she spoke, her eyes would widen and her voice become hushed. 'There are some that are good, like human folk, just living out their lives. And then there are the other sort; the evil whisperers.' I could see fear upon her face. 'If those come near, things start to change as they did with my friend Bashira years ago. Her eyes turned from brown to grey. And she started speaking strange and foreign words. She wouldn't leave her room.'

Ma said her friend would bark and scream at night, and

also in the day if anyone came near. She'd throw things around, but even worse, 'If you pressed your ear against her door at night, you'd hear her talk as if there was someone in the room with her. Chatting and laughing with unseen things.'

It terrified Mama. The *pirs** and other holy sorts came to send the djinn away. But the djinn decided to stay. And Bashira was never the same.

Every day Ma would pray to protect us from such things. She'd cast the prayer upon us by a *pook,*** blowing the prayer she'd mouthed upon us like blowing candles out at night. My eyes would flicker just like the flame.

Later that night, as Nu and I lay in bed, Mama prayed hard over us, laying a gentle hand upon Nu's sleepy head. Nu fell asleep, but I lay awake listening for Papa's footsteps in between the chirping of the *jhingurs*** in the dark.

* A spiritual guide or saint.
** Transmitting the blessing of a prayer on to another by blowing on them after recitation of the prayer.
*** Night insects.

Chapter Ten

Words

Hours passed, and still I lay awake. Then I heard a voice in the courtyard.

'Did you never think about this before, Nafsi? Did you not suspect?'

It was late, and Ma and Nu were fast asleep. The voice was deep, and when he spoke, I felt our walls vibrate. Then I heard my pa.

'Why should I?' he said. 'Look around. We've all got different-coloured skin. Why should that mean anything?'

I crawled out of bed and crouched down by the door, turned my ear towards a crack where a line of light spilled in and broke the room in two.

'Nafsi,' the deep voice said, stretching out my papa's name. Then he paused. 'Don't be a fool. Look at yourself, and at Baji Hira too. And do you see another boy as fair as Nu?'

Then I heard a different voice, the high-pitched whine of someone who had not spoken yet.

'You've heard how Hira's cousin earns her keep. Her family never told you that, of course. She's a prostitute, a Hira Mundi girl, and I hear she's worth her price.' Then a rocking laugh. 'I say it's in the blood.'

'No,' said Papa. 'They're just rumours, lies.'

'How can you be sure?' the high-pitched voice replied. 'And many Englishmen want Hira Mundi girls. Perhaps that explains—'

'Relax, Nafsi, it's clear what must be done,' the deep voice said. 'Such women and the creatures they birth have evil flowing through their blood. They bring only shame and dishonour on the family.'

'Don't think of them as human. They are more like flies, not worthy of the name *insaan*,* the high-pitched voice said.

Then the deep voice, with a swinging tone, sang in broken English, 'Fee fi fo fum, I smell blood of Englishman.' A hiss of muffled laughter.

Papa said, 'I have to go.'

I leapt back into bed. Closed my eyes and with deepened breaths made out that I was fast asleep. I felt him walk up close to Nu and me. The scent of onions and spice upon his clothes filled my nose. I clutched myself to muffle the growl of hunger I could feel. He knelt down on the floor. I saw him in a slice of light that entered through the door. He looked sad and angry all at once. The light upon his sweat-glossed skin shifted back and forth with the clenching and releasing of his jaw.

He reached his hand down slowly to Nu. I stiffened with fear. Then he softly stroked Nu's hair. Gently. Tenderly. I'd never seen his love before. He breathed in crookedly. I think there may have been a tear in his eye, but I couldn't see it properly.

* Human being.

I don't know when he stopped. When next I opened my eyes, it was already day.

Next morning, I was tired as I played with Nu. I'd hardly slept.

'Mani, come over here.'

Nu was whispering. We stepped with care so as not to scare the creature away. Nu watched it with an intense glare, tilting his head slow and steady as the lizard stopped and started and stopped again. The raw pink beast charted a crooked path down a stony broken wall and ran towards our feet. As I leapt away, Nu moved towards it so slow and confident. He stroked it gently on its back.

I watched Nu carefully after hearing the conversation last night. Stared at him to see if there was evil turning, curling blackly in his eyes. Nothing. There was nothing bad that I could see. The men who'd whispered in the courtyard must be wrong. I didn't fully understand, but I knew that Nu was good.

Nu spotted Naboo walking towards us from afar, his arms raised and the usual frown upon his face as he looked about. We crept nearer to him, then hid behind some boxes on the left of the entrance to the Arc. When he was close, we shouted his name and watched him turn to his right and search for us on the wrong side of the path. We laughed out loud before jumping into view and running to him, burying ourselves in him.

'I heard your cheeky plan inside my hearing ear before you even saw me come,' he said.

We laughed again, and apologised. 'Sorry, Naboo, *maafi*,* *maafi*, forgive!'

* Forgiveness.

'Remember, Mani, Nu,' he said. 'God can hear every thought you have. And thoughts and words are real things, like the things we do. So always choose them well, my little ones.'

We walked with Naboo to our home. When we opened the door, we saw Mama kneeling on the floor. The room had fallen down, with pots and pans strewn around and bedding heaped in piles. Ma was sobbing silently, dabbing the *dupatta*, the one with purple dots on it, upon her eyes. When she saw us, she rushed to make up busyness that wasn't really there. Naboo made us go and play in the courtyard and closed the door. We ran away, then, like magnets drawn to secret things, we edged back to the door to listen in.

'Naboo, help me. Nafsi's not himself. He must be possessed by djinns. He thinks I'm a Hira Mundi . . .' Mama was saying as the door opened. Nu and I were squatting either side like guarding lions. We both looked up, too surprised to move.

'Go and play,' I said.' Naboo stood within the frame, no surprise upon his face. We skipped away and he closed the door again.

'What is Hira Mundi?' Nu asked.

'I don't know,' I said, holding back from saying what I thought. We spun upon the dried earth, arms outstretched until we made a muddy cloud of dust rise up. Then we ran to climb Mr Singh, the banyan tree at the centre of the Arc.

'Let's play jungle,' Nu said.

'OK.'

We ducked down with arms raised, creeping forward through grasses and trees that only our minds could see.

'There's a tiger on the right,' I shouted. 'Quick, Nu, I have to save you from his teeth.'

I pulled him to an imaginary cave and we hid until the danger passed. Then we carefully stepped out.

'Oh no,' Nu said. And there before us we saw a fierce river raging past.

'We need to drink to keep up our strength,' I said. We crawled on hands and knees and slurped.

Then Naboo appeared, and our jungle vanished.

Chapter Eleven

Fabric man

The day that Nu turned nine, Mama and I were washing clothes in a bucket in the Arc. I liked her scarf. It had purple dots that became indigo when wet. I made it catch a bubble of air, and when it ballooned, I squelched it down into the suds to flatten the bubble. After washing the scarf, Mama helped me squeeze the water out, twisting it so tight it looked like a rope. It was my job to hang the clothing out to dry on the flat roof of our house. I climbed up the ladder and laid the scarf on a string suspended between two lengths of wood. The sun was hot and high, so I knew it wouldn't take too long to dry.

Later, when I was playing in the Arc, a gusty breeze blew the scarf down off the roof. It snaked and rippled as it fell. I ran to catch it like a cricketer lining up to catch a ball before it landed on the dusty earth below. My fingers grasped the muslin as it floated down, but Imran with his short, fast legs, sped past and whipped it out of my hand.

'Give it here,' I said.

'Come and get it then,' he shouted back.

I lurched towards him, making out that I was chasing him. But I knew I couldn't catch him even if I tried. He kicked up a cloud of dust as he teased me with a dancing dodge from afar.

'I'm telling my ma,' I said. 'Give it back right now.' But it was too late. Imran sped away.

Later that day, Naboo came to visit us. He spoke quietly to Mama for some while, so quietly we couldn't hear his words. Nu and I were running about like puppies ready for a walk.

'Naboo, Naboo, tell me what you hear today,' Nu said.

'Child, I hear the frying of a delicious dish.'

'No, Naboo, I want to know if you can hear some whisperings.'

'And if I could, would I tell you that?' I saw a smile hidden behind pursed lips. 'But I would watch that family across the way.' And he put his finger to his mouth.

'Why, Naboo, why?'

'Enough,' he said. 'It's time for me to go.' But as he left, he held his hand up to his ear, and I was sure I saw a shadow cross his face.

After Naboo left, Ma spoke some thoughts out loud. Things that Naboo had talked to her about. She never did that normally.

'I fear that djinns have whispered evil things to Pa.'

She didn't look into my eyes, and she seemed to speak more to the air than to us. I didn't know what she meant, but I had seen darkness growing within my pa with every day that passed. And other things as well. The street had eyes, and the traders stopped their smiles, stopped speaking to my ma. They didn't want to serve her or have her in their shop.

Two days earlier, Ma and I had gone to Anarkali to see the fabric man. He sat upon a platform like a king, directing his workers to fetch the fabrics and the trims. That day he wore a flat cap with coin-like mirrors sewn on it. Mama was distracted by a blue silk she hadn't seen before. An assistant caught the fabric at one side and threw it up into the air. The silk unrolled and spilled like a river flowing from his hands and pooled on the platform. Just then another stall boy spoke to the fabric man, who was stacking trims upon a rack.

'Look, Uncle, there's the whore.'

I spun round to see who they were pointing at. The only person standing there was Ma.

'Her cousin's a Hira Mundi girl, and they say she is as well. She even has a bastard son she hides away at home.'

They didn't see me watching them, didn't know that I could hear. I was just another child at the bazaar. Mama walked towards the fabric man and spoke.

'I need the red sequinned trim for a *dupatta* I've forgotten to bring.'

The fabric man looked at her and his face turned strange, as if he'd smelt a foul and fuming thing.

'It's out of stock,' he said, even though I had seen him put the trim high up on the rack.

My mama knew, but she just walked away. I chased after her holding her *dupatta*, which swayed behind her with each step.

Not long afterwards, Nu and I were walking home from school. As we entered the Arc, Imran came towards us. We both smiled, and Nu ran to him to play. Imran stopped so fast his feet kicked up a cloud of dust. He picked up a stone and threw it at Nu, and although it missed, a liquid fury rose in me.

'*Haramzada*, go away,' Imran shouted. Then, to me, 'We don't want your bastard brother near us any more.'

'Hey,' I said, running after him, both fists balled, blood surging up my neck and thumping in my skull. Imran turned and ran away into his house.

'Why did he do that, Mani, *baji*?' Nu asked.

'It's nothing, Nu,' I said. 'He's just being bad.'

But a tension in my tummy started to grow.

As time went by, every time Papa looked at Nu, his staring eyes would slim and I could see something icy and distant in them. Afterwards, he would leave and not come back till late. Words were not shared much between my ma and pa, except to deal with practicalities, but I could feel an agitation growing. Pa backed away a little more each day. I could see that Papa's doubting heart had hollowed him away until an ugly shell remained where Papa used to be.

One night, Mama pleaded long and hard. 'Nafsi, Nafsi, don't say these things. These are the words of evil djinns. There is no truth in what they say, don't listen to their words.'

Papa grunted, and Mama pleaded once again.

'Thank God that you have a son, Nafsi. They lie.'

But the troubled look on my papa's face remained the same. As questions over Nu's whiteness grew, the shadows on Papa's skin seemed to seep within. He began doubting things.

I didn't know that two days later my world would tip so that everything I knew would lie broken on the ground.

Chapter Twelve

Fear

'Hira from the Hira Mundi,* my diamond from the diamond market, that is what you are.' Papa's face was stern, his eyes a spin of terror. 'Now your secret's out.'

It wasn't late and Papa shouldn't have been home. I was teaching Nu some new words that he hadn't learnt so far at school. We scratched chalk upon a board of slate, *ishk*, *mahaabat*, *pyar* – so many words for love.

Mama didn't speak at first. Papa closed the doors so it was dark inside the room. Then they talked of things I couldn't fully understand. Pa was loud and Mama cowered away, pulling her *dupatta* low upon her head as if to hide in it. I'd never heard some of the words they used before. Pa's face was puffed and angry, like punched dough. He said, 'I always thought something wasn't right. And now I know.' He glared at Ma. 'Now I understand your name, I know everything. Sultan told me.'

'What do you mean?' Mama said.

'Meaning you're no different from Shamim.'

Papa seemed to grow as he stepped closer to Ma.

* Red-light district in Lahore (literally: diamond market).

'You went to him.' He paused, then arched over her, shouting up against her ear. 'Didn't you?' He slapped his hands on the wall either side of her. I could hear her breath, jagged and short. 'His wife has passed, so now you're offering yourself.'

'He lies,' Mama whispered, her voice shaking as she spoke. 'You know that I . . . I . . .' Her voice petered out.

Papa's eyes slid to Nu.

'If that is true, how is it he has proof?' He pulled a scarf from the pocket of his *kameez*. The scarf with purple dots on it that Imran had swept away some days ago.

'But Papa,' I said. 'It was Imran. He took the scarf from me.'

He wasn't listening. I ran to him and pulled at him, repeating what I had said, but he brushed me off and I fell to the floor.

There was a knock on the door. Papa opened it and Sultan walked in.

'Now let's separate lies from truth,' Papa said. He held the scarf up and away from him.

'Don't make me shame you in this way, brother,' said Sultan, his eyes upon the ground.

When Papa looked away, Sultan looked at Ma, pursed his lips and motioned out a kiss.

'It's like I said. Baji Hira came to me.' Half of his face smiled as he spoke the words.

Papa threw the scarf on the floor and stood motionless inside a dim pool of light from the window. It reflected off his sweat so I could see the pounding of a vein at his temple and a shade of purple rising underneath his skin. Sultan opened the door and Papa left with him. I shouted after him, 'Papa!' but he was gone.

Chapter Thirteen

Alone

The door swung open hard and banged against the wall. Papa stepped in slowly.

Mama pressed her back against the wall, her face a sideways silhouette. I knew she saw a djinn in him the moment he walked in. I held on to Nu and hid his face in the circle of my embrace. Papa grabbed Mama by her upper arm and took her outside, leaving me and Nu behind.

I knew that things were bad, as once, way back, I got a slap from Ma for saying 'Hira Mundi'. I didn't really understand, but Mama said to never say those bad words again. She talked about markets like Anarkali but where only men would go.

'There are no fabrics, sequins or beads; only women on the streets. The men are shopping, looking, touching things for sale. They buy a woman's flesh, the size and colour too. They take her to a room where no one else can go.'

I was shocked to hear these words. One thing we knew without ever being told: there was no greater shame for a woman than being touched by a man before her wedding day.

At first we didn't move, Nu and I. The pair of us wrapped about each other as one. The room felt eerie with Ma and

Pa both gone. I was scared that a ghostly djinn would walk in. The night grew big and crept in at the edges of the room.

'Where are Ma and Pa? Why did they leave us all alone?' Nu asked.

'It's nothing. I'm sure they'll be back quite soon,' I lied. My arms tightened around my little brother.

'Are you scared?'

'No. Why should I be? We're home and safe, aren't we?'

Throughout the night, we sat on the floor holding each other, watching the door. The darkness grew complete, and it became silent outside as the world about us went to sleep. Still Ma and Pa didn't come home. I lurched a little as a sob inside me tried to escape. But Nu kept glancing at me so I didn't let it out, but kept it tied in knotty lumps inside my throat.

The night passed and Ma finally returned. I couldn't help but glare, wide-open eyes, lips tight with fear. I'd seen the look before on people sitting beside the road, all skin and bones, hungry and afraid. Nu had tucked himself into me as deeply as he could, his ghost-white face framed between my swelling breast and my arm, which held him tightly round his neck. His eyes were wide and hollow too, his mouth a little 'O'. The cold of the Lahore night had seeped into my bones, and I felt so stiff I wasn't sure if I could move. Ma picked Nu up and wrapped him around herself as she sobbed into his neck and swung him left and right. When her face emerged, she placed him on the bedding on the floor. She glanced at me but nothing more. No hug, no kiss, no sobs or wetness at my neck.

We waited with Mama for a while, huddling in the corner. Then we heard a noise. Ma scanned the room as if to work out where to hide. I grabbed Nu and held on to him, not knowing what else to do. The door opened slowly.

Naboo. Relief. He ran to us. I'd never seen him move that fast before, although he still looked forgetful and confused. He handed Ma a bundle wrapped in newspaper with dirty string knotted around it. I knew it was rupees. I'd seen the traders at Anarkali exchanging packages like that.

'It's set,' he said.

Mama took a cream-coloured fabric bag, its edges turning grey, and placed it on the bed. Like flies she and Naboo buzzed about the room, collecting items and dropping them into the bag.

'Naboo, Naboo, what are you doing?' I said.

'Shh, shh, Mani, you have to go away. Just help Ma pack.'

'But I don't want to go away.'

I was ignored.

Nu's fear had made him whiter still. He lit the darkened room, his eyes confused and darting. Without thinking, I ran to stand on the chair beneath the high shelf where Papa's watch and special things were kept. I gently lifted the picture by its bamboo frame, the picture of the Englishwoman in a summer dress. Jumping off the chair, I slid myself underneath the bed. I wasn't going anywhere. I would stay here until Pa got back. Nu saw me hide. I put my finger to my lip to motion not to give my hiding place away.

I liked that I was invisible. That I could see feet scurrying about but no one could see me. I thought I'd been so clever, that I was staying here, but when Mama opened the door to leave, she reached under the bed, grabbed me by the hair and pulled me to my feet.

Before we stepped out of the door, Naboo called us back. He held both Nu and me so tight that I couldn't take a breath. When he released us, I could smell Surf and green cardamoms. His frown was more intense and his little beard was trembling.

'Remember,' he said, 'no one can protect you but the One above, so ask protection from the Lord. And take care of your ma for me. I know that you are *bahadar** *bachay*. My bravest little boy and girl.' He closed his eyes and mouthed a prayer. 'Everything will be OK, my little ones. You're going on an adventure with your ma, that's all.' He turned to me. 'Please be good, Mani. Remember too that God doesn't see the way we look; he only sees our deeds. And deeds, like seeds, start off as ideas in our minds.' I could tell he held a sob inside his throat, but he wouldn't let it out. He screwed his lips into a ball.

'Hira,' he said, as he took out a *taweez*,** a prayer he'd copied down from the Quran, folded up and squeezed into a locket on a string. He hung it round her neck. '*Inshallah*,*** this will protect you from danger and harm.' He cocked his head. 'You must leave, they're coming for you now; they're on their way.' He held his hand beneath his ear as if to pour the words he heard into his palm. Back then it seemed a normal thing, that Naboo's deaf ear had made the other bear a secret gift.

* Brave.
** Amulet.
*** By the will of God.

'Naboo,' Mama said, her eyes round, terror loosening her jaw, 'who will protect my Nu if he finds us and you are not about?'

Before Naboo could reply, I shouted, 'Me, Mama, I will I will I will. I'll protect our Nu.'

Ma and Naboo looked at me, disbelief on their faces. I didn't understand it then. I get it now.

'Who will find us?' I asked, but we were already rushing out of the door, and no one replied.

I didn't realise then, as we ran from everything we knew, that I would not see Papa again, except for one time, and then for many years repeatedly as an apparition in my mind.

Chapter Fourteen

You: bus route 23 to the Royal Courts of Justice

30 November

My dear,

My friend and I met up today. I wanted to tell her I was meeting you like I did last time. Back then she said to me, her curls scruffy around her face, 'Stay away. Don't meet him on the bus, my lovely, it's too dangerous.'

Doesn't that make you laugh? She's telling me, don't go, be safe, when home is where the danger is. The old dear hasn't got a clue. That's why this time I didn't tell her that we're meeting on the number 23, by the Royal Courts. I don't want to worry her.

I love that building on the Strand, don't you? It's so proud and tall, with its grand arched entrance topped with towers pointing to the sky. It makes me think about the lore of love and wonder at the things that most people never get to understand.

You say I'm brave to meet you this way. But my love, it isn't courage I feel, stealing secretly away from *him*. No, I'm still afraid. Courage isn't real. I know that now. It's just desire rising higher than the fear we hold inside. And I desire you, my love, of that you can be sure.

I know you feel the way I do. And though I've told you many times before, I need to say it once again, shout it out so everyone can hear. I AM MEXX AND I LOVE YOU!

I'm feeling better now.

But, honest now, it's more. This isn't normal love, a lightweight teenage thing, and I have a feeling you agree. I love you desperately and I cannot help myself. I have to write to you, see you, be with you. I know it's not right. But you consume me. I think of you all day and night, and every moment is better with you inside my heart.

Does that make me bad?

There is something else you should know. I can write it down, but don't ever speak to me of it. I cannot voice such secrets aloud. It's this.

Don't think that things are completely bad. They're not. I know a part of him does love me. The bruises are proof of that. Does that sound strange to you? Perhaps it does. You see, that's why I stay. Why I haven't run away.

I feel ashamed. Don't get me wrong, I understand. It shouldn't be that way – woman hurt by man. Most people think it's bad. And so they should, but I would be lying if I denied that there's goodness in it too. He needs me. Only I can help him. And isn't such intensity another face of love? Passion. Proof that I matter very much. Perhaps it is the darker side of love; but dark or bright, at least it is that rare and precious thing that people seek.

Back then I loved him too. Deeply. Then one day I saw a change in him. The wedding date was set and arrangements were in place. It was the smallest shift. If I had mentioned it back then, before I realised what it really meant, you'd have told me not to be paranoid. It was the way he clenched my wrist. He was annoyed at something I'd said. I thought nothing of it then, but deep inside I wondered at the vice-like feeling of his grip. And his sideways glance, his look, the subtle shifting of his brow. All things so easy to ignore. And why should it matter? I was saved, could hardly sleep or eat, so consumed by blinding joy that – well, I couldn't even think. How could I then note such a tiny thing?

Back then, and for some while, things were fine. Fantastic, actually. We went places, spoke almost every day and stared into each other's eyes. That was before I knew what was going to happen next. I don't really want to tell of the violence and the hurt. But I promised you, my love, and so I will. You know you are the only person I will ever tell my secrets to.

And don't worry about my friend. Nothing will stop me from meeting you, but I will take care. After meeting you last time, I took steps to cover my tracks. Secreted groceries in the bin to justify this trip to him, disposed of my bus tickets afterwards and made sure I was back by 5 p.m.

You should have seen me dashing through the aisles at Sainsbury's, grabbing randomly at things. With shopping bags pulling on my arms, I stepped inside. My heartbeat split apart as I saw he was already home. I felt his eyes on me, watching me.

'We needed groceries,' I said, walking casually past him. As I spoke, I kept my eyes averted. It was a lie. My first. And I'd only just begun.

With all my love, until next time.

Mexx

Chapter Fifteen

Escape

My feet were covered in dust as I ran. It formed a ghostly pair of shoes with the rhythmic padding of bare feet upon dry earth. Pale upon my chocolate-coloured skin. The scent of earth about us everywhere. It was getting dark, but still I noticed all this as we moved.

The heavy heat had made the world about us *soosth*;* drained and throbbing, people lying suspended in roped hammock beds. Our neighbours in the Arc were unaware. They sat reclined and hypnotised inside their single rooms, waiting for the cool of night to come. Swatting at fat flies that floated in the air about their face, missing every time.

Mama pushed us out so fast, I left my *chapals*** in the house. As I ran, I felt every grain of sand beneath my feet. I turned back to fetch them, but Mama hauled me back.

'Too late, Mani, it's not safe. We must leave now.'

I wanted to know where we were going and why we were running, but I just followed on as any child would do. Mama held on to Nu like some shoplifter's loot and left me clutching

* Lethargic.
** Sandals.

her sari as it billowed reds and yellows with each stride. We hunched down low, like tigers on the hunt, as we passed the doorways in the Arc. Every door was open wide, with ragged muslin hanging from the frame, waving slowly as our movement stirred the air. The light began to wane and the world was greying down. Mama led the way, her wide white eyes shining in the dark as she scanned the terrain. Something wasn't right. Something I felt I knew, like the feeling in the air before the rain falls in *bersaat*.*

We hunkered down at the corner, breathless, desperate to make it to the main street unseen. Me, Ma and our baby Nu all huddled on the ground. I quieted my breath. I didn't want to make a noise and give away our hiding place. My eyes were blurred with tears.

'Mama, why are we leaving like this?' I whispered.

'Be quiet, child, we can't speak now.'

'I'm scared,' I mouthed in her ear. 'Why can't we just go home?'

'There's something you don't know,' was all she said.

Mr Singh, the banyan tree, shuddered as we crouched, and a shadow escaped from his upper branch. I think Mama saw it too, because she pulled Nu closer, then took her sari – the part that rose from fan pleats on her waist, arched over her shoulder and tumbled to her feet – and cast it over him, like a fisherman netting fish at sea, hiding him away.

She covered him, not me.

'Let's go,' she whispered. With that, we ran, like animals being chased, casting backward glances all the way. Across

* Monsoon season.

the open space before the road. And then together, in a line, we crossed the road, Nu in Mama's arms, his legs around her waist, and me behind, holding her sari. Three slum boys sitting on a low wall to our left watched us as we ran. The middle one had mousy hair that clashed with the darkness of his skin. We paced along the roadside between the crowds. The sounds along Lahore's roads were always deafening; every car seemed to honk its horn for no reason. Horses clattering as *tangas** passed. Dust thrown up in clouds, the smell of burnt petrol fuming in my nose. But that day I couldn't hear the sounds, only the pounding of my fear within my ears. We were lost amongst streams of people walking on the street. As we curved along the outside of the Arc, I kept my face and feelings down. As if my lowered eyes would hide me from the crowds.

Rain had started falling, fat, warm drops that mingled with our sweat as we made our way. In moments we were wet.

Mama added speed into her stride. She put Nu down and held on to his hand. She ran, and as I followed, I saw Nu bumped by her hip, his hand released. In that moment he was thrust into the moving traffic right in front of me. Mama screamed. Nu had fallen into the middle of the road. His lips apart, tears glassing up his pale-green eyes, his blood-red hair swept over to one side. He sobbed. A giant multicoloured truck was coming right at him. The details of it hit me all at once, as if I saw without the need to look. Nu was too small, too low on the road, invisible. The truck was an immodestly jewelled and decorated beast with a baubled

---

* Horse and carriage.

fringe swinging at the front. A giant bride amongst the other vehicles on the road. It was domed up high in front, and its bonnet thrusting out seemed like some great open mouth about to eat Nu up.

I ran into the road and called to him.

'Jump, my Nu, jump, my little one,' I said, just like in the games we played. 'I need to save you from the tiger's teeth.' We often rescued each other from the terrors in the jungle of our minds. The survival games we played in the dusty courtyard right in front of our house.

He looked directly into my eyes, his lips went tight and with one giant leap we caught each other in mid-air. Wrapping him in my arms, I swung around just as the truck swept by. Its force and speed thrust us off the road. The two of us entwined upon the dusty earth; a rolling wheel of flesh, half black, half white.

Mama grabbed Nu from me and squeezed him tight. Then she slapped me, tears streaming from her eyes. Still holding Nu, she started running again. I followed. Our caravan was out of sync, jostling unrhythmically with every step we took. But we carried on. We ran as if the devil followed us. Ducking and hiding at every twist and bend.

As I ran, I scanned the crowds. I saw Papa. A brief flash between the crowds, between the raindrops streaming down my face.

'Papa!' I shouted. 'We're here. Papa, come to us.'

Mama turned to me and screamed: '*Allah bechow*!'* There was terror in her face. Instead of waiting for Pa, she grabbed

* God save us.

me by the arm and ran even faster than before, bumping into people on the street.

I wanted Pa and I didn't understand why Mama didn't wait for him. What had she done that we had to run this way? Whatever it was, it seemed to me that we were paying for her sins. She sliced through the crowd without a care until we reached a drab old rickshaw hidden off the road. It had our luggage in. We got in and it sped off, dodging and curling through the madding traffic in the centre of Lahore.

Chapter Sixteen

Clerkenwell

My memory from here is blurred and the sequence is confused. I recall Ma's eyes, white with fear, firmly fixed upon Nu the whole way through. When we entered the airport, on the plane and as we were led to our new home in this grey and cloudy land. She never really looked at me that day we left Lahore. I trailed behind like luggage, tired and ignored.

I mostly kept my gaze on the shoes the rickshaw man had stopped to get me from the store. Although they were a little big, they were pink and shiny. I liked them. There were too many people hurrying to get somewhere. Taking giant strides. Everyone was in a rush, and if I looked up too much, it made me dizzy and afraid.

Many hours passed and every step beneath me changed. It started with the reddish dust of Shad Bagh, then turned to stony tiles that made my shoes click. That was where Mama handed our bags to the lady sitting at the tall desk. Tarmac that we walked across to reach the metal steps and ramps of the plane.

In the lounge where we waited to board, there must have been a hundred seats. I had never seen so many seats before gathered in a single place. People dotted here and there sat in wait, ignoring people next to them. I took in each in turn. The pretty lady reading a magazine with another braced beneath her arm; the frowning man who was unaware that I was watching him; the sleeping man, his head lolling to one side. I hid behind my ma whenever eyes started lingering on me. I saw a poster on the wall with a picture of a man who looked a little bit like Pa. I smiled at it as I quietly wiped away a tear.

Then we were afloat. The plane took off into the air.

We had never been on an aeroplane before. When it rushed down the runway, I was so scared, I unlatched the belt round my waist, slipped on to the floor and curled myself into a tiny ball. Nu cried, 'Mani!' so loudly and urgently, I'm sure he thought there was no floor and I was falling down towards the escaping land below. It took some while to calm him when later I emerged.

Hours and hours went by on the plane. Nu and I both fell asleep, and when we woke, we played together nervously. I was afraid to look outside. Nu told me we had climbed above the clouds.

The first thing I noticed when we stepped off the plane was the cold, and that the clouds above had fallen down. They were so thick, they blocked the sun. I couldn't tell the time of day.

We were driven in a taxi along roads very different from the roads I'd seen at home. They were clean and dark and had edges that were high. The land beyond them was wet and brown and green. And from the window I could see many trees batched together like a single giant thing.

★ ★ ★

When we arrived in London, I saw the strangest thing. The clouds above had broken up and were floating down and landing about us. They were even falling on us. I looked at Nu and he looked back at me, and then we both looked up. We stood and stared, our mouths ajar. Nu's red crown of hair was quickly framed by little tufts of white.

'It's snowing,' we heard someone out of view shout. Mama rushed us both inside the place where we had come to stay, afraid of what she saw. Nu and I raced straight back out again. We stood with arms outstretched, staring at the sky, and let the snowflakes melt upon our faces. They vanished on our lips the moment they touched, cool and fresh on our tongues. There was something in the swirling movement of the snow; it was as though time itself had slowed. We stared and stared, bemused, until Ma came out to drag us both away.

We stayed with Naboo's friend in Clerkenwell. He had a maisonette inside a block the council owned. It was flat-roofed and square, surrounded by pretty mini houses squeezed together side by side. On the right, St John Street snaked gently down and out of sight.

Abdul was a slight old man; his wife Dalal was tall and wide, with thick lips and deep-set eyes. We sat together when we met. In the corner of the room there was a TV set. Abdul crossed his legs. He was so thin, I was sure he could cross them over yet again. He sat upon an old brown sofa, balding here and there just like his head. As he talked, he stroked his wispy wise-man beard and adjusted the flat cap upon his head. Dalal hardly spoke. She was mostly still as well, her thickened arms in straight lines down her side. She lifted the scarf circling her neck up on to her head as she looked at us in turn.

Abdul whispered something to Ma and to Dalal. Then he voiced a prayer, '*bismillah*' – in the name of God – and then '*la hawla wala quwwata illa billah*', just like Naboo used to say. I stared at him, and my eyes filled up with tears to think how far away Naboo was. Abdul said, 'I know of Naboo's gift. That he can hear beyond the workings of the human ear. No one who knows Naboo well ignores the words he hears inside his hearing ear. The unspoken, hidden ones. And that is why you're here, isn't it?'

Abdul proudly showed us around their maisonette. It was small, with printed paper on the walls that clashed with carpets in an orange tone embossed with swirls. He took us up the stairs, which led to two sleeping rooms and in between them, behind a slatted wooden door, the biggest cupboard I had even seen. There were shelves inside where Dalal neatly piled folded sheets and towels. The first room at the top of the stairs was ours. Abdul said he would get a bed for us in time, but for now we'd sleep on the thin brown carpet. The room was small. The walls were cream and cold, and in the corners the paint had curled and flaked, like white bread-crumbs on the floor. The smell of old *masala** hung on the brown striped curtains. Ma emptied our little bag of clothes and placed them in two piles along the edge of the wall.

The window looked out on our strange new world. The buildings opposite were different from Abdul's flat. It felt

---

* A generic name for Indian and Pakistani spices.

like we were on a ship wrecked upon the shore of a rich and built-up land. There was a street of slender houses stacked together in a row. They had shiny brightly coloured doors. Green and blue and red. Short-haired men and women wearing suits and holding leather cases would come and go through the doors at the same time almost every day.

I crept around the flat for weeks, hiding from our hosts. One day I asked, 'Mama, why did we come so far away and leave our pa behind?' There was fear and anger on her face at once, then she shouted in a whisper, 'Be quiet, child.'

Nu started to cry. 'But Ma, I want Pa,' he said. Mama left the room, unable even to comfort Nu. He ran to me and I wiped his tears and calmed him in my arms.

Mama never spoke a word about Pa or our life before. She spent hours on a prayer mat, praying silently for things she never shared. Something had punctured holes in her where happiness usually went. No joy could ever stay; it always drained away. I wondered if one day Pa would join us here in Clerkenwell. But Mama made me fear. Without the need for her to say, I knew we weren't to speak of it. I knew she'd never tell us why we ran away.

That night, when it was quiet, I heard Mama sobbing, and as she did, she whispered, 'Nafsi, Nafsi, why?'

A few days later, Mama put the TV on in Abdul's living room. A man wearing a suit and tie spoke of devastating things somewhere far away. And then a picture of some starving people came on to the screen, children with pot bellies, mothers watching their babies die before their eyes. Mama, Nu and I were horrified. We cried, reaching out to touch the screen. We felt helpless, weak.

We didn't switch Abdul's TV on much after that, but chose the radio instead. Except after a month, I turned it on and there was a man on the screen who had nearly died in some accident. He lost his arms and legs, but instead of being left an amputee like the ones we saw in Lahore, he became bionic man. It cost six million dollars to make bionic man. They replaced his missing parts with better man-made ones; bionic ones so he could run really fast and, like Naboo, hear things it was not possible for human ears to hear. I wondered quite a lot about bionic man. About how, after mending his broken parts, he became so much better than he started out. I wondered if Naboo had bionic ears. I wanted to ask him, but he wasn't near us any more. I thought, if he did have bionic ears, then he could hear me anyway. So I asked him right from where I sat. I wondered if he heard.

Chapter Seventeen

Want

Many months went by. Nu still asked me why we'd come here and where Papa was. There was nothing I could say and so I lied. I promised that one day Pa would join us here in Clerkenwell, but for now he had to work. Nu searched for Papa everywhere, thought he saw him in the streets, visiting him in his dreams. Part of him was constantly in wait. He would often think of Pa and cry. Not me. There was no trace of sadness in my face. It's true. I hated Ma for taking us away without a reason. And part of me grew cold for knowing only half a truth. It felt like a lie. I didn't know back then that life was filled with broken truths given out in parts. And that things mostly never turned out as you planned.

Mama came to Nu. She embraced him and said, 'It's sunny out, let's walk to Upper Street and I will buy you sweets.' She stroked his hair, smiled and kissed him on his cheek. I ran in front of her.

'Can I come too?'

Her face went straight. 'No,' she said. 'Be good and help Dalal.' She frowned. 'The sun will only darken you more.'

She walked past holding Nu's hand. I saw his hurt. As he passed me, he clasped my hand and dragged me with him.

Ma separated us and closed the door on my face.

A cold and hardened anger grew in me. I wanted to be home, wanted things back the way they were before. Nu and me under a scorching sun, playing jungle in the courtyard of the Arc, having fun with sticks and stones on the dry, dusty earth. But most of all I wanted Pa. I didn't want to be here in someone else's home in this wet, cold land. There was no cricket being played here on the streets, or marketplaces selling multicoloured sweets.

In the house one day, Ma was cooking away, the wideness of Dalal blocking out the light as she moved about. Opening this, chopping that, sprinkling things. The smell of frying onions, garlic, melted butter everywhere. They didn't notice me. Ma had taken off her ring. The gold upon a silver sink. I put it in the bin when she looked away. It felt good. And then I left.

I remembered in Lahore how when Mama took a break, she'd turn and twist her ring. And so I rushed back to the kitchen to get the ring and place it back upon the sink. But the bin was empty. Ma and Dalal were searching everywhere, in the drawers, on the floor and around the sink. Searching for my mama's ring. My tummy started feeling funny. I didn't like what I had done. But I couldn't tell. I couldn't say that I had thrown the gold away.

Chapter Eighteen

Bersaat

Each week we spent in Clerkenwell felt like a whole year. It was as if time was stuck somewhere in the clouds and cold. Nu and I didn't know what to do. Ma would say, 'Go out to play,' but we were scared and there was nowhere to go. So mostly we'd listen to the radio and sometimes watch TV.

One time, after the show was over, we stepped out into the small square garden space behind Abdul's house. We crept warily, as if we were afraid a leopard would leap out and maul us on the lawn. Nothing came. Nu crouched down and stuck his fingers in the ground but couldn't find a stone. Instead his finger caught a lump of sodden earth.

'Do you think it's *bersaat*?' he said.

'How do I know? Perhaps.'

'It must be, it's so wet.'

'But I've not seen the sun at all. Perhaps it's always rainy season here.'

The patch of grass was thick and deep dark green. Nu ran to a small tree and touched the trunk.

'I miss Prince Charles,' he said referring to the young peepal tree in the courtyard of the Arc. I smiled; I'd heard that the real Prince Charles lived in this land.

Nu started searching for stones. There was freshness in the air, and at the edges of the garden there were hedges growing spiky and wild. Something broke the green like a single speck of leaf floating on a golden sea of tea. I picked it up and wiped it with my sleeve. Nu came running over.

'It's a watch,' I said. 'You know, like Papa had.' Papa never let us touch his watch. He'd take it off when he got home and place it carefully on the high shelf that we couldn't reach.

'Mani, Mani, give it to me.'

The watch was round and scratchy gold with no strap. The hour hand had fallen free from time's demands, though it was still trapped within the face. Nu took the broken watch and examined it, turning it round and round. He wound it up, then smiled.

'It has a heart, Mani. Listen.' He held it to my ear and moved his head from side to side. His face grew calm. 'Can we keep it, can we keep the watch?' he asked.

'Why not,' I said.

Nu cherished the watch, hiding it in his pillowcase. He took it out each night to listen to its beating heart. And when he prayed, sitting on a prayer mat on the floor, he always held the watch face in his hand, even as he'd lay his forehead on the ground to supplicate his yearnings to the Lord.

There was a knock on the door, and Mama went to open it.

'Hello, my dear,' said the visitor, looking at us one by one. 'It's nice to see some more of your sort here.'

It was old Mrs Lane from next door. She had purple see-through hair. She sat with Dalal and Ma in Abdul's living room and spoke about the weather and her shopping at the supermarket that day. She examined me carefully.

'How lovely your hair is, Mani,' she said. 'So thick and curly. I wish mine was like that, but I have to put rollers in each night.'

Dalal brought in cakes and tea. Everybody chatted about nothing in particular.

'My doctor, Dr Raj, is from India,' Mrs Lane said, looking once again at me. 'He's been here five years now, I think, since the late seventies.'

I smiled and nodded. I couldn't help but stare. I was sure the purple colour in her hair must have seeped on to her eyelids too. Mrs Lane had pale, silky, ruched-up skin. Her lips had trouble closing over her front teeth, and she had a lisp. She wore a net upon her short, tight curls, which looked as if the rollers were still there.

Mrs Lane took some sugar from Dalal and left. After that, every second or third day, she would come and join us for tea and a chat. I always looked forward to her company.

Ma was fussing over Nu. Again. I felt a gnawing ache. After we went to bed that night, when Ma and Nu were nearly asleep, I sat up. Took a deep breath in, then screamed.

'Mani,' Mama said, 'what's wrong, why did you scream that way?'

'I think I saw some dark smoke seeping through our bedroom door.'

I knew that Mama feared a visit from a djinn above all things. I felt a longing to be loved by Ma the way she loved

Nu. And so, though I don't know why, I hatched a plan to tell a lie.

'*Ahya khair*,'* my mother cried out. She opened the bedroom door, afraid to close it after what I'd said. Then she pulled us closer to her and I could hear her whispering her prayers in fear as we huddled in the sheets. I knew it was wrong, but I smiled a little when the thing was done.

That was when I first realised it wasn't difficult to lie.

* Colloquial expression meaning 'may God bring good'.

Chapter Nineteen

You: bus route 17 to Ludgate Hill

7 December

My dear,

It's only been a few days since we last met, and yet I ache to see you once again. We're meeting on the number 17 by the great domed cathedral of St Paul. It reminds me of exotic lands with the way it curves and peaks and turns. As I write, I'm thinking of your face, the curl of hair that sways upon your brow, the way you worry about me. You must know how much you mean to me. The intensity of it. You see, the love inside me nestles like a tiny bird. A second stomach I think most people just don't feel. But it makes me sick. And I need to let it out. To set it free to take flight upon the wind. That's why I must tell you how I feel. It must be done. Just as a bird will land one day, it cannot fly on endlessly. My love has landed on your heart. I know you feel it too.

Last time we met, I promised I would tell you what happened after *he* proposed to me. But first, my darling, you must understand, things were different at that time.

I thought I knew him, had the measure of the man, but thinking back, perhaps I'd misread the signs. Isn't life a strange amalgamation of such things: portents, pointers, warnings (call them what you will), all hinting at unknown times ahead. One time he and I sat together under the stripy green and cream awning of a café that looked towards a park. We'd sneaked away from school that afternoon. We often did that.

It's sunny and cold. A crisp brilliance in the air with the earthy scent of fresh green shoots breaking through old bark and dark winter earth. Waiters blur back and forth from a kitchen where two rounded, red-faced cooks are busy at their work. Each time the waiters fly around, a cloak of coffee and sweet croissants follows them.

Two waiters come over and start chatting with us. Serving small talk with pricey coffee and the house special: carrot cake. Waiter no. 1 winks at me and then, with an Italian lilt, says, 'Shouldn't you be at school, you pree-ti girl?'

I nearly glance behind, wondering if it's me he means. *He* smiles and answers in my place. 'Perhaps.'

I smile as well, but I can see that he's uncomfortable.

'Your secret's safe with us,' waiter no. 2 replies as he places a finger to his lips.

'Enjoy,' they both say as they scurry away.

He looks away, scratching his head. He is embarrassed, and instinctively I mirror him. It was like that between the two of us. Me watching him, following and copying his every move. When he smiled, I would carefully observe and then smile as well. And so it went.

Now I notice something in his eyes as waiter no. 1 approaches us again. Something urgent and intense. Protective. The waiter places a little ball of chocolate by my mug.

'Treat for the pree-ti lady,' he says.

I am flattered, and it shows in the smile I squeeze back into pursed lips. Just then, *his* arms reach forward like a barrier in front and to my rear. He throws a brief smile to the waiter before looking away. The smile is wrong, forced and wide. His way of signalling: *leave us to ourselves*. I see it now. How I mistook possession for desire. For love. I didn't understand. Nor did I guess where it was leading.

Do you believe in premonitions? Because something in me knew I'd find you on the bus the first time we met. Just like I knew that being caged by *his* embrace in the café meant something. Something bad. I felt a worry in my stomach that wouldn't go away. Dear God, how I wish I'd trusted what I felt, trusted that little bell my grandfather told me about. I am a fool. Sometimes that is the only explanation I can find.

With all my love until we meet next time,
Mexx

Chapter Twenty

Normality

Abdul put us into school, a bleak, grey place. Both of us mastered English. Abdul said it was because we were young. New words could more easily form upon our tongues. After school, Nu and I would play inside or on the street outside Abdul's maisonette, on the green or on the pathway by the road. Sometimes other local kids would come and play with us. They taught us hopscotch and we took them to the jungles we made up inside our minds. The place where rivers raged and tigers prowled.

The day we started school, as we were standing by the door about to leave, Abdul said, 'Remember always, children, the pen is mightier than the sword.' And then he handed us each a plastic pen with the word *BIC* etched into the side. I loved my pen and kept it safe. I noticed as he looked at me he frowned, sweeping his hand over his gaunt face, right down through the wispy beard on his chin.

A year passed and still I missed my life before. There was something simple about how we lived now. So few people that we met, groceries purchased from a single store, and everything was neat: food packaged up, streets swept and people well dressed. Routines were the norm, unlike in Lahore, where one day randomly I'd run around all day and stay up till late, while on another I'd siesta through the afternoon. When we shopped there, we went to several market stalls, and school wasn't always every day. Everything was dusty and we bought vegetables with roots attached, carrying them in our arms wishing we had a basket or a bag. But there was another reason I was sad. Despite the good and bad of Clerkenwell, I never really fitted in. I was a stranger in a foreign land, and people noticed me. Sometimes when I thought about Papa and Lahore, I cried.

By now I knew our ma would never tell us anything of why we went away or why Papa could not come and join us here in Clerkenwell. And anyway, I knew she never really loved me. Not the way she loved Nu. Back in Lahore, perhaps she had to protect Nu with the way he looked, but what did it matter here, since almost everyone was fair? The anger in me hardened, so whatever Ma did, something in me wanted her to hurt. I often whispered to myself, *I hope you hurt, Mama, just the way I do.* I thought of ways to annoy her. I pretended that I didn't hear her when I did, I refused to help and sometimes I purposely made a mess.

One time Ma had told me off for something I had done. When she left, I started peeling blistered wallpaper off the wall. Abdul caught me doing it. He took me and Nu into the living room.

'Mani, Nu, take a seat,' he said, looking just at me.

I perched on the sofa arm, refusing to sit down.

'Life is a test,' he said. 'Respect your mother and God will be happy with you for that.'

I looked away.

'You must bear patiently with life. With the difficulties you face. Trust God, the kind and merciful Lord.' He cleared his throat, then carried on. 'Some things are not for you to know. Just know that things happen for a reason. God wants to see the choices you make.'

Nu nodded dutifully and listened carefully. I started swinging my legs back and forth.

'Mani,' Abdul said, in a firm voice, 'you know the angels on your shoulders make a note of all your deeds. The angel on your left records the bad. The other one your good. Let's make sure the angel on the left has nothing much to do.'

I got up and left the room.

Life rolled on endlessly in Abdul's house. Days and nights added up. The months passed. One morning when I woke to go to school, I calculated we'd been in London for just over three years. And in that time, Lahore had gone quiet in my mind. I still felt like a stranger in this land, but I had learned how to blend in. Sometimes Naboo phoned, but his voice was an echo, crackly and distant like my fading memory of the place where we first grew. Slowly Clerkenwell began to feel like home.

Nu was in the junior school, and sometimes through the fence between the playgrounds I spotted him playing hopscotch and football with his friends. He blended in well.

As a senior in my school I made a few good friends. My best was Jasmine. She was half Jamaican and half something else unknown. We got along and she liked Nu too. We'd go to shops to stare at bags and clothes we couldn't ever own. Still, it was fun. We'd also look at boys and share our dreams of men with whom we'd spend our lives in time to come. We dreamed the dream of every little girl, Jamaican, Pakistani and British too. We dreamed of marriage, romance and kids. And we planned the flowers for our wedding day, the dress and the other things we wanted after that. The house, the garden, the dishes, the bedding. There was very little detail we left out.

I learned, unlike in Lahore, to need so many things. Need became a part of who I was. It made me feel poor. I didn't know back then that all I really needed was some tenderness and love. But our neediness increased. Lipsticks, bags, clothes, boys – and so many other things. The list grew and grew. And we wanted to be beautiful. We bought girls' magazines with pretty faces in and tried to look the same. We started using make-up. Mama told me not to, but I didn't stop. A little lipstick, eyes outlined in kohl and blush upon our cheeks. That was when I noticed something change. I noticed how men's eyes would linger on my made-up face.

Chapter Twenty-one

Shopping

One time when Jas and I were wandering around the shops, testing lip gloss at make-up counters with school books tucked under our arms, I saw a boy, not so different from the many others about. I stopped to watch him as he stared at the display inside a shop. He was holding a large, round Nike bag. He didn't notice me. His hair was dark and flicked back, his face quite slim, his chin a rounded square. And as I stared, I had a strange feeling. It tingled in me scarily. I badly wished to speak to him. Instead I watched a breeze flap his jacket and his hair as he turned and walked away.

In that moment, crazy as it seemed, I thought I was in love. Was this the feeling I had wondered hard about?

Jasmine saw me staring. 'What are you looking at?' she said.

I lied. 'I like the sporty bag that boy's holding.' She started messing with her hair. Then her eyes rose and followed my gaze, landing on the boy.

'Adam, hey, Adam,' she shouted after him. He ambled slowly towards us. Panic tumbled through me and I turned to face a plate of glass, the shopfront to my right. My skin aflush with blood, I was a juicy purple plum. The perfect plastic beauties in the window looked back. Tall, voiceless, white. Angled poses on their slender lengths, and at their side, as if to warn me what I lacked, reflected back at me, my dark and rounded self.

'Adam, how's my favourite Irishman?' Jas said. Then, waving at me, 'This is Mani, aka M.'

'Hello, Mani, aka M,' Adam said, moving towards me, his hand outstretched.

'You're not supposed to shake her hand. She's a Muslim, don't you know,' Jas said.

'I see,' he said, his eyes hypnotising me. He clenched his hands behind his back, leaned in and kissed me on both cheeks instead.

His lips upon my skin, his hands released. He must have felt my heat. I could smell his spicy neck. Felt his hand rest gently on my shoulder. I couldn't breathe or speak. As he pulled away, I nodded. 'Hi,' was all I said.

My lips had brushed against the stubble on his face. I licked them for the taste. Salt and warmth and muskiness. And like the snowflakes months before, his saltiness, his warmth was in that moment gone. But he tasted good. I craved more of him immediately. My jaw relaxed; wetness had pooled in my mouth, as in the urge for food.

'Where've you been hiding this one then, Jas?' he said, a lilting rhythm in his voice. He gazed at me like a tasty morsel on a plate. 'You've got gorgeous hair,' though as he spoke, he wasn't looking at my hair. His eyes in motion moving back and forth between my eyes and lips. 'I'd like to take you out sometime,' he said after a while.

'Don't be silly, Adam,' Jas said. 'She's a Muslim – hands off, you're not allowed.'

'But . . .' I said, and then felt gagged. I hated Jasmine at that moment. Adam's eyes held back, and as he pulled away, the little flutter in me died and in its place there was an ache. I yearned for him to keep on looking at me as he had before.

He mumbled something I couldn't hear, and then he said goodbye and left. I couldn't calm myself for quite some time, and even then he'd often enter uninvited into my mind. This boy called Adam that I'd met by chance.

The next morning when I woke, I could hear leaves rustling in the trees and thoughts of Adam came. And of Layla and Majnun. Naboo used to say, 'Majnun would see her beauty in the rustle of the tree, in the eyes of wild and dangerous animals that he'd befriend, and in the sky at night. Her beauty even humbled down a diamond moon.'

When I thought of Adam over and again, thoughts of Layla and Majnun always came to me.

I got ready for school. I was meeting Jasmine early by the gates before maths. I did well in my classes. I worked hard and it made sense to me. I loved maths the best, especially geometry. Shapes. Circles, pentagons and triangles. And when I learned these things, mentally I sectioned everything I saw. Flowers had six-point symmetry, the leaves upon the trees held circles at their base, and everything had beauty and balance in its form.

At school, in the break between maths and history, Adam came to speak to Jas and me. I noticed how his gaze lingered upon me. Could it be that he liked me as well? Afterwards,

I mustered all the courage I could find. It was so hard to do, I felt my hands go limp and my heart begin to race.

'Jas,' I whispered, looking down, 'do you think Adam would ever be interested in someone like me?'

'Don't be silly, M,' she said. 'You're not his type, and he has a girlfriend anyway.'

Of course, I thought. Why did I think it could be any other way? I would always be a stranger in this land. A different kind of human that no one really understood.

During history, a lecture on kings and queens, I found myself thinking about my own history. About how since we'd left Lahore, life had shifted in such a dislocated way. It was as if the story of my life back there had ended half told. And since that day I had been spending my time searching for ways to make it whole. I licked the strawberry-flavoured gloss, silky on my lips, and thought of Adam once again. I often looked for him, in the crowds at break and when Jas and I went to get our lunch. When I spotted him, every time I'd find that he was watching me.

Chapter Twenty-two

Phone

The phone rang in Abdul's place one day. I picked it up, as Ma and Dalal were out and Abdul was resting in his room. The voice was faint. It said, 'Hello, my *sammili*.'* No one had called me 'mid-brown of skin' since Lahore three years ago. Something in me knew – the tone, the sound, the familiar ring to him – though I couldn't say for sure.

'Do you know who I am?'

'No,' I said.

'*Sammili*,' he said, chiding through the crackles and the hiss. 'Where do you live?'

'We're in Clerkenwell. Flat 9 in Wynyatt Street,' I said, a rising sense of pride that I had given the strange-sounding address in well-formed English. The voice faded away, but the crackles carried on. 'Hello, hello,' I said. And then the phone went dead.

I felt a little strange, but thought no more of it. I straightened the curled and twisted wire of the handset and put it back in place. I told no one of the man who had called or what he had said.

After that, my whole world changed.

---

* Mid-brown of skin.

Chapter Twenty-three

Dead

Don't tell anyone you were there.
   Only God knows.
And Pa.
How's anyone ever going to love you now?
You see, my mama's dead. Nu hardly lives.
It's because of me.
I didn't save my ma or Nu. I hid myself away to save my own skin. It was me, just me, that did the killing in that room.
Don't make me think of it.
Let me believe it isn't true.
Forgive me, God, for what I am.

Chapter Twenty-four

Aftershock

With Mama's passing, something in me changed. Something died and something else became. A curled and darkened voice that mocked me everywhere I went. A sadness searing through my blood.

It's true that with certain things, words run out.

I've nothing more to say.

Chapter Twenty-five

Investigations

The police asked their whats and wheres and whens. They came in pairs. The ones I remember best were the last that visited. Before that was a blur. The older one was fat; he widened at the middle so folds of him completely hid his belt. That was Jim. Or John. His partner was tall and thin with translucent grey skin. He had moles and the slightest stubble on his chin that looked like dirt. I don't recall exactly, but I think his name was something like Tom.

They looked nervous. Treated me as if I were an injured animal. If they spoke too loud or fast I might attack, or more likely crumble up.

'My name is Tom,' the tall one said. 'We are so sorry for your loss.' He motioned for me to sit. I ignored him, kept staring at the ground. 'You will be contacted by Victim Support and also by our counsellor for youth bereavement. And as you know, Abdul and Dalal have agreed to become your legal guardians.'

Then Jim or John spoke. 'We are going to ask you some questions about what happened. Do you feel up to that?' I nodded, with eyes averted. Abdul stood next to me. 'Where were you when this took place, Mani?'

'I'm a senior, sixteen years old,' I said, 'so I often stay at school quite late, much later than our Nu.' I paused, then added, 'He's twelve.'

'You were at school,' Tom or Jim or John said. 'When you returned from school, what did you see? Did you see anyone inside the house?'

'No,' I lied. 'When I came home, I found Nu and Ma alone.' How could I tell the truth? That I was there, and instead of saving Ma and Nu, I chose to save myself? How could I admit my cowardice? And if I told them Pa was there, what would become of him? What would that do to the fractured remains of who we used to be?

I knew that no matter how I felt, I had to keep my eyes still, stop my feet from shuffling, in case in movement my lie would wordlessly reveal itself. No, I would not say. Something wasn't right. I could not link the killing with my pa, no matter how I tried; couldn't reconcile it with the good in him I'd witnessed all my life.

Tom, who did most of the questioning, spoke again, scratching the stubble on his chin. 'Mani, do you know who could have wanted your mother dead?'

I dipped and shook my head. I don't think he believed me. His stare was icy cold.

'Was your mother's behaviour different in any way in the weeks before this happened? Can you think of anything at all?'

I answered with raised eyebrows and a small jolt of my head. They watched me carefully, then stepped inside the room where Mama died. I stood on the landing with my back to the airing cupboard door. Hiding it. Fearful of its testimony; that it could bear witness against me. From where I stood, I could see them in that room.

Tom asked me, stepping out again, 'Is there anything you want to tell us, Mani? Did you hear or see anything as you entered the house that day?'

Perhaps they knew.

'I . . . I . . .' was what I replied. Words and thoughts refused to form.

'It's OK, *beta*,' Abdul said.

I left. Walked away, stepping slowly down the stairs, resisting desperately the urge to run.

They questioned Abdul and Dalal again, then went back into the room. Measured things, touching the floor and walls around the protected zone. I heard them speaking, saying things like 'culture' and 'their ways', as if that made it OK. Every now and then they frowned.

Eventually they went away.

The police never caught Ma's murderer despite everything they did. They never knew that it was Pa. And when reporters came, hiding in the bushes, cameras hanging from their necks, the smell of wet and sweet and smoke about them like a cloak, Abdul sent them off. I'd see his skinny bearded silhouette chasing them and swatting after them like flies. Eventually it seemed the newspapers had nothing more to say.

There followed days and nights that merged into one. Abdul and Dalal watched me carefully, wonder, shock and pity about their eyes. They wouldn't touch me. They kept away in case that rare and vicious germ of tragedy could spread.

I understood.

I felt it too.

★ ★ ★

After a week, Naboo came to the UK. He flew in from Lahore a broken man. He kept touching the flat cap upon his head as if to check it hadn't gone. He wasn't as tall as I recalled from years back. He had aged so much. His hair had gone and his skin looked like a brown paper bag that someone had screwed up then flattened out again. I was so happy to see him. He hugged me hard into his doughy flesh as he cried. My tears made a scatter pattern on his white *kameez*. The smell of mothballs mixed with Surf and cardamom filling up my nose. He told me that everything would be all right, that God would make things good again. I listened, nodding, not believing anything.

I became a hollow thing. And a few weeks on, when immigration sent Naboo home, I cried endlessly. Throughout the day as well as the night.

One day, Abdul called me to the living room. He struggled hard to say anything at first. I stared at him, the muscles in my face all weak.

'*Beti*,* everything will be all right in time. Let me teach you something of life. There are reasons why things happen,' he said, almost whispering, 'that we cannot ever understand.' He sighed a deep breath slowly out.

'It is like when *Khidr*** with his inner eye saw things that no one else could see. One time he punched a hole inside a boat.

---

* Daughter.
** A mystical figure widely known as the spiritual guide of Moses (literally: the Green Man).

His companion saw the damage, not the calamity he had saved the boatmen from. Later, the king ordered the seizing of all seaworthy boats. You see, *beti*, we just don't know.' He came and sat beside me. 'There is a reason why this happened. Trust in the Lord.'

I didn't nod, or smile or say a single word. I stood and walked straight out of the living room.

Chapter Twenty-six

You: bus route N38 to Buckingham Palace

14 December

My dear,

Every now and then I worry that *he* may suspect. My love for you is a grand palatial thing. So big that sometimes I fear it will spill right out of me. Today I'm sure he monitored me walking round the house. Staring like he hoped to catch a sign of us, some evidence: coy smiles perhaps, or dreamy eyes. But my love is hidden deep where he can't find it. If he had X-ray eyes, he'd see it like rainbow-tinted butterflies filling up my heart. But I promise you, he will never know. Our secret love is safe.

I've been telling you of him. What I haven't got to yet is what happened next. After those little signs I told you about last time. The signs I didn't note. My friend suggested that I tell him straight, and so I did.

'I have a job at the local library, two hours a day,' I say.

He flicks his eyes away as if I'm an unpleasant thing to see. Funny, that's the bit that hurts the most.

'What's the point?' he says. 'You've got me to earn money for us.'

'But—' I say.

That's when he huffs and walks away, shoving me to the side. Hard. I ricochet against the wall. There's more shock than pain, and then a thrumming in my flesh that creates an off-beat rhythm with the thumping of my blood. I feel jumbled up and out of sync.

'Sorry,' he says. 'It was an accident.'

He moves to me, concern distorting his face. I'm shaken, of course. But then I make a choice. I choose his version of events. I don't argue or resist; I feel limp. I know now that it's because a part of me, somewhere deep inside, knew that I was lying to myself. A lie that started changing everything.

And now.

Well, it's just a way of life. The hurt. The hate. And it's not like I'm blind. There are times I see it too. Like when jumping on the number 17, I caught a glimpse of skin reflected in curved steel. It was warped and bent, but even then I saw the cut on my cheek and the purple shade beneath.

Look. I know what you're thinking. And you're not alone. Last time on the bus, I knew that everyone was staring at me. The young woman to my left, throwing sideways glances when she thought I was looking away. The old man across the aisle making out he was stretching his neck to see the tall buildings as they passed. Even the little girl sitting in front who turned round, perched up on her knees and stared stonily at me as kids do.

Their eyes all asked me the same thing: why do you stay?

That's so tough to explain, my darling. I am afraid. Not just of him, but sometimes, it seems to me, of everything. I cannot picture life beyond him. Will I crumble and die, or become some echo of a person once alive, like a dried-up daisy pressed between the pages of a book? And so it goes . . . and I stay. Does that make any sense to you?

Don't worry about me, my dear. People hate bad things happening to them, but they really shouldn't. You see, bad things lead to good. Let me explain. There's always been a you-shaped hole inside my heart, my missing part. I've known your scent, your feel, that we were meant to be together, before we even met. That may sound strange, but it's true. And stranger still, I know there's a reason for the bad things in our lives, the things that slice us half and half. They're growing pains that stretch the heart to let our truth fit in. And you are my truth. You see, my love, do you see? *He*'s the one that's slapped me straight to you.

Until next time, near the Palace's grand and ornate gates on the N38.

Forever,

Love from Mexx

Chapter Twenty-seven

After

I sat with Nu in hospital. He was unconscious, cold and still. The doctors said there was much to do. Bones had to be reset and internal bleeding kept under control. There was no certainty he would survive. I didn't fear the words they spoke; it was the things held back that filled me with dread. I saw thoughts begin to form inside their heads, which in a moment's indecision they'd swallow back again.

Endless hours ticked away, and Nu didn't move at all. I'd watch him, sitting close but careful not to touch his damaged flesh. Then something sharp would stab me from within, and I would lean and hover fingers underneath his nose. The precious rhythm of his breath upon my fingertips. Warm and moist. Then I'd sit back again and wait.

The floor was white, with multicoloured speckles caught within, and when I tired, the speckles danced about for me. Nurses and doctors came and went. Shuffling through the pages of the red file hanging at the foot of Nu's bed. Some of them were nice; they would smile and ask me if I needed anything. Others kept their faces straight and acted like I was invisible to them. There were lights and LEDs on a screen beside Nu's bed. I'd stare at them until they blurred into a smudge of red. Often I would sleep. A jagged, dreamless sleep from which I'd wake more tired than before.

Nu looked like a puppet whose strings had been abruptly cut, slumped in the bed, his head angled to the side. His skin was red and blue, with stitches holding parts of him in place. For weeks and weeks I sat with him as others came and went. I never tired of watching him. It was as though somehow my watching eyes were keeping him alive. I also watched the patients in the other beds, the visitors who came and went. Not just Abdul, Dalal and Naboo, but others I had never met before. Widespread news of the attack had attracted spectators who came to gorge upon the white-skinned Pakistani boy; the one who'd managed to escape death. Some brought flowers; others came with good wishes and their prayers.

I also stared randomly at things inside the ward with the time I had to kill. It was the window that I gazed at most. How drops of water gathered on the pane from a misty rain. Occasionally they flared up orange and alive as they caught the headlamps of a car going by. They trickled in a stop-go way, then, after resting for a while, they'd join with other drops, growing heavier and big. Eventually they'd lose their hold and race quite suddenly down towards the sill. It reminded me of when, some years before, Nu and I had crouched to watch a lizard chart a crooked path upon a rock. And the path my tears would take as they moved jaggedly towards my chin. Was it all connected? Was it all one thing?

As I sat with Nu, I learned that silence was as real as the sounds that filled our ears. At times it was so loud, I had to leave the room. As I waited endlessly, Nu seemed to grow. I was sure that he was getting bigger day by day.

* * *

I jolted in my seat. Realised I must have been asleep. The air smelled sour, and for a moment I didn't know where I was, or why. And then, perhaps it was the nap, but something seemed completely out of place. I scanned the ward. Everyone appeared to be asleep. As I breathed in deep and raised my arms to stretch, I saw that the way Nu looked was wrong. I stood, afraid that he was leaving me behind. Panic pressed upon my throat and I ran into the corridor to find a nurse. I found I couldn't form words. Instead I held on to the nurse's arm and pulled at her to come.

'Don't you touch me, girl,' she said, repulsed.

'My brother, he's . . . he's . . . Please come quickly now.'

With wide and steady strides, she paced too slowly over to Nu's bed. She checked him and the monitors, then pursed her lips. 'He's fine,' she said. 'Who are you anyway?'

'He's my little brother, Nu,' I said.

'He doesn't look much like you,' she said with a frown of disbelief. 'Now go home to your parents. I'm sure they'll be worried sick. You shouldn't even be here anyway.'

When she had left, I sat motionless for a while. A single teardrop left my lower lid and pathed that jagged line down to my chin. She's right, I thought. That's exactly where I should be. With my ma underneath the earth, a cold, breathless, buried thing.

In the many hours that I sat with Nu, I caught the eye of a new nurse. She came up to me and said, 'Visiting time is over. You must leave.' I heard the words but they made no sense to me. She may as well have asked me not to breathe. I wasn't going to leave, no matter what she said. She must have thought I didn't understand. She gave in with a huff and let me stay.

As the days and nights went by, I watched the light about me change. It rolled endlessly, like a lighthouse beacon on the sea. Bright, then dim, then fading grey before it brightened up again. I lost the sense of time as if I were lost at sea, floating wearily, never knowing if I'd feel again the firm earth beneath my feet. Days flashed by and nights vanished in a blink. Weeks turned into months and time ebbed away, and a realisation came to me with total clarity. My purpose on this earth was Nu. What God himself had appointed me to do. The meaning of the devastation that I felt.

Nu was unconscious for many weeks. As if a part of him wished to join our ma. Eventually he began to wake, left our Ma and came to me instead.

The day he first opened his eyes and looked at me, I held his hand and told him everything was fine. When the medics came rushing to his bed, I left calmly. I walked into the corridor and went into a storage cupboard with linen on the shelves. I closed the door behind me, paused, then heaved and sobbed tears of relief and joy mixed with agony. I fell on the shelves and clutched on to sheets, landing on my knees, a mess of linen before me on the floor.

'Dear God,' I cried. 'Thank you for saving my Nu. Thank you thank you thank you.'

I lay prostrate upon the sheets in the shape of a *sujood,** my

---

* Prostration, where you kneel and place your forehead on the ground.

forehead pressed upon the floor. I cried so hard I couldn't stop.

'Dear God, I promise to take care of him. Thank you for giving me a reason to go on.' With the breathing of my precious Nu, my own breathing could continue too. 'Forgive me my sins, the things I did to harm the ones I love. I love you, God, for granting me this, even though I'm not worthy of the gift.'

When my sobbing calmed, I wiped my face to hide my tears from Nu, breathed in deeply and returned to his bedside.

At first as he came to, we spoke of silly little things. The taste of orange juice, or the trees framed by the little window next to him. When fast asleep he often held something: a crushed plastic cup or a spoon from the lunch he'd hardly touched. I brought him his watch face, the broken golden thing he clung to night and day.

I never spoke about the night Mama died. I hid my shock and grief inside. Away from Nu. I wouldn't let him see me cry. The only thing I knew was that Nu must come home. I had to be the person I had always been. There was nothing I wouldn't do for him.

But I noticed something change. Nu became increasingly distant. He never held my gaze; his eyes would flutter off another way and refuse to meet mine. He started saying strange things. Speaking of the taste of sadness and the scent of joy.

'People with different-colour skin have different-colour feelings,' were the words he said the night I knew that something wasn't right. He smiled at me as if it made perfect sense. As if he was talking about the weather or the healing of his wounds.

After that, he lost his need for words. Just like that, my brother became a mute, a silent soul. I pictured words trapped deep inside him, trying to escape. They never did. He sat quite still, eyes averted, tranquil. It seemed as if the real Nu was curled up in a ball, hidden deep inside the body I could see.

I noticed other changes. He started tapping randomly at things. Two fingers of his right hand moving rhythmically. *Tap tap* pause and *tap tap* once again. A book, an envelope, or his other hand if nothing else was close. With me he was calm and still; he only tapped when others were about. Mostly he would tap on his watch, the little broken face we'd found in the square of grass where we played, matching his fingertips to its ticking. Did it remind him that he lived despite what he'd endured? Despite what I had let Papa do? And when the watch stopped, he'd wind it up and carry on.

Chapter Twenty-eight

Silence

Nu was in hospital for months, even after he came to. In that time I tried so many times to talk to him. To hear his voice reply to me. I missed the company of words. But when I spoke to him, lashes all aflutter, he would lift his eyes and look away. I felt a sinking despair, a place where even tears refused to go. I had lost my ma and part of Nu as well.

One day I gazed into his face. I said, 'Nu, please look at me.'

I moved across the room to where his eyes had flown. He was focusing intensely on some distant space. When I tried again, his eyes took off once more, landing somewhere else.

'Why won't you speak to me, my Nu?' I said. 'Please look at me. We can talk about things you'd like to do.'

Nothing. Just a boy who acted like I wasn't in the room. And then I said, 'I brought your stones.' He turned to me. Our eyes momentarily met, and then his fell away to where he thought the stones would be. I showed them to him. He picked one up and examined it. A dark, smooth, rounded one. He looked at the stone the way I wished he'd look at me.

And that was when I could finally see.

His silence spoke. It spoke so loud it drowned all noises

out and I heard its words. It was in things that he placed his trust, not people; not even me.

I had to write the silence down. I had to write what I had said to Nu so many times before. For months my words had gone unheard. I felt so alone. The love he pushed away, the many things I wanted him to know. I had to crystallise my thoughts into a solid form. I took a scrap of paper from my bag and wrote: *My darling Nu, you know I love you.*

I loved him deeply, even more with the constant hurt inside for what I'd let Papa do. I prayed he didn't love me less.

He picked up the note and examined it just as he did his stones. As if he saw the paper, ink and letters but not the words. And then with a stone in hand, the way he used to scratch in the dirt, I saw him write. He didn't look at me – there was no warmth or familiarity – but I could make out the dents and rips and gentle folds the stone had marked upon the paper. Tears upon my cheeks. My darling Nu, my companion by night and day, had in his childish hand written: *Love Mani.*

That was when I knew what I had to do.

Chapter Twenty-nine

Writing

The first was very simple.

> Dear Nu,
> You know I love you very much. Do you remember when you were four, or was it five, how you'd jabber on as toddlers do about your toys and favourite food (carrots with a yogurt dip). And how you warned me not to touch Mum's lipstick when I went through her things. You told me it had insects in because you heard her say it gave her bee-stung lips! And you always loved 'and-gels'. Said you saw them everywhere. You loved my 'el-la-bows' too. You still like elbows now, don't you – moving the loose skin at the bend, examining them and reading them the way a gypsy reads a palm. I wonder what you see within the folds and dents and peaks. I wish you could speak to me, my Nu, like you used to.
>
> Love and kisses,
> Mani

I handed it to him, and he held it to his face, too close. Then he swung his head from left to right, a playful cartoon reading scene. He looked into my eyes. And he smiled. It was his special smile, the one that filled a room. I felt conscious of myself. As if I sensed a stranger's stare. A swell of joy rose in me.

Then, as if he'd done it many times before, he took up the pen and wrote in his childish hand, *I am 7* – the 7 back to front. He must have been confused, because he was twelve.

I felt a strange and special warmth. I knew right then that somehow things would be OK.

Like pen pals sending notes from distant lands we shared ourselves through ink and pen. And that was how the letter thing began.

I sat at home on my bed that night, staring at the dull colour of my bedroom wall. There was mould creeping up from the skirting board and the wall had bubbled like boiling water frozen in time.

It doesn't matter, Nu, I wrote. Pencil on a torn-up envelope. *Words are only little puffs of air, just momentarily there. Much better that we scribe them down so we can once again hear their sound. That's not so bad a thing for me and you, my darling Nu. That the words we share can live again on other people's breath.*

Love you Nu.

I never gave it to him, though. I folded it to the size of a two pence coin, then squeezed it into the crack where the built-in wardrobe met the wall. And when I looked at the crack, I felt the muscles in my body relax a bit. I knew this was a sign that maybe things were going to be OK.

Part Two

Chapter Thirty

Arranged

My full name is Rahman although everyone calls me Mani. It means 'mercy'. And mercy finally found me in my sixteenth year.

Over six months had passed since Ma had left, and Nu was close to whole again. He attended a special school with speech therapists on site and saw a doctor at the hospital each month now that his diagnosis was confirmed.

Naboo and Abdul made plans for me to marry in a hushed and hurried way. They failed. The news spread fast. In the local Sainsbury's I bumped into our neighbour, batty old Mrs Lane. This time she had pink tint in her hair.

'So you're to marry Khan,' she said. The constant tremble in her chin made her seem much sadder than I think she really was. She hesitated. 'I've known him many years, you know. He's a darling, good as gold. Such a shame about that dad of his; he was a nasty piece of work.'

I dipped my head and smiled.

'How wonderful for you, my dear,' she said as she smiled at me.

Naboo wanted desperately for my marriage to be confirmed so he could be relieved of the burden of an unwed orphan girl and know that I would have a home of my own. He said there was to be no delay for fear that things might turn, minds change. It was the only thing to do now, with Mama gone and, except for Abdul and Dalal, no one here for me or Nu. He came to me in the living room when I returned from Sainsbury's that day.

'People,' he said, 'are looking for bad words to say of us.'

He wouldn't stand for wagging tongues, not after what he'd seen. Every day he wept for Ma.

'I keep thinking of the twisted words and evil hearts that led Hira to flee. Leave her home because her son was fair.' He frowned. 'She had to leave to save our Nu,' he said, then added as an afterthought, '. . . and you.' I watched him carefully. 'And now I've lost my girl.' He sobbed in a quiet, breathy way. 'My good *masoom** girl, innocent of the thing they accused her of.'

He looked so desolate and lost.

'Your father said that he would do it even if she ran away. That he would find her. But we never really thought he would. I can't bear to think of what that *shaitan*** did; what that man became.'

Naboo hugged me in his arms and reached for a letter beside him on the sofa.

'And Nu. See what that monster did to Nu,' he said.

He held the letter up to me. It was from the hospital.

* Innocent.
** Satan, devil.

Dear Guardian,

We have been working with this patient for some months. Nu is a strong young boy who is tall and well built for his age of thirteen. In group sessions he has tended to be withdrawn and does occasionally isolate himself socially. This patient was not born mute. His condition came on after suffering severe trauma that left him in a coma for some months. Since then he has suffered total mutism with no partial speech ability or whispering-style communication observed. Following extensive tests and examinations and despite a presentation of auditory neuropathy, we are satisfied that Nu does not suffer from this condition, and therefore his auditory physiology and ability to hear remains unimpaired. There does not appear to be any physical disability, although we have diagnosed a degree of social anxiety, particularly in loud or crowded environments.

There are episodes when this patient rejects auditory stimulation. We are not clear as to whether this is voluntary or involuntary. Speech perception ability becomes poor to non-existent at these times and the patient loses understanding of spoken words. Studies highlight that commonly such individuals may be able to hear sounds, which we believe to be the case here, but during such episodes they have difficulty recognising spoken words; sounds may fade in and out and speech can seem out of sync. Of particular interest and unique to this case is that this patient during such episodes remains capable of reading communications and can even respond in writing, notwithstanding his rejection of auditory stimulation. Rejection of auditory stimulation (as is the case for most patients with trauma-related mutism) is indicated by an inability and/or refusal to maintain eye contact.

We should add that we have observed extreme episodes on two occasions. At such times the patient freezes, standing motionless, and is incapable of communication of any sort, including written. We are encouraged that this has not been a frequent occurrence.

We are satisfied that his overall physical recovery from trauma is excellent, but this does not indicate possible recovery from mutism. It is our experience that if a patient suffering from trauma-related speech loss and mutism does not regain speech ability within a period of six months, the prognosis for recovery of speech becomes increasingly unlikely. As we discussed, the six-month anniversary of this patient's loss of speech passed a few weeks ago.

Mr El-Amin

Consultant Neurotologist

I handed the letter back to Naboo. He folded it and flicked away tears at the edges of his eyes. I didn't want to think that I'd never hear Nu speak again. I steadied the wobble in my chin, pursed my lips and breathed in extra deep. Naboo spoke.

'Your marriage will fix a little of the damage to our family.'

He was trying to rebuild our lives.

'*Inshallah*, if God wills, Khan will be a good match. He's quite fair; a handsome man as well. I think you'll like him, *beta*.'

I nodded, saying nothing. I knew I simply had to do as Naboo said. 'It must be done,' I'd say aloud and in my head, ignoring the trembling doubt inside my breast.

Chapter Thirty-one

Breathless

I met Khan first at Abdul's flat, the place we called home. Tradition asked for many things, but most of all a chaste and modest girl. So contact was supposed to be controlled.

I wore a black *choori dar** with a red and gold *dupatta* round my neck. I liked the way the fabric of the leggings ruched and gathered tightly round my legs. And how the flowing long *kameez* was cut from the knees, a slit that travelled confident and straight right to my waist. I tamed my curly mess of hair and tried to brighten my dark skin with blusher. I touched my lips with gloss and trimmed my eyes along the rim with a black liquid line, which I lifted at the edges for a movie-star effect.

Khan came with his mother and uncle. I held my breath. He was a blend of East and West. Princely, hazel-eyed and tall. All golden dimpled cheeks and sandy hair. Could it be that he was interested in me? I thought as our eyes met. Abdul's living room seemed in that moment far too small. We sat together speaking about Islington and Clerkenwell. There was laughter in the room.

* A traditional dress worn with tight ruched leggings.

Nu came in with biscuits on a plate just as Khan looked at me, an angled glance, his hand before him like a mask upon his nose, as if hiding in plain sight. His eyes were wide and steady. He smiled. It was a luscious private smile that he pulled back when Abdul looked at him, as if to guard it like a gift for me alone.

In the background, like the chatter on a radio, I heard Naboo say, 'She's so much better than someone raised here in the UK. She knows the traditions of her land.' Then he turned to me. 'Did you know, *beti*, Khan's doing A levels at the same school as you.'

Leaning towards me, Khan cut in. 'This is strange,' he said.

'What do you mean?'

'We need to lose these guys.'

'OK,' I said, looking at the floor.

'Let's do it,' he whispered, as Naboo asked if we'd have some tea.

'Yes,' he said, 'for both of us,' not even asking me. It set a flutter free in me. Our eyes met, then, in a flash, he pulled both his eyes towards his nose just as Naboo spoke. A clown with wobbly eyes. A lurching laughter rocked me back and forth. I morphed it to a cough and ran out of the room.

Naboo, still chatting, called after me, 'Get some more biscuits, *beti*.'

Khan and I disappeared together, along the corridor and out. We ran on to the green, the patch behind our maisonette, and sat on the cool spring grass in the sunshine. For the longest time he gazed at me, a small smile upon his lips. His eyes had me falling into a deep abyss. No one had looked at me that way before. My own eyes misbehaved and I couldn't return his gaze. They leapt around the scenery, landing on the privet, grass and bricks. Anywhere but Khan.

He told me his dreams: the house he'd one day own, his desired career, how he'd save up to pay for university and his love for Rumi and Shakespeare. He had a lot of dreams and hopes stacked up in a row. I nodded every time he paused. I didn't tell him mine. I didn't mind. My dreams weren't long enough to queue. I would have finished very quickly. The dream that Nu would speak and Ma could be with us again. Or that once, some time ago, I'd felt a strange but real love for a boy I'd never met. And on that day I'd found my secret dream of perfect love, I'd felt it on my skin, that gentle, soft and rounded thing.

The pull of him disrupted everything. My thoughts. My focus and my breathing too. A little whirling feeling turned and turned inside until it grew so big it crushed me. I had to stand and concentrate on breathing. I moved away. He slowly stood and stepped towards me. Hesitation. A moment's pause. My breathing growing deep. Another step. He reached for me. His thumb, it seemed by accident, swept upon the meeting of my parted lips as he reached to touch my face. I stepped backwards, still facing him, abrupt and awkward, and then walked away. He ran to me and took my hand.

'I'll meet you tomorrow after school – don't tell, and I won't either.'

I ran back to the flat, my heart a rhythmic drummer, a beginner learning how to play. I felt a mixture of fear with strange, unsettled tinglings. I controlled my deepened breath and walked into the room where Naboo was speaking in detail about things my racing blood wouldn't let me understand. I drank my tea and didn't look up again.

When the visitors rose to leave, I noticed that Khan stood close to me, his arms spread wide about me like a cage, a guard against the world, a sort of ownership. As he left, he swung back to glance at me as if to claim me for himself. Something of his that he'd come back to take away. It made me feel I mattered in a way I'd never felt before. As if the world itself now turned because of me. Excitement rushed around me and then forward out of sight, to some faraway unknown. A dream began to form. A future that was mine, a life I'd care about. I felt a rising joy.

Perhaps the hard and hollow times would now shrink away. And though I didn't know if it was love, I felt it must be something close. Like a movie scene with a couple in a pose. Khan had eclipsed my world. Everything that went before was blinded by his brightness into something very small. Even Adam shrank away, an infatuation I could now ignore; small and monotone before the multicoloured Khan.

My time with Khan felt both wrong and right at once.

But it felt good.

As good as I had ever known.

Chapter Thirty-two

Sleep

That night I couldn't sleep. A sparkling, pleasant anxiety was swirling and dancing inside me, like something twisting and turning in the sun. It just carried on and on.

The next morning when I woke, I couldn't put my mind to anything but the vision in my head of Khan waiting for me at the school gates. I dropped my breakfast cereal on the floor, couldn't pack my bag and nearly walked into a wall. A lovely sickness rolled around inside me that made food tasteless on my tongue. I looked at my reflection in the mirror for a long, long time. I put some balm that smelled of mint on my lips. Pressed down my bumpy hair, lifted the corners of my mouth to smile a bit. By the time I had to leave for school, I thought I looked fine.

Later in the day I asked Jasmine for some gloss to brighten my lips. A little colour to enhance the shape. She smiled, her eyes nearly closed, and said, 'Who is it then?' She held her make-up bag away. 'You have to tell me, or no lipstick.'

I looked down, holding back a smile. She noticed and latched on to my arm.

'Tell me, please, please,' she said.

'It's nothing really, just a boy who came to see us yesterday. He wants to meet me after school. At the gates.'

'Oh, I see,' she said. A smug and knowing smile across her face. I couldn't hold it in.

'Jas, I have to tell you. He wants to marry me!'

Jas breathed in deeply, then screamed. I screamed as well. We grabbed each other's hands and started jumping up and down.

'God, that's amazing, but . . . but you've just met. And don't you think you're too young?'

'No,' I said, 'it's the best thing for us, with what happened to my ma.' I hesitated. 'And with Nu the way he is.'

Then she made me up. When she had finished, I examined the result in the bathroom mirror. I looked like a clown. A pretence of beauty with me hiding underneath. I hated it and washed it off at break.

Chapter Thirty-three

You: bus route 78 to Tower Bridge

19 December

My dear,

I'm writing as I wait for the number 78 at Tower Bridge where we plan to meet today. Sitting like a princess waiting for her prince, back straight and nose a little up. Sparrows hop near my feet, hoping tensely for an offering.

I wonder, do you ever see people, my love, with those almond eyes of yours? I don't mean look. I mean really *see*. See them as more than just people on a bus going from A to B. Take the man who sits beside me on the bench. Grey hair and tired skin. He reads a paper, but when he looks up, do you wonder what he thinks about? I don't believe he's only looking at the buildings and the street. I am sure he's thinking of the love he left behind on holiday more than fifteen years ago. And how his heart shattered when he left, unable to confess his love for her.

As I stare at Tower Bridge, its colour merges with the sky. It's as if it wants to hide. Like me. The towers look like something from a fairy tale. I think about

Rapunzel trapped in the upper room of the tower nearest me. What if the handsome prince was trapped in the other tower, so they could never meet? What would they do then?

I'm so glad that you are free, not trapped in some tower far away from me. You are the prince I've been waiting for and you're coming here for me.

Last time I told you about The Push. After that, something in me changed. My friend kept asking, 'Why are you so jumpy and unsettled? Is something troubling you?' As she spoke, her lower jaw would shake.

I was afraid. Afraid that I would set him off again. That I'd step out of line and lose his love. And I started doubting everything. But then he brought me tulip blossoms wrapped in green tissue and tied with silver ribbon at the stems. How fickle I am, because those flowers brushed away my fears. He's fine, I told myself. (Silly me!)

How wrong could I have been? Since then the dark-ness and the bruises have been growing by the day. Until you. You've changed everything. Now when I close my eyes I see my vibrant times with you. It fills me with such joy. It's only when I open them that I find I'm alone with nothing but a creeping fear. It's the fear of hidden things. Things you'd never guess at, like words, and looks, and what they can become. I am terrorised by normal life. Thank goodness I have you to soothe me and take away the ugliness I feel.

With love,

Mexx

Chapter Thirty-four

Gates

History was the last class of the day. Thoughts of Khan, imaginings, streamed like a movie in my head. Everything else was simply interrupting that. Pauses in my private show.

Excitement squeezed my stomach small so nothing could fit in. But I felt hollow too. Sleepy. No. Weary perhaps. Worn down by the anticipation of meeting Khan again. I hated history at school. Grey-suited Mr Martin, with his spiky fading hair, his sunken eyes, his monotone drone about the history of a world that was not mine.

'Your grandparents may remember this,' he said.

Not *my* grandparents, I would find myself thinking. Naboo couldn't tell me about the Blitz or rationing or the bomb shelters they slept in until dawn. I was an alien from a different world. A guest to smile and nod at, which Mr Martin often did as if to excuse himself from the need to understand exactly who I was, what I was doing here. I had no interest in his stream of words, like a TV left on after the show had ended. Today, with Khan in mind, I was also aware of the classroom's dull and constant smells: fabric mixed with the sweet and sickly adolescent sweat that hung in pockets here and there.

There was still an hour before Khan was due to arrive at the school gate to collect me. I liked the word *collect*. I whispered it silently within the cavity of my mouth – *collect, collect, collect*. I had mastered English within months of moving here. I mastered elocution too. Softened my d's, made clear distinctions between w and v, and whispered out my t's. And I never lost my fascination for some English words. Just the thought of them could twitch my tongue or a muscle in my face. Like so many words I liked, this one had other meanings too. *Collect*. It said I belonged to another, was being taken away, gathered up. Perhaps, I thought as I watched Mr Martin's lips move, it could mean even more.

My thoughts would roll along like this, but equally I could stop them dead. That was something I'd learnt to do since the day Mama died. Now the scratch of chalk on board jolted me back into class again.

I brushed my hand along the smooth grey laminate of the desktop and trailed my hand downwards. The pale wood was almost completely blue, inked with protestations of everlasting love mixed in with obscenities and doodles. I ran my fingers over the nicked and dented wood. Every time I looked, it was the love hearts that caught my eye, with names of unknown people scratched or penned on either side.

When it came to four o'clock, I felt faint as I scanned the crowds around the ornate school gates. There was no sign of Khan, only the usual din of a thousand voices speaking at once, punctuated by shouting and laughter. A momentary thrill rushed over me as I saw his face flash in the crowd, but then it dissolved away again. I looked around frantically, not sure if I was seeing things, hopes and dreams creating made-up scenes. My stomach shifted, a hollow squeeze as I felt someone stroke my arm from behind. Khan stepped up and smiled. He looked like a caramel dessert, tall and slender in sunshine that paled and shone his hair to gold, his curled black lashes sprinkled around his milk-chocolate eyes. He had on jeans with a pale blue shirt. Jasmine looked at him with rounded eyes and smiles she pulled away then gave back out again. Jasmine was usually so confident. I'd never seen her act this way.

'Hi, I'm Jas, Mani's best friend,' she said. He looked at her, then straight away turned back to me.

He said to Jas, his eyes still on me, 'I've come to kidnap Mani, hope that's OK with you.'

'Only if you take me too,' Jas said, then giggled something else I missed. I was breathlessly in awe of Khan. I couldn't hear or see things properly. The crowds, the building, even the sky was a single blur of everything that wasn't him. Even though he stood some distance back, his musky scent wrapped itself around me.

Jasmine giggled, her head cocked sideways, fingers interlaced, arms swinging side to side. When Khan looked at me, I found myself smiling at the tarmac at my feet. He placed his hand on my lower back and guided me delicately through the school gates. Jasmine shouted her goodbyes and walked away.

We went to a café. I sat in silence, feeling stupid. Khan said, 'I've been really looking forward to seeing you again.'

'Really?' I said, raising my eyes but not my head.

'Don't be shy,' he said. 'Or I'll have to leave and write to you instead.' Could he know that I wrote to Nu?

His face relaxed, his focus gaining strength.

'Ah, I am relieved,' he said. 'It's nice to see your eyes. And I'd rather speak; I'm not the best at writing things.'

I smiled. 'What do you want to know?'

'Let's start with your favourite things.' I held my breath, as I knew I couldn't tell the truth: that my favourite thing was him.

'I like good food, with lots of chilli in,' I said.

'Ah.' He smiled. 'I'll bear that in mind, especially as I like my food mild. Come on, what else? I want to know all about you. What's your favourite colour, your favourite films, what are your dreams?'

'I don't know,' I said. 'Favourite colour, red, perhaps.'

'I see.' Khan sat back in his seat and stretched. 'You want me to make your mind up for you? Tell you what you like?'

I laughed. 'Perhaps,' I said, thinking of the colour of a wedding dress.

'And films, do you have a favourite one?'

'We don't watch too much TV,' I said, 'but I quite like *The Six Million Dollar Man*. It's about this man who nearly dies after a fatal accident and gets rebuilt into a superman with robot parts,'

'Ah, I see you have high expectations of me,' Khan said.

He made me laugh and we shared so many thoughts. He told me how he'd waited for that special one to call his own. 'I knew I'd know immediately when I found the one for me,' he added, winking a gentle half-wink. It made my stomach turn and then constrict. As he spoke, he touched and tapped me on my hand. His goldenness upon the plummy purple of my skin. It sent electric warmth up my arm and made me want to touch him too. I didn't. I knew it wasn't the thing to do. I was from Lahore, and I knew some things as naturally as parched earth knows how to drink. I knew of purity; the primacy of chastity. I knew it not through words but through the world in which I'd lived. Purity was a woman's gift. I had to save myself, make sure that I was chaste for the man I would marry. I really hoped that it was Khan. And somewhere deep inside, I knew my feelings also had to do with Ma.

'Mani,' he said, 'I've never told a single soul this thing I want you to know.'

I felt flattered by his words.

'My father beat me every day until he left when I was twelve, and I've never seen him since.'

I was surprised at the rise of feelings in me. I was equal parts angry and upset at the thought of someone harming Khan.

'That's terrible,' I said. 'It must have been a relief when he left.'

'That's the strangest part,' he said. 'I miss him terribly. Wish he'd stayed.'

As we walked home, darkness was creeping in at the edges of the day. Khan stopped abruptly a street away from where I lived. I thought at first he'd dropped something. I stopped with him and looked around our feet. But then I felt his hands on my elbows. He paced me gently backwards to the wall. I felt it cold and hard against me as he pressed me back. Force and hesitation equally. He smiled at me and tucked a stray curl behind my ear. I didn't know what was happening, but I felt powerless, possessed. His breath had deepened and he seemed to struggle with himself, certain and reluctant both at once. I couldn't breathe, and there were pounding sounds in my ears. I didn't understand the way I felt. Couldn't comprehend the power of Khan's touch. He leaned in to me. Without a moment's thought I moved my face away.

'I can't,' I said.

His finger trailed up my neck and ended underneath my chin. He lifted my face. He was so close, but holding himself away. He slowly breathed in, breathed me into him. I could smell his musky skin, felt his breath upon my skin. Against my will, I leaned forward, reaching up to him. He held me back, a prisoner, my passion contained. He smiled, then stroked his thumb across my cheek right to my ear and gently down my neck. He skirted round the fabric neckline of my dress. My breath deepened. He stroked my face, four flat, broad fingers making a circle around the heated roundness of my cheek, then ran a finger in the rising and falling of my lips. I licked them for the taste of him. All muskiness and salt.

Something in his face had changed, his brows buckled up, something pained and frantic in his eyes he struggled to contain. He seemed to breathe in endlessly. I thought I might die, my own breath so deep and ragged, my heart thumping erratic drumbeats in my chest, all my strength deployed to keep myself stone still. And then he slowly stepped away. Bowed like a prince and rolled his hand. 'Beautiful Mani. Come, let's go.'

As we walked home, he caressed my hand. 'Mani, you did nothing wrong,' he said. He must have seen confusion in my eyes. There were so many feelings within me. The greatest of them being my need for more of Khan. He had me mesmerised as he winked at me, then smiled and led me to my door. 'Let's meet again,' he said.

'How about tomorrow?' I suggested too fast.

He pulled his lips back tightly in a smile and nodded, proud of something I didn't understand. Then he placed his hands on both sides of my neck and kissed me gently on the head.

I watched him as he walked away, his form contracting in the dark, but then he swung round and came back to me urgently.

'God, Mani,' he said as he took my hand, 'I'm missing you already and I haven't even left.' His eyes kept poring over me as he cupped my left hand with both of his, then raised my palm to his mouth and held it there. His lips against my skin, so soft and warm, sapped the strength from my legs. 'I'll see you sooner than you think, Mani, perhaps even at school.'

I smiled at him, unable to respond. He was the prince I'd been dreaming of. And then he left for real.

I was distraught. If I had not been brought up in Lahore, I would have run behind him begging him for more. But I had never learned to act upon a want. I needed him, needed more of this strange magic that was Khan. For once I knew that someone saw me before the colour of my skin, made me feel as if I belonged for the first time since I came to the UK. I didn't chase him, though. Instead I went straight up to bed and laid the palm that he had kissed upon my lips. I couldn't sleep or think or eat. From that day on, I could do nothing but dream.

Chapter Thirty-five

Love?

In the morning when I woke, Nu was sitting next to me. He knew I was distracted. Full of the anxiety of possibility. He looked sad, his head hanging down as he leaned on his hands. It was cold, and my breath made a little cloud of fog as I sat up in bed. We hadn't put the heater on and the room looked drab. The balding brown carpet curled its corners up as if it too felt the cold.

'I'm so happy, Nu,' I said quietly, feeling the ache for Khan gnawing at me hard. It was as if I hadn't said a thing. I took my pen and the brown envelope he held in his hands and wrote:

> My lovely Nu,
> You know I love you. I am so happy and I want you to
> be too. It's Khan. I think he is the one. I wonder if you
> prayed for him to save us from our misery. A silent
> prayer that no one else could hear. From you to the
> Lord, my darling Nu.
> Mani

I handed him the envelope. He dropped it to the ground,

then fell off the bed and knelt on the floor.

'What is it, Nu?' I said, kneeling next to him. He took my hand and reached my fingers up to the air before us. 'What do you see?'

I feared this was another strange and different behaviour in Nu since Ma left. That was when I saw the golden circle shining on the floor. A blinding shard of light had entered where the curtains didn't quite meet. It made a slender run of sunshine that ripped across the room and split the place in two. Silver floats of dust were dancing in the spotlight that it made. It took my breath away.

I thought perhaps he hadn't read what I had written. I picked up the envelope, thinking I'd throw it out, until I saw, scribed in his crooked childish hand, the words *Nu happy too*. He must have done it when I looked away.

He took the envelope from me and, turning it around, my words facing down towards the ground, started tapping it with two fingers. Nu had developed other senses too. I knew his tapping was a warning sign that someone else was close at hand. His agitation grew and the tempo of his tapping increased. I opened the bedroom door to find Dalal bent forward, ear pressed against the wood. She nearly fell. She looked at me and I looked back at her. She left. Even if she had bionic ears like the man on the TV, she'd never hear our thoughts, the silent messages we wrote to one another in place of spoken words.

Nu was still kneeling on the floor, his arms outstretched to where the light had been, as though in supplication to the Lord. He turned to me, and both at once we silently laughed, our hands upon our mouths, our shoulders juddering.

I took his hand and kissed it on the back, then placed it on my cheek.

Chapter Thirty-six

New universe

Things were moving fast. The phone call came a day or two after I met Khan at the school gates, although it felt more like an age. It seemed as if he'd meddled with the universe, slowed the pace at which the planets in the sky created time. Each second, like a reel of film repeating round and round, ballooned into a tortured ball filled with the time he held me up against the wall. I yearned for the freedom I had felt at that moment. The strange and contradictory calm of loss of all control, both in my body as he held it back, and in my soul as I became possessed. A bystander in my blood and bones. I yearned for the rhythms of this love, the musicality of breathing, blood and thumping heart. When, I wondered constantly, would I see Khan again? He had created something new, an urgency in me. I felt distracted, weak and urgently in need. It was so much more than mere desire, this need to breathe him in. Water, oxygen and food would no longer suffice.

'Of course, next week on Friday will be fine. We'd love to finalise the plans.'

It was Naboo. That morning, as I was about to leave for school, I heard him on the phone. I dropped my school bag on the floor and hid behind the door.

'I am happy if it happens soon. We'll be with you next week at six.'

He called to me. 'Ay, Mani, *ither ow*.'*

I appeared so suddenly from behind the door that his eyebrows jerked up.

'Are we going to Khan's next week?' I said, too casually, annoyed immediately that I'd revealed I'd been listening in.

'Yes,' he said, his eyes exploring me suspiciously. 'They want the wedding date to be set and they want to make it soon. Make sure you're ready, *beta*. It's great news.'

'OK,' I said, hiding my excitement as I skipped out of the door. I wondered how I could manage one more moment without seeing Khan.

School in the morning was a blur of lessons that meant nothing. As Jas combed her hair in front of the mirror in the washroom, she asked for every detail of what she referred to as my date with Khan. I refused to let her call it that and said I'd just met up with him. I flushed a bit as I wondered what the word 'date' meant anyway. We walked along the corridor towards the school canteen, the smell of boiled cabbage and chips hanging in the air.

'Did he kiss you?' she asked as she set down a plate of chips we'd agreed to share.

'Don't be silly,' I replied. Then I looked away. My words were not a lie, but they didn't feel much like the truth.

She tapped her fingers on the table and pursed her lips.

* Come here.

I knew that no one in her family had ever married. She'd told me about it once on a break as we combed our hair to try and make it straight.

'Did I ever tell you,' she said now, 'about my aunt who lived with this man for years? Ironed his clothes and cooked his meals. She even bore him several kids. But he never married her. He took off a year ago with a girl half his age.'

I picked up a chip and chewed on it even though it burned my lips, not sure what to say to that.

'So your grandpa wants you married, then?' Jas said.

'Yes, it looks that way,' I said, holding back a smile.

'Why do you think Khan is interested in you? I don't mean to be rude, but look at him.' She eyed me up and down. 'And look at you.'

I knew exactly what she meant. But, I thought, it could be that he liked girls who were different from the way he was. Perhaps, like birds of paradise, I was the plain female and he the magnificent plumed male.

'I had the sense you liked him too,' I said to Jas.

'Not at all, I was just being polite,' she said. 'I just mean don't let his good looks fool you.' She flashed her eyes at me. 'I forgot to say, Adam's coming round my house later today. You should come as well.'

But Adam wasn't Khan. And only thoughts of Khan now circled inside my head; endless daydreams in which I was powerless, possessed and in his arms.

'I can't come round, Jasmine.' I took another chip and added, 'Anyway, it wouldn't be right.'

History with Mr Martin was next, and I wished that lunch would never have to end. I put two chips at once into my mouth and listened to the drone of braided voices, the clattering of cutlery, the mesh of echoes sounding out at once. As I looked across the room, my mouth overfilled with chips, there was Khan leaning against the wall with a friend on either side, staring straight at me. It was the first time I had seen him at school, as the sixth form had their own classrooms and canteen. I nearly choked. I dropped my eyes and let my curly mess of hair fall down and veil my face. I started examining my nails, then flicked my hair back and shot another glance towards him. He was still watching me. The ache of shyness overtook me and I looked away again.

'What's wrong with you, M?' Jas said as she slathered ketchup on the plate. 'Aren't you hungry any more?'

I reached for a drip of ketchup that was hanging off the plate and swiped it up with my index finger. I sucked my finger nervously, thinking of Khan's eyes upon my skin.

'Jas,' I said in a hushed tone. 'It's Khan.' I motioned with the slightest tipping of my head. 'He's over there and I think he's watching us.'

Jas looked up. She smiled her widest smile and waved high and wild towards Khan and his friends, beckoning to them to come to us.

'Don't, Jas,' I said, but she carried on. My stomach closed and blood burned underneath my skin until I knew my cheeks were turning burgundy. He was walking towards us with one friend in tow, the other still leaning on the wall. I breathed in, filling my lungs, and started fidgeting, not knowing where to put my hands and feet.

'Hi, Mani, Jas. How are my favourite girls?'

'We're great, aren't we, M?' Jas replied on my behalf.

'This is John. He's doing A levels as well, another wannabe engineer like me.' I weakly nodded my hellos.

'Wow. There's too much brainpower on this table,' Jas said. 'No, wait. Mani and I set that right.' She juddered out a raucous laugh.

'Speak for yourself,' I said, feigning offence.

Khan ducked his head to examine me. 'Are you blushing, Mani?'

I shook my head as nerves and streams of heat took away my ability to speak. I hated the crippling effect he had on me. Khan was a drug that seized me up but of which I could never get enough.

'You *are* blushing, M,' Jas said, making a show of my embarrassment for everyone to see. 'You look like a juicy plum.'

'Plum,' Khan said. 'The perfect name.' He cocked his head a little to the side and teased, 'My juicy Plum.'

'So now I'm fruit to you?' I answered back, stretching a thin-lipped smile across my face. 'Is that the best you can do?'

'Well that depends,' Khan said, rising to the challenge. He crossed his arms and leaned back in his chair. 'I have to spend more time with you if I'm to find a better name.' The chair was small against his broad, angular back, and when he spoke he had mischief in his face; his tightened smile, his half-moon eyes.

'What are you guys doing here anyway?' Jas said. 'Why aren't you in the sixth-form canteen?'

'They do better chips here,' John replied as both he and Khan snatched a handful from our plate. Jas slid it away.

'I see,' she said, smiling widely and nodding suggestively

as she swept her eyes from Khan to me. She looked up at the canteen clock. 'Come on, M, we have to go, it's nearly time for history.'

I moved to rise too fast and caught my foot between the table leg and my chair. I stumbled awkwardly. Khan lurched forward and I broke my fall upon his arm.

'Are you all right, Mani?' he said. He kept his hands around my waist even after I was balanced once again.

'Fine,' I said, feeling like a fool, not knowing where to look. When Khan released his hands, Jas was some way off with John.

'Why don't you come with me this afternoon?' Khan whispered. 'You can catch up on history another time.'

I hesitated. One part of me, the good girl, felt the urge to scurry to lessons. The other part, the unfamiliar me, was magnetised, an explorer drawn to unknown lands.

'I'm not sure that's something we should do,' I said.

'Come on, Mani, let's have some fun.' And even though I hadn't yet decided what I should do, he shouted out: 'Jas! We'll see you in a bit.'

Jas waved from the far side of the canteen as she left through the double doors. Khan winked, then reached down and took my hand. In that moment, my resistance fell away and I was shot through with currents of electric joy. I smiled a bashful smile. I had stepped upon a boundary and crossed the line. I knew right now that I would do things I shouldn't really do. And so I nodded and said, 'Where are we going, then?'

'You'll see,' Khan whispered in my ear. 'We'll have some fun and I'll get you home at a sensible time.'

The warmth of his guiding palm upon my lower back tingled through the thin fabric of my shirt as he led me to his car and took control.

Chapter Thirty-seven

Cambridge

Khan reversed into a space between two cars, hoisting himself up to look behind as he did. It was an expert move, the way he spun the steering wheel and measured distances and angles in his head. He leapt out of the car, and before I released my belt he was already opening my door.

'Come, Mani,' he said as he held an upturned palm to me to help me from the seat.

Cambridge had ballooned unexpectedly, a city cast between so many fields and tagged by an endless road named the M11 motorway. Approaching, I had opened my window a little and noticed the rising scent of citrus freshness in the spring air as it lapped my skin. I could smell the greenness of the fields and trees, and instinctively I sucked it in. The radio played music and there was a talk show afterwards. A woman by the name of Joan called in complaining how her husband never took her anywhere. Then a man spoke of how his lover had saved him from his misery.

Khan took me by the hand and led me along a cobbled street, pointing out the buildings and the colleges around.

'Cambridge is my favourite place in the world,' he said, 'and that's why I brought you here. Did I ever tell you that I hope one day to study the engineering tripos here, although I'll take a year or two to work and save a little first.'

'No, I didn't know,' I said. 'How amazing that would be.'

'I'm starting work in engineering after my exams. It's happening so fast, and then you can give up school and I'll look after you,' he said.

'But I'd like to stay at school,' I said.

'No need, my Plum, you've got me,' he said.

We approached St John's College from a busy street. He took me to an arched entrance with a church-like feel; inside, I was surprised to see great grass lawns caught like wildlife within stony walls. Walking back along the street, we reached a marketplace. There was a scent of waffles sizzling inside a tent: vanilla, cream and dough. It reminded me of cooking sweet *paratha** on a scorching *tava* in Lahore.

'That smells like something I remember from back home. Have you ever had sweet *paratha* fried in butter?'

'God – that was my favourite. I remember it from when my father was around.'

We bought waffles and chewed on them amid the tourists and the shoppers. I was transported to another world, a world previously unknown to me. Tense and joyous at once. As we walked across a field called Jesus Green, past children playing chase and couples lying on the grass, knees up and elbows splayed, he turned to me, his eyes fiery.

'Let's sit down for a bit,' he said.

We approached a grand old tree that cast a skirt of shade. It reminded me of Mr Singh, the banyan tree in the courtyard

* A type of flat bread.

of the Arc. I had the urge to greet the tree the way Nu would do, but I held it in. Its branches formed a ragged dome of secrecy. We ducked underneath the boughs and I sat with my back against the trunk as Khan lay down propped on one elbow facing me. There was a scent of earth and mashed-up grass. The ground was freckled by dappled sun.

'Mani, I know I've not mentioned this before, but I think I should . . .' His voice trailed away.

'Go on, Khan, what do you want to say?'

'I know our marriage is being arranged,' he said, 'but I am a person of both East and West, and it matters that I speak to you as well.' He leaned towards me. I had the urge to press myself into the security of his chest. As if he sensed it, he kept his distance as he searched for the words he wished to speak.

'I just want you to know that I can't imagine how difficult life must have been for you after you lost your ma, and with Nu hurt so bad.'

I looked down, unable to reply.

'I want you to know that I feel for you with everything you've been through.' He lightly touched my leg. 'And I will care for you.'

Recollections of the past year came to me and I hugged my knees to my chest, buried my face and curled up into a ball.

'Mani, I've thought hard about the things we suffer in this world.' He paused and edged closer, his voice dropping to a whisper. 'And I think mending is the point.' I raised my head. 'I believe that when we break, and then we mend . . . we're stronger at the joins.'

He ran his fingers through my curls, looping one around his fingertip.

'I'm not saying I could ever understand what you've been through. But I know about the mending of our brokenness.'

'Khan . . .' was all I could say as I wiped misbehaving tears from my eyes. 'God must have sent you personally to save us.'

He smiled.

'Since we arrived in the UK, I've always felt out of place,' I said, 'as if I don't really belong. My accent, my appearance.' I paused to look at him. 'Since you've been in my life, everything has changed. For the first time ever, I feel as if I am exactly where I should be.'

Khan said nothing. Slowly, slowly he moved towards me. I didn't know what to do, so I froze. I could smell his muskiness, and it was as if the park around us had disappeared. He stroked me on the cheek, then kissed me lightly on the lips. I could never have guessed what would happen next. An electric shock, and I gasped as if the air around had disappeared. Blood rushed to my face, and I leaned further in to him. I felt his palms upon my cheeks, anchoring me. I clenched his wrists instinctively and my body tensed itself.

'Steady,' he said. There was a wolfish look, a pleasant fury in his eyes as they raced wildly about my face. I gathered myself up. Remembered I was in Cambridge, on a green. I pulled myself away, clutched the grass to calm my dizziness.

Khan smiled and edged back, staring up at the sky while hanging on to his knees. 'That was . . . interesting,' he said.

'Hmm,' I replied, averting my eyes.

He lay down on the grass and closed his eyes. I watched broken sunlight washing back and forth upon his chest with the gentle stirring of the leaves.

A couple walking by raised their hands to motion hello as they passed. I wondered if they saw my joy. The world poured into my eyes, brilliant and bright, as if I was seeing things for the first time. The sky was blue and high, the air alive, and the sunlight magnified the glory of buildings framing the green some way away. Three children played tag, a mother pushed a pram and a small group of people picnicked over to the left, handing out sandwiches and drinks. I wondered then how it was possible to enjoy the company of people I'd never meet.

'Come on, Mani, enough sitting around,' Khan said. 'I want to show you something else.' He jumped up and slapped the grass off his jeans, then took my hand and helped me to my feet.

We ambled through parks and greens, past threads of people wound around the cobbled streets. We paused before King's College Chapel, rising up with its narrow symmetry and grace. Inside, standing in a liquid pool of light, I marvelled at how like love it seemed to be; so cavernous yet intimate as well. Khan stroked my cheek.

'Remember what I said to you.' He tipped his head to see the great fanned arches up above. 'It's a sort of vow, Mani, a promise to my Plum.'

I looked up. I thought of all the promises echoing eternally above, cupped inside great embroidered palms and witnessed by the stony fingers pointing to the Lord. The filigree reminded me of henna laced upon a hand. The hand of a bride-to-be.

Afterwards we wandered to Parker's Piece, with its stretch

of pathways cutting out a lover's kiss. I sat down in the open space and Khan sat facing me. The clouds above were making shapes. I saw a fish and a mountain range with many peaks, before they folded to a mass of nothingness. Things are and then they're not, I thought, thinking of Ma and life the way it used to be; that must be the way it is.

'First,' Khan said, 'I have a treat for you.' He rustled the brown paper bag that he'd been carrying. 'As any decent Eastern man knows, mouths must be sweetened on the announcement of good news.' He opened the bag and held up a doughnut. 'We're in Cambridge, not Lahore, so no *ludo*,* I'm afraid. Now take a bite.'

I closed my eyes and bit. Some jam squelched out and dripped down on to my chin. I reached for it, but he stopped me; with his other hand he scooped at it, his eyes focused steadily on mine. My heartbeat quickened as he licked the jam from his finger and ate the remaining doughnut in two bites.

'And be ready,' he said as he wiped his mouth. 'There's more.' He lifted a fine gold chain with a charm attached from the pocket of his shirt. The gold reminded me of Mama's ring. I closed my eyes and squeezed the thought away.

'That's beautiful,' I said as he handed it to me. 'Thank you.' I lifted it up high to take a better look.

'It has an eye on it,' Khan said, 'to keep you safe from *nasr*.'**

---

* A sticky round golf-ball sized sweet made from lentils, milk and sugar.
** The evil eye.

I thought of the tradition from Lahore, where people believed that a jealous glance could harm. *Nasr*, the evil eye, was said to be banished by the wearing of a prayer scribed down and folded into a bead or amulet.

'Here,' he said, as he clasped the chain around my wrist.

As I watched him, I did something I never thought I could. I reached to him and with my fingertips I stroked his face. I felt it then, so slight I could have been imagining it. He shuddered at my touch. His slow intake of breath confirmed the tremble I sensed. Then I felt his fingers lightly trail a disobedient path along my thigh. Instinctively I pulled away.

Khan stopped abruptly and contracted back into himself.

'I'm sorry, Mani,' he said.

Something in me lurched as he backed away. I longed for his attention, though in equal measure I feared the power of his touch, feared the boundaries he made me want to cross. And so I spoke.

'When I was a little girl in Lahore, I used to play Naboo's *bansari*. I was quite good at it. We used to sing, too, Nu mostly, with me playing the flute. I liked to draw pictures in the sand with Nu as well, though his were always much better than mine. I was better at "jungle", a game we used to play. I loved Lahore, and I miss it, especially the warmth, although it's mostly too hot there . . .'

I couldn't stop myself even as I knew I wasn't making sense. I was casting words at him to haul him back to me. Khan shifted closer, his eyes intense upon my face. I spoke of Mama and our school and the trees inside the courtyard of the Arc. And as I spoke, I picked a daisy from the grass and sniffed at it.

He gently took the daisy from my hand and smiled. He picked a couple more. Something in my random words, it seemed, had pleased him very much.

'Did you know that I'm a man of many skills?' he said.

'No,' I answered.

He started linking the daisies into a chain, focusing to prick a tiny hole in each stem.

'Well I'd have never guessed,' I said. 'You can make daisy chains.'

'I know,' he said. 'You tell anyone, you're dead.'

When he was done, he placed the chain on my wrist.

'You could say that chaining daisies is an engineering skill,' I said.

Khan huffed a gentle laugh. 'Yes, I like the sound of that. Perhaps I'll put it on my application to this place.'

Was it the sunshine magnified upon pale ancient stone, the scent of grass and muddy earth, or was it Khan? I don't think I'll ever know. But I do know something in me changed. That afternoon in Cambridge, the girl in me curled up and in her place a woman started to emerge, confident and sure.

Chapter Thirty-eight

You: bus route 43 to Monument

My dear,

Last time as I went to catch the number 43 to Monument, I nearly lost my letter to you. The bus arrives and I step up and miss. I slip. My letter floats upon a breeze. I run for it, leaping up as if I'm trying to catch a butterfly. The driver of the bus shouts, 'Watch out, there's traffic coming up ahead!'

I don't care. I mustn't lose this note. It lands by the kerb, in a patch of wet on the other side of the road. I pick it up and wipe it on my coat, then race back to the bus that will take me to my love. To you.

Eventually I see the Monument itself between new buildings either side. It rises like a finger pointing to the Lord. Its golden tip makes me think of the many banks surrounding it. Why do people hanker after gold? No one ever seems to have enough. Don't they know? It isn't gold that glitters, it's the heart.

On the bus, the upper deck where I always sit, there's an old lady walking up and down the aisle. She speaks to any stranger who will hold her gaze. She has a woolly hat on her head, pulled down low over grey and dented skin, and she's handing out tiny purple sprigs, then reaching out her hand to take a fee. I can smell the lavender. It smells so sweet, with just a hint of savoury. As she approaches, I jerk my face away before our eyes meet. Too slow. She knows. She puts a posy in my lap and says, 'No charge to you, my love,' then walks away.

I wonder if she pitied me. Could she see the hole in me that yearns for every part of you? Did she feel my sadness too? My hurt? You see, it has to do with *him* and what came next. The next part of the sorry story I've been telling you.

To hurts, he started adding threats. Mostly things he could do if he chose to: divorce me, dump me on the street and so on. They always got me panicking. Funny how his threats often hurt more than his blows, although they also carried on. One time he was angry for a reason I didn't fully understand. He threw a small frying pan at me, and where it hit, it grazed my skin. Then he slapped me, flat palm upon bare flesh. And so it went . . .

You were upset with me last time, though you tried to hide it. I know why. It was the bruise on my cheek. You asked me again: why do I stay? I've told you of my fear, but there's something else. Each time I'm hurt, every time it happens, I forgive. Who am I to judge? I think. And anyway, isn't forgiving another way to love, another word for it?

There's more, something I've not shared with you so far. It's this. The way he treats me could be my own fault. I'm not going to talk about it, but I did something wrong, something you don't know about, and so it's possible that my suffering is payment for my misdeeds. That's just the way it is, or could be anyway.

On the flip side, my love, you are my reward. For my patience and the suffering that I've endured. You know, as I left last time we met, the sun laid down a palm of heat upon my face. It made me think. When gentle sunlight warms our skin, we never think of how it came about. The blazing fire reaching us through the dark, cold void. My love for you is the same. It travels endlessly to you, through loneliness and pain. It's a Great Fire consuming me, though you only feel my tenderness and warmth. But you should know, my dear, love rages fiercely in me.

Love always,
Mexx

Chapter Thirty-nine

Guilt

It had only been a few days since Cambridge, but I missed Khan terribly. Things were moving fast, plans were being made. Soon we'd make a formal visit to Khan's family. I thought about the outfit I should wear, running my hands over the options in the drawer. There was a dark red velvet *shalwar** kameez*, or a black one with a camel-coloured scarf. The velvet felt soft against my palm, and I touched it to my face, thinking of Khan's finger tracing a line on my cheek. Life was about to change, and perhaps because of this, thoughts of the past filtered through my mind. There were things I'd never said to Nu. Things I'd never asked. Things I hadn't been able to face until now. And so I took a pen and wrote:

> Dear Nu,
> I've wanted for so long to speak to you about that day, but I never knew the way. I don't even know if you remember it. Do you remember it, dear Nu? I don't want you to hurt, but do you recall the things you saw,

---

* Loose leggings worn in Pakistan.

the things that happened? And do you remember who was there? It's just that since that day, I've never had the heart to ask these things of you. First you were unwell, and then . . . well, then my stomach felt so sick every time I even thought of it.

But Nu, things are changing now. It's hard for me to hold the secret privately, and harder still for you and I to never speak of it. I know I go round acting like nothing ever happened to our family, but the truth is a dagger sitting deep inside me, and I must be sure it never moves. Knowing what I know and keeping it inside hurts me like a stabbing in my gut. And I feel it every day. I made a decision, you see, my Nu. I made it alone and now I have to live with it. But I couldn't see another way. I still can't. I am calling all my courage to my pen, and hoping through my words that my courage will extend to you. So here it is.

It was Pa. Pa was there, do you remember that? And it was Pa who took away our ma and injured you. Will you forgive me? Because, my darling Nu, what I've never said to you is . . .

I was there too.

I can hardly write the words, tell you of the shameful choice I made. My Nu, I hid myself away when Papa did the thing he did. Forgive me that I didn't try to save you from his hate. Believe me, it's hard to live with it, my cowardice. But I made my choice and every day I am ashamed of who I am. A girl who saved herself and let her loved ones suffer and die.

But then things followed on. They always do, don't

they? And I knew I could never tell. Never name our pa. And so I made another choice.

I lied.

The secret cut itself a deeper hole inside my gut. It burrowed down, a creature that I have to keep inside. Nu, I know I stole the truth from you and Ma. But what was I to do? We must be loyal to our own, protect the remnants of our family. I don't want the world to think badly of Pa. Perhaps he wasn't well. Perhaps he was possessed. Either way I couldn't see him locked away, with Mama gone as well. And so I covered it up: that Pa, the man who cared for us before our world turned upside down, our own flesh and blood, did that thing he did. And you mustn't ever tell on him. It would be wrong to splinter what's left of who we are. No matter what, he is still our pa.

We never need to speak of it again, my Nu. I just wondered if you knew. And I want to share my guilt with you.

Do you forgive me? Please, Nu, I so hope you do.

With all my love to you,

Mani

I folded the page in half and went to Nu. He was in the bedroom. Slowly I opened the door. He smiled at me and held up a picture of a horse.

'Wow, Nu. That's amazing,' I said. 'You're such an artist.'

Behind me, my hands unthinkingly folded the letter once again. It was in quarters then in eighths. I kept on folding until it was a little square in the centre of my palm.

I walked to the window and looked outside. I couldn't bring myself to give the note to him. I opened my mouth to speak, and then closed it again.

I watched the trees in the distance. Their branches waved gently as if to say hello. They calmed my troubled soul. As I looked down, I saw a gap between the windowsill and the frame. Nu was focused on his drawing on the floor. I slid the folded letter deep into the crack, using my fingertips to wedge it firmly. Back at the door, I rested my eyes upon both the windowsill and the trees. I couldn't focus on them both at once, but I didn't care. I enjoyed the blur of comfort as I thought of my note nestling deep inside Nu's bedroom wall.

After a week, we set off to Khan's family home. Naboo, Abdul, Dalal, Nu and I. There were many pleasantries, tea was served with pastries and plans for the wedding were put in place.

As I got up to take a teacup into the kitchen, Khan called me over to the door. We stepped out on to the street and he took my hand. 'How is my Plum today?' he asked, his eyes scanning my face.

'OK,' I said, 'but can I ask you something?'

I told him that I didn't really care about rings or romance. But there was one thing.

'Khan,' I said, 'can Nu come to live with us as well?'

'Yes, of course. I wouldn't have it any other way,' he said without a pause.

With his words, I knew that things would finally come right. Nu would join us in our life ahead.

I smiled and breathlessly placed a kiss upon Khan's hand.

He leaned into me and kissed my cheek. I couldn't breathe and pulled away.

'We must wait,' I said, anxious not to break the rule of chastity and worried that we'd be seen. Khan smiled and slowly stepped away, running his finger down my cheek.

'OK, my Plum,' he said. 'It's not long now . . . it's not easy, but I'll wait.'

At home that night, through the open window of my room, I stared up at the midnight sky. I was sure the stars were shining brighter than I'd ever seen before. I thought of the beauty hidden from our eyes. Like the stars in daytime and the clouds at night. And then I thought of Khan and the hidden kindness in his heart.

I was overcome with joy. But it felt wrong to feel so good after the devastation only twelve months before. So I expressed my joy with nib and ink. Took a pen and wrote: *I'm getting married. I'm so happy I could scream.* Then I folded the paper small and squeezed it into the crack between the fitted wardrobe and the wall; my personal wailing wall. I sat back and looked at it, a smile upon my face. Then I pinched my fingers deep into the crack and pulled it out again. Some brittle paint flaked away. I opened up the paper and added: *Thank you, Lord, thank you so much and I love you too!*

Then I folded it again and pushed it back inside.

Chapter Forty

Nerves

My dear Nu,

Our world has changed.

Again.

It's my wedding day. My head says I'm a fool to feel this way, but my joy has morphed and now my heart is full of fear. Why do you think that is? Seems mad to even say. I know it must be wedding nerves. I am so lucky that I have Khan and that he wants me too. We have a way out of our perpetual misery, my darling Nu; I can see the future, my life ahead of me.

Mostly I think I just exist. Like a molecule or a mouse, being, eating, drinking, seeing things as nothing other than the next thing lined up in a queue. The next thing I need to do. Not now. I feel so different now. It's a little like the times you show me things. I never know if it's what you mean, but when we are alone together, I am so rooted in the moment; present with all things.

Everything has moved so fast, and I feel so much for Khan. But don't forget, we only met a few short weeks ago. So of course, I understand that I'm bound to feel anxiety and nerves. My Nu, can you believe it's only been a year since Mama left . . . and soon your sister will be a married girl. Khan and Mani. It feels so good to write our names together side by side. How amazing it will be when I'm actually at his side and we're together, a real family again.

I feel as if I have superhero senses, as if I know everything there is to know. My future. But all I see is darkness. How silly I am. Even though things have finally come right, and the bad stuff's in the past, I cannot feel that things are looking up.

Ignore these words. They're confused and born of wedding nerves.

Love you, Nu.

Mani

I folded the letter in half and looked in the mirror. The wedding dress looked back at me. By tradition Khan had handed it to me, the blood-red silk and gauze barely visible through embroidered colours, weaves and golden threads. My heart began to race and I felt the prick of heat beneath my skin. Something in the colours reminded me of Ma all redly mangled up on the floor. The sequins in the dress like the play of light on the creeping bloody circle around Nu. The ornate latticed gold that pierced my nose and ears and rose and fell upon my collarbone an echo of Mama's golden ring. The ring I'd secreted in the bin. I calmed myself, told myself the scarlet slash across my face was just my painted lips.

I missed my ma. I felt such sadness when I thought of her. I wished that she could see me in this room. Small and dark, a mirror on one wall. A long pine-framed thing that Jasmine had brought. She said I needed something big to see the full effect as I dressed for this momentous day. I imagined Ma looking back at me. Seeing the beauty I could see. And then I saw her shake her head and tut, and I looked away, averting my eyes from what wasn't really there.

A sparrow landed on the outside windowsill. Its fawn feathers such a contrast to my multicoloured self. A pointy wind lifted dents into its perfect plumage here and there. It hopped staccato steps and took up a sideways stance, then shot a cocked-head glance at me. I obliged and moved so it could see my bridal form in full. I was a rainbow creature, part me, part something I had never seen before. I wasn't quite ready to depart yet. To leave my life with Nu in Abdul's house. My face was only half made up. One eye confident, lined and shaded with the blackest kohl, the other nude and vulnerable, searching the room for answers that I couldn't find. A sudden flap and the sparrow flew away. I wished that I could take flight too.

And then I saw Mama again. She stood behind me as I posed before the glass. I was a darkened shadow; she was the light that cast my form. I saw the beauty that she hid away each day. It shone. I had the urge to pray *namaz** and send my wishes to the Lord. Pray that our future would be good. I laid the prayer mat on the floor, then sat down carefully to supplicate. As I gazed at the carpet – not grey, not green, not brown, but somewhere in between – I thought: I am resigned. Life pretends to hand us choices, but in no single moment did my life give any real choice to me. Today I surrender;

---

* A term for prayers.

there is nothing I can control. Nothing I can do. I am a leaf upon a river flowing into a great cavernous unknown. Can a leaf turn and swim away? No. I could land upon the bank, but fate has thrust me to the centre of the flow, and I'm set to land wherever the currents lead. But it's OK. It's the *qadr*, the path that God and circumstance has planned, the way of truth, the way it's meant to be.

I folded up the prayer mat and placed it on the bed. Then I opened the letter I had written to my Nu. I paused, and with great force crushed it firm and fast into my henna-patterned hands, a kernel disappearing deep within fruity vines on fleshy palms.

'Mani!' Jasmine entered out of breath. Her hands balled up under her neck as she looked at me. She didn't need to speak. The look on her face spoke for her. She breathed in deep, then ceremoniously took the veil that rested on the bed, cradling it in her arms like a baby. In a single move she tumbled it down. Spirals of green embroidery turned and danced on every centimetre of the scarlet veil, interrupted only by the inset mirrors looking back through threads along the way. The violent bloody red fabric cooled by verdant green. I was a heavenly virgin. Pouting lips and dark *houris** eyes veiled in innocence and restrained smiles.

Jasmine raised the edge of the veil and with ceremony laid it like a crown upon my head. She brought the sequinned edges down and round to frame my face. It fell straight to the floor, curving across my shoulders as it went.

* Virginal companions in Heaven.

'Wow,' she said.

As I finished off my other eye, Jasmine placed an orange Sainsbury's carrier on the bed. A thorned stem punctured a hole in the bag. Jasmine pulled out a bunch of flowers she had brought for me to hold. I could see it was a home-made job, well meant but the heads misaligned, stems roughly bound by foil.

I picked it up. Held it so the flowers seemed to bloom out of my waist. We looked into the mirror. Me in front, Jasmine behind, her hands resting on my shoulders.

'Mirror, mirror on the wall,' she said, 'who is the . . .' and then a pause, 'most gorgeous of them all?'

I held the roses up. Their curled beauty looking back at me. They were the darkest burgundy, bright red veiled in black. Three beads of water made a trail upon the petals of the biggest bloom. Perfect motionless spheres, like teardrops refusing to fall. I thought of Ma. She never said much to me, but my mind landed on a distant memory at a wedding in Lahore. The scent of jasmine filled the air from the ringlets on our wrists. The smell of beauty in my nose. She said, 'In Heaven there is no time. Past and future are created things.' She paused to turn her ring. I had no idea what she meant. 'Time,' she said when she saw me looking perplexed. 'Time will sometimes misbehave. It slows itself or speeds up really fast.' Our eyes met. 'And sometimes past and future merge into one and the future can reveal itself.' Still her words made no sense. Then she whispered, 'I saw my death that way. It happens before your wedding day.' Her face so still as she turned the golden ring upon her finger as she always did. Her eyes towards the bride, but seeing something else besides.

I felt that stillness now. And I was sure the future came to me, like a memory. Time seemed to still, and I saw my death like Ma had said. There was no blood, or eulogy, or tears, just the end of things held dear. Hidden things that mattered more than life or death itself. I brushed the thought away and reached out for the kohl to perfect the lines around my eyes.

I was done. The mask upon my face now fully formed, my perfect hiding place. I looked out of the window but couldn't see the sparrow anywhere. Jasmine pulled and pinched the pleats and folds here and there until finally I was set: a delicious raspberry feast.

I was ready.

Chapter Forty-one

Bride

I'm thinking back to my wedding day. I was so excited I could hardly breathe.

He's sitting on a golden couch dressed in ivory silk. The hall is big and smart, with great arched windows to the side. There is a crowd of people in the room. His jacket has a Nehru collar and golden buttons running down the front. He's talking, sprawled across the couch, his fingers proudly pushing up his chin, his *shalwar*-covered legs crossed at the feet. On his head he wears a turban, which rises to a fan and folds and rolls behind him as if unravelling, although it doesn't fall away. His hair puffs out along the edges of his face. He's sitting there as if it's any other day.

His eyes lock on to mine. I feel the balling of my cheeks. Is this the moment? Is this it: the time I start to realise things? I search his face for signs of happiness. A smile, a raising of inviting arms. Nothing. Instead he frowns and with his eyes directs me to look down. I ease the worry rising in me. Tell myself I know this game. He wants me to look sad. I saw it before in Lahore. The tear-filled bride distraught upon her wedding day. Bashful chastity. No sinful, brazen joy for what her wedding night might be. I do as he directs. I'm looking at the pitted parquet floor. Sequential slabs of dark and golden brown, like the skin of mostly everyone around. I dare a sweeping glance around the room and see my Nu, a moon amid great earthy mounds. I see fear within him.

I know it's wedding-day nerves; I have them too. And although something in me wants to run, I hold it tight to suffocate the urge. It's hardly a surprise to feel this way, with me on full display, so many people watching me. How could I feel any other way?

The air is heavy with the scent of cardamom and spice. It makes my mouth well up. Jasmine and Dalal on either side are holding on to me. They lead me from the small private room towards the couch and Khan. The room is full of strangers, still and staring, and yet there is a resonating drone of sounds that don't add up to words. And I cannot see the movement of their lips.

Now I'm sitting next to Khan. I want to look at him, to have him take me by the arm, but he gets up and starts to walk around. Slow and lazy weighted steps across the parquet floor, his hands joined together at his rear. He turns to me and with his right hand sweeps the hair back off his face, then very slightly he winks.

Sometimes it is the smallest things that make the biggest difference. His wink sets me free. A bunch of butterflies released in me. I can feel my sweat begin to bead and can hardly wait for what this night is promising. The scent of chicken korma with pilau is now making me feel sick.

I'm still sitting on this golden throne. I feel awkward and alone. But then from the corner of my eye I see that Jasmine is approaching. I heave a deep sigh of relief.

'Hello, Mani. You're like a great raspberry pudding sitting there,' she says. She makes me laugh.

I study her a bit. The pale-blue sari hangs off her hips and the plunging neckline of her blouse is wrong. It's shameless, brazen and too loud. Adam appears and grabs her from behind. They laugh in unison. And then he kisses her right on the lips. It makes something inside me flip. She sees the look on my face.

'Adam and I are together,' she says. 'Surprise!'

I don't know what to say, so I just smile.

'I thought I'd save it for your wedding day.' The expression around her eyes and lips is wry, and then she turns and walks away. I look at Adam, and an inappropriate yearning turns in me. I hope he cannot read my feelings.

Maybe this is the point at which my whole world shifts.

Adam's eyes grow round and soft, and like a swooping bird he falls on me. Before I even know what's going on, he's kissing me on both cheeks.

'Congratulations, Mani,' he say. 'Khan's a lucky man, the bastard! I wanted to go out with you, but Jasmine told me you weren't interested. I guess I get it, what with your religion, the customs of your land.'

I cannot believe what he is saying.

As Adam pulls away, Khan comes into focus between the guests in front of me. His lips are pursed. No expression on his face, his eyes small and round. I smile at him, but he turns and walks away.

Then the moments blur. An imam sits before us on the couch. He is wearing a flat cap. He has black hair, I think, but I can only see the greying in his beard, which reaches to his chest. He is portly and small. The room is silenced as he recites a special prayer. I am soothed by the familiarity of the Quranic chant, although I do not understand the words.

'Will you marry Khan?' he says.

'Yes,' I whisper so quietly that I can barely hear myself.

'Will you marry Khan?' he repeats.

'Yes,' I say again, a little louder than before.

Then he asks me once more.

'Yes,' I say without a thought.

And the deed is done.

We are married.

I feel no different from the unwed moment before.

Khan holds my hand and I am filled with joy.

The guests begin to leave, full-bellied and in need of rest. Khan is leading me away. He whispers in my ear that I am ravishing. He's taking me to the room where I waited when I first arrived. The day is gaining colour and my head is light. The world around me spins. The spinning isn't stopping even though the crowds are filtering away.

It starts like this.

'Mani.' He takes my hands in his.

I feel his heat. He's standing far too close to me. I'm breathing him, his warm and earthy scent. He pushes me away and looks me up and down. 'You are gorgeous,' he says. He pulls me back to him, my forehead in his collarbone, and starts to rock me side to side. 'And you know it,' he carries on. He takes my chin and raises it. I am magnetised. I feel a tingling. Large square hands are creeping around my waist. He seems restrained, as if he wants to hide his aim. His fingers spread. He owns me totally. My breathing starts to race all by itself; my limbs begin to loosen at the joints. I think my knees might just give in.

In that moment, wrapped in Khan, my life before this day seems insignificant and grey. Ahead, colours line up; a rainbow starts to form. I have been colour blind, seeing only black and white and grey. Now I am real. I am alive, in bloom, no longer a seed of possibility buried deep inside the ground. I mouth a little prayer that nothing will ever change. But best of all, something I can hardly believe: the feelings of this day are carrying away the darkness hidden in my heart since my ma passed.

Things have finally come right. That much I know for sure.

There is a knock on the door and a crack begins to appear. In one unhesitating move, Khan thumps the door closed, swoops to wedge a chair beneath the knob. In that instant, a strange vision forms. I'm looking into Adam's eyes instead. A yearning curls inside me. I shake away the thought. And then Khan turns to me again.

I did not anticipate the rising tension in my stomach. The nausea of joy. Or the shyness of my eyes as they flicker into his like a lighted candle wick. That is when, still in a spin, I land with a thud. Buried in a tumble of gauze and blood-coloured silk. I've been swallowed by my dress. Left cheek stinging raw and red.

The strike was neat, precisely aimed. It feels like a well-rehearsed scene. And slowly it comes to me; I realise what is happening, and as I raise my head, he falls to his knees. Head buried in his hands, his turban tumbles off. His brow is rippling, a tortured moan pushing out.

'God, Mani. Oh my God. I'm sorry, sorry, I . . . I don't know what came over me.' There are pauses between his words. He holds me in his arms. 'I saw you flirting.' He takes a deep breath and holds it still at its tip, then releases it into the words. 'You made me mad, jealous . . . How could you let him kiss you on your wedding day.' A juddering breath. 'Mani. God, forgive . . .' and then a sob. A pause.

'I don't deserve you,' he whispers.

My mind goes blank, then pours out a memory. The day I tucked myself away hiding from my pa. My secret scratches its way out. And I see it again. I see the deed that sent Ma away and silenced my dear Nu. The pain is searing, deep and harsh and punctures something soft within. The hole it makes is where the taste of Khan starts to seep away. And then numbness rises.

The world appears to me again, the present time. Embarrassment, confusion and some shame.

I smile. 'No, no,' I say, my hand on my cheek. 'I'm fine, it's OK . . .'

His body jolts before me in a rhythmic sob. Lunging forward, squeezing me, he yearns into my ear. 'Mani, please forgive me . . .'

'Don't cry,' I say. 'I'm fine. I understand.' And I did, I got it bright and clear. It was what I deserved. It was my worth.

'I love you so.' A pause. A sob. A lengthened breath. 'I want you to myself.'

I warm to his possessing me. Needing me. It's only love's intensity. How could I hurt him so? I cannot bear to see his pain, and this upon his wedding day. How terrible I am. I know right then that I will make things right. For him,

I'll do my best. I'll fix it and everything will be fine.

I smile again, numbness masking truth from lie.

'Khan.' I decide it was right. That it was meant; things were just as they should be. 'I love you too,' I say.

And even with the hurt, I feel the strangest calm. A joy, an ugly small atonement.

I know there is a wrongness too; a snag, a pull, a tiny pinch upon the skin. But some part of me has disengaged and I have a role to play. I have to practise hard, the part of newly-wed and wife, suffused with happiness and joy.

I play it well.

Chapter Forty-two

First: just married

That night at Khan's flat, our new home, when I see that Khan is leaving our bedroom, I find a pen and discarded envelope. I write with hasty hands:

> My dear Nu,
> I am afraid, but I can't say this to anyone but you. We have to carry on. Where can we stay now we have no Ma or Pa? I don't know what to do. My hands are shaking.

I hear Khan calling out to me, but I cannot stop. I carry on in a great rush.

> I know he loves me really. And he is so kind to save us from our plight. Please pray for me. Pray that everything will be OK, that things will turn out well for you and me.
> Don't worry, Nu. I think I'm just tired after this big day. Please ignore these words today.
> Love,
> Mani

I read it to myself, then screw it up and throw it on the floor.
I find a scrap of paper and begin again.

My dear Nu,
Don't worry about me, I am fine. Everything is really
great and I am sure you can't wait to settle down at our
new home. I am happy. This is all so good. How lucky
are we.
Pray for me, my Nu.
Love,
Mani

I hope he doesn't hear the lie between the words.

I hear Khan walking to our room. I pick both letters up
and push them in between the mattress and the base. He
comes in, takes off his raw silk jacket, throws it on the bed,
then leaves again. I run to Nu's room. He's sitting on the
mattress on the floor, examining his hands. I hand him the
second letter. Nu looks at me and smiles a little artificially. I
go back into my room and take out the first letter. I read it
carefully, then screw it up and put it in the bin. I walk around
the room, but something isn't right and I can't settle down. I
fall to my knees to retrieve the letter from the bin. I straighten
it and press it flat upon the floor. I fold it in half and then in
half again. And then once more and once again. I squeeze the
square into the crack between the flooring and the skirting
board. A corner still sticks out. I stand up and breathe in
deep. I run my hands along my wedding dress to straighten
out the folds and find that Khan is watching me. I sit down
on the bed. I cannot say when he entered the room. I keep

my eyes still and steady my breathing. His eyes are slim and sharp. Intense.

'What are you doing on the floor?' he asks. I don't know what to say.

'I thought I dropped my earring clasp,' is what I reply.

He says nothing, just frowns a bit.

'But . . . but it's right here,' I say, then look away.

He's walking slowly towards me and bends down to the floor, not taking his eyes off me. My breath won't leave my chest. I watch him carefully. He glances at the carpet, momentarily sweeping his eyes from bed base to skirting board. I jump a little as he reaches for my brocade veil, which trails upon the floor. He steps away, still holding on to it. It slides slowly off me and spills on the floor. A bloody river in the land of Khan, curling between the two of us. He stares at me, not just my face but every part of me. I will myself to feel the way I felt back at school and on Jesus Green. I don't. I'm conscious of my dress, which is too tight, and cross my arm about myself as if I need to scratch my neck.

I hear him breathing heavily as he walks slowly up to me.

'I'll never hurt you again,' he lies beautifully as he undresses me.

Chapter Forty-three

You: bus route 205 to Marble Arch

My dear,

Finsbury Circus was so beautiful last time we met on the 205, with that brilliant winter sunshine glossing up the ice. The iron railings set the garden in its place like a treasure locked securely in a safe. And on the railings here and there frost had melted into points of light. Like the light you place inside my heart.

After you left that day, I met my friend to shop at Marble Arch, though we never bought a thing. As we're about to leave, I walk up to the Arch itself. It looks forlorn standing on its own. I cross the road to take a closer look. I rush a little because I must be home before *him*. I remember wishing badly that you were there. Holding my hand. We would be like tourists from a far-off land. As I wander round the Arch, I see it straight away. A carving. It draws me in as if it speaks to me. Between carved horses, angels and ladies decked in drapery, I see you and me. I know it is us, the lovers posing on the left. You wear a helmet, though you bare your chest, and I am draped in silk; its pleats and folds caress my arms and legs. I know that you'll defend me to the end. You even hold a sword to do it with. And I am good again. You're so brave to be with me. Valour and virtue side by side. As I look at them, the figurines in stone, I stand a little taller, throw my shoulders back. It's a sign. A message from above. We were meant to be and here's the proof, the two of us set in stone.

I hope your life is beautiful and my love for you is part of it. Something I love about you is how gentle you are. Even in the way you speak. Even just to think of you transforms how I feel. Gentleness is a form of beauty, isn't it? Mild-mannered sympathy. I know it from its opposite. Aggression. Violence. Hatefulness. *Him*. They're ugly, don't you think? You are a gift to the world, to me. Stay gentle.

Take care, and be sure to carry my love with you.

Love,

Mexx

Part Three

Chapter Forty-four

Sauce: two weeks married

It took less than fourteen days before I saw that part of Khan he promised would never return.

The three days after the wedding were the best days of my life. Khan held on to me so tight, as if, like some bird or butterfly, I'd fly away if I were released. And then he left. A business trip that meant he'd be away for several days.

His maisonette on Essex Road in Islington was three flights up and a thirty-minute walk from Abdul's place. The road a mix of shops and houses unhappily pressed together side by side. Antique auction rooms, cheap cafés, smart stucco flats.

Nu had a room of his own for the first time, and he started spending more time alone. It was so small, Khan had to wedge the mattress in on the floor without a base to make it fit. But Nu seemed comfortable enough. And he had a window overlooking a patio some way below, and further out a narrow lawn.

We didn't have a honeymoon because of Khan's new role as trainee engineer. Khan had insisted I give up school. He said he'd take care of us, provide for us just as a man should. But with Nu at his special school, I was mostly alone with time to occupy.

When Khan returned from his business trip, I was so excited, but he was distant and removed. So I hatched a plan. A way to win his love for sure, despite the pressure of his work. I went shopping the next day, selecting ingredients from several different stores: shiitake mushrooms, tomato sauce, skinny chillis from the Caribbean store, cumin seeds, fenugreek and a clutch of coriander that left the scent of fresh air in my hands. I loved this dish I'd watched Dalal teach Ma to make. I set the ingredients in a row upon the kitchen top to start the perfect meal. I focused hard on making it taste right.

The kitchen was melamine and gloss and merged into the living room; the carpet cut abruptly into tiles. There was no flame to cook upon; instead a pane of glass mysteriously heated up. From the kitchen I could see the front door opening. Khan was home from work. Outside it was overcast. Heavy, dirty clouds weighing down the sky.

'Hello, stranger,' he said. 'Seems like you've been cooking away today.'

'You're here at last,' I said. 'I was worried you'd abandoned me.'

'Are you being mean?'

'No . . . no,' I said. 'I . . . I didn't mean it in that way. I haven't seen you in a while, that's all.'

'Whatever,' he replied, staring through slit eyes. 'I'm going to bed.'

'But it's early and you've just got back . . . Khan, I've not seen you much this week.'

He started climbing the stairs.

'I've cooked a special dish for you,' I said as he stepped on the treads.

From the lower steps he raced towards me and in a single sweep knocked the pan off the stove, spilling the contents. A ripped artery of sauce snaked across the floor. I caught my breath. He had struck me too with the swinging of his arm, although I couldn't tell if it was meant. My eyes wide open. Disbelief. Relief it seemed in Khan, his expression calm. Or was it satisfaction I could see? At first I willed the food back up and into the pan again. I think I even tried to catch it mid-fall. It took a moment more before I felt my skin stinging with heat. My arms were covered in noodles and tomato sauce.

'You should be more understanding,' Khan said, an accusatory finger stabbing at me. 'Now I'm off to bed.'

The sweep of his arm had pushed my fingers back, and they were sprained and sore. The skin on my arms throbbing with the burn. I switched on the tap and buried my arms under the cooling flow. Where the pan had hit the tiles, a spidery crack had formed: round centre, eight legs radiating out.

Above the stony spider, reflected in the gloss, a solitary pendant shone its chilly glare.

I switched off the tap. The shrill scent of balsamic vinegar filled the room. The shock and hurt consumed me like fire. I tried to hold the sobs inside, but they escaped. My lurching lungs would not obey. Wetness formed inside my eyes as I tried to rationalise. I saw every version of the man he was even as I thought of what he'd done, the wickedness of it. I saw the dreamy man beyond my reach and could not align him with the man upstairs in bed.

I put the pan into the sink and started scrubbing it. Ran the tap to muffle my whimpering. My arm and fingers hurt. I put too much soap in, so bubbles filled the sink. As I washed the dish, a misbehaving tear formed in my eye and balanced at the rim. I blinked to let the tear drop. That was when Nu came to me, transfixed. I think he must have been partway down the stairs, watching silently. He didn't seem to notice the food strewn across the floor. I almost moved away, afraid that he would see my brimming eyes, but he wasn't looking at my face. He focused on my arm, slowly lifting it.

My body tensed and I nearly pulled my arm away. Why did he watch me from afar and not do anything? I held my anger back, because I saw what he was showing me. A ray of angled light had landed on my wet and bubbled arm. A carnival of purple rainbows streamed and curled and swirled on a bubble near my hand. My breath held still, my eyes thrilled as the dancing rainbows circled round and round. And then the bubble split, the rainbow flew apart.

Momentarily I felt at one with everything. The speed of life turned down a notch or two, past and future vanishing away.

I squeezed more Fairy into the sink and made a million bubbles rise and fill the air. Nu and I ran about the room, leaping to burst them as they rose. We didn't even see the food we stepped on. And when we were done, we laughed like children playing in a park.

Nu helped me clean the floor. All that remained was a faint red stain upon the carpet of the living room. It was hardly visible. But sometimes you could see it clearly when the angle of the light was right.

The memory returned: the hurt, my special meal wasted

on the floor. A shot of pain. I felt soreness on my arm again.

I thought about the sadness in Khan's eyes and the way he was with me before our wedding day. Kind Khan. Pressing on burnt skin, I decided I must make things right. I had to take away the sadness in the man, make him happy once again. Do better so that things would be OK.

Chapter Forty-five

Sharp things: five weeks married

I ripped tape off the box as I counted to my left the five remaining wedding gifts still hidden under wrap. I lifted out a dancing figurine frozen in white porcelain and set her on the mantelpiece, snipping off the label strung inside her arm. I moved her to the left and then to the right so she looked away from me. It wasn't right. I couldn't have her dancing in plain sight. I moved her down on to the hearth and hid her behind a pot. Perhaps it was the sofa angled too steeply at the fireplace. I pushed it back a bit. But still it looked wrong. I couldn't make the place feel right no matter what I did.

I pushed the unopened wedding gifts under the sofa for another day and pulled up my sleeve. The skin on my arms was still burnt and tender from the hot tomato sauce. I sighed as I switched on the radio and stared out on to the street through the three square windows of the living room, which formed a shallow bay. I'd caught the middle of my favourite show, where random callers phoned the host. They were laughing at something I hadn't heard.

'James,' the host said, 'do go on.'

'Like I said, I'm overcome by her. When things were bad,

I mean really bad for me, she put me right. Cheered me up and made me feel loved,' James explained.

'That's wonderful to hear,' the host replied.

'And no matter what she's suffering, she spares a thought, kind, loving words for me. I feel quite inspired, actually.'

'Well, James, it is inspiring indeed. What will you do now?'

'I'd like to say how much she's done for me. Tell her I love her too. That's what I want to do. And I want to tell her to take care.'

'And that's exactly what you've done. Let's hope she's listening today. Hope that goes well for James . . . James from London speaking of his secret lover on air . . . Now, the weather . . .'

The caller made me smile. It was his willingness to tell so many strangers on the radio how he felt. I switched off the radio and sat on the sofa with crossed legs. On the street there was some kind of Labrador. Beige and glossy. I couldn't look away. It hung around sniffing at the ground. It froze, alert. Then suddenly it moved, legs jigging back and forth, and disappeared. It made me think of how I felt with Khan. Unsettled. Wrong. Like how part of you knows when something's out of place: a smile, a door, a banister support.

There were things I should have known after my wedding day. Consequences that likely follow on. But I couldn't see it then. So how could I have guessed what was going to happen next?

I went upstairs to Nu and sat with him in his room. Paper and pencils scattered on the floor. We wrote occasional notes and doodled random pictures on the pages here and there. I'd noticed since the wedding that Nu had started to withdraw into himself and was writing to me less. I stroked him on the head, pushing back his hair. I yanked at his shirt and pointed at the buttons, which he'd done up misaligned. He smiled a little as I helped him do them up again.

I heard the jangling of keys and the front door open. Khan was home. I ran down the stairs.

'Hello, Khan,' I said. There were lines on his brow and his lips were pursed. He held on to my arm and took me up the stairs into our bedroom. His grip hurt, his fingers pressing too firmly into me.

'How was your trip? Better than the last?' I said, too quietly, aware that something wasn't right, trying not to cry. He looked sad and angry at once. Then he pushed me down on to the floor and held me there. Bearing down on me; dead weight that I couldn't shift no matter how much I wriggled underneath.

I told him no as I held a sob within. He carried on.

'Please, please no,' I said.

But it was as if I wasn't really there. He looked at every part of me except my face. I felt his slap. It stung a bit. I felt his joy as well, even though he tried to hide it. A rising secret thing. Sordid. Wrong. He hid it in the straightness of his face. But faces lie. At the edges here and there I could detect a stifled smile. I fell into line. I knew I shouldn't have. I should have let him know what I really felt. But I wanted things to mend. To win his love, make things like they were before we were married. I had to kill this madness so we could be like normal loving newly-weds.

The carpet rubbed my hair into a matted mess. And the cowardice in me filled my belly. I moaned, a little cry, and then I turned my face to the side. Ignored the wetness in my eyes. I saw the golden carriage clock I'd found at a car boot sale some while back. It told me it was three o'clock. It lied. It never worked. He slapped me again. It hurt a bit, nothing I considered to be pain. It tingled out. And then he was done. I curled myself into a ball on the floor, knees drawn up, and leaned against the bed. I saw his face. The shame it held within the shaping of his brow, the slightest slant upon his lips. I knew he hated himself just as much as I hated my cowardice.

And that was the reason I felt for him. Why, despite the things he put me through, I stayed, couldn't run away. He battled with the demons in himself every day.

As Khan moved about the room, I rehearsed how much I owed him, how much I had to be grateful for. I rationalised it carefully. He'd given Nu and me a life despite the devastation I'd caused. Perhaps this was the way it was supposed to be. Sometimes.

I closed my eyes and ran through memories of the Khan I knew before to fix them in my mind. The first three days, the canteen, our trip to Cambridge, the way he held me against the wall. My love for him was crashing into misery and disbelief. I must believe this was an aberration, not the real him. As I recalled the tremor in his limbs when I touched his face on Parker's Piece, three things became clear. Firstly, his love had changed me radically and permanently. Secondly, there was a part of him, a part I didn't understand and was entirely unable to deal with, that wanted to hurt me. And thirdly, I was completely and irreversibly in love with him. I knew right then that no matter what it took, I would wait for him, the man he really was, to return to me.

* * *

I left Khan in our bedroom and returned to Nu, lying belly down on his mattress drawing pictures. I saw he'd drawn a butterfly, a boat and a giant eye with tears inside. 'Are you OK?' I asked. He nodded, eyes averted, focused on his work. *Sure?* I wrote on the page. *Yes*, he scribbled. Then he picked up one of the pebbles he kept in a box beside his bed and examined it. Through the wetness in my eyes I neatly coloured in the blurry butterfly to the gentle pattering of rain upon the window pane. Its pale wings morphed to purples, oranges and greens. Inside the box of waxy crayons my fingers touched a metal thing. A hair grip. I picked it up and pressed its sharpness into my fingertips. Scratched a snaky shape on the pale skin on the inside of my arm.

I rose and went slowly back to our bedroom. Empty. I ran down the stairs. No one. Khan had left. I ran back to the bedroom, stepping stealthily. I crouched down by the bed and pressed the hairpin between the mattress and the frame, making sure to hide the silver under sheets.

That night I lay in bed, lonely in Khan's company, the smell of Surf on the sheets reminding me of Naboo's *kameez*. I stroked the hairpin with my fingertips; firmly wedged but within my reach. Cold, metallic, sharp. I drew my hand away. It's OK, I thought. I know he didn't mean it. I think he needs some help. My help. I should be more considerate. My skin was soft from the shower that I'd taken. I'd stood under the scalding water for too long and scrubbed hard to wash away the hurt. When I got out, I saw something on my thigh. I thought it was some body wash I hadn't properly rinsed off.

It didn't wipe away. It was a cut upon a rise of swollen flesh, though I couldn't exactly recall how it had happened. It didn't matter, though. I knew I could hide it under clothes.

I told myself that tomorrow things would be all right and denied the hurt Khan had forced on me. I focused on the good days in the past, and dreamed of all the loving he could give. Fixed it in my mind.

I was nearly asleep when Khan whispered, 'I'm sorry, Mani, for being such a fool.' He wrapped his arms around me, strong and firm, and I felt his breath begin to jolt. I pulled back.

'Are you OK?' I said.

Khan pulled me back to him and buried his face in my neck. He began to weep.

'Please forgive me,' he whispered. He sat up in bed and switched on the bedside lamp. 'I don't want to hurt you, Mani, it's not the person I am.' He took me in his arms.

'I don't know why you get so angry out of the blue,' I said, lowering my eyes.

'I don't know what comes over me. I don't want to be a monster,' he whispered. 'You have to help me, Mani. You know I love you very much. Tell me you know it's true.'

I nodded out a feeble yes. I didn't want to see him sad.

'Are you OK? Tell me I didn't hurt you.'

I didn't answer him.

'What's wrong?'

'I'm fine,' I said, then paused, not knowing what else to say. To fill the silence I added, 'I'm just a little peckish, that's all.'

Khan leapt out of bed. 'Wait there, don't move,' he said.

He ran downstairs and returned with a mound of yogurt with fresh fruit chopped on top. I reached for the bowl, but he held it away.

'No, no,' he said. 'Open your mouth,' and spoon by spoon he fed me the dessert.

When he was done, he wrapped me in his arms, my head against his chest, and stroked my hair until I felt the urge to sleep. I smiled. I knew that things would be fine. And I remembered something Naboo often said: 'No man is all good or all bad.' He'd say it mostly when our ma became upset. I gently laid my palm on Khan's chest, and as I did, some sort of night bird called out, *caw-caw*, at a distance.

I didn't understand back then that something had begun. Something mysterious, powerful, unknown. Like dripping water piercing holes in stone. And it would carry on and on until it burrowed down deep, a cavity inside me.

When I awoke the next day, my smile was gone. I hurt a lot. My left arm mostly, the bruises blooming blue. Nothing natural should be this blue, except a pansy perhaps, I thought. My right cheek was rosy red with a scratch across the top. I dabbed on foundation to hide it. It was a shade too light and afterwards it just looked more prominent. Out of the window I saw Khan walking down the street to work. No sign of the Labrador. I didn't really mind bruises or the scratch on my face. I knew it wasn't me that cared. It was the child I used to be. She said to me, *The dreams we hold dear as children never leave*. I told her, *It's the child that never left. You really should go now.*

She didn't.

And so it was her, the child, not me, that hurt so bad with every strike. I, the woman, picked myself up and carried on. I was fine. It was the nine-year-old who lay smarting on the ground.

She lies there still.

I rose to leave the bedroom. Each day I walked Nu to the bus stop to catch the bus to his special school; a school for children who'd been traumatised. Some children were in care, some wouldn't engage with anyone, and others, like Nu, had lost their words. As I walked towards the door, a glint of metal caught my eye from underneath the mattress. The sharp hairpin I'd put there yesterday. I slipped it further in and out of sight before I left.

Chapter Forty-six

Heaven: seven weeks married

I was ironing clothes and folding sheets when it occurred to me I hadn't seen Nu for a while. I ran to his room, and checked the bathroom too. I couldn't find him anywhere. He seemed to hide himself away a little more each day. And he wasn't writing to me much. I found him finally sitting on the floor behind the sofa in the living room. He wouldn't look at me and so I wrote:

> My darling Nu,
> Is there something troubling you? I notice you don't write to me so much as you used to. Is there something you want to say to me?
> Are you thinking of Ma? And Pa?
> I think of them as well. I think of Mama very much and I still feel the pain. Is that it, my Nu?
> Let me help you, my darling Nu.
> Love,
> Mani

Nu took up a pencil and drew a star high in the paper sky. Above it he wrote *Heaven*. No other words, except for *Mani* and *Nu* at the bottom. Then he drew tears falling from the star high up in the sky. The tears fell to the paper earth upon the words *Mani* and *Nu*.

We sat silently listening to the hiss of traffic sweeping past our home.

Chapter Forty-seven

Fists: nine weeks married

I told Khan that Jasmine would be visiting. Something in him snapped.

It had happened several times before in the last few weeks. Like a dormant firework, he sometimes stayed benign. But then, quite unexpectedly, he would explode. The scars on my skin were testament to this. I never knew what I had done wrong. And as I tried to make things right, there was something I'd begun to see. Khan was a good and honest man. It was just that there was this evil man who lived within him too.

That day he said to me, 'So Jasmine and that Adam are coming to see you.' And then he said some things I'd rather not repeat. He said that Jasmine reminded him of the slutty thing I was. And in a whisper underneath his breath I heard him say, 'You bitch.'

I should have been angry at the hurtful words he hurled at me. But all I could think was that he might be right. I am my father's child and I know exactly what I did.

I said, 'Shall I call and tell her to stay away?'

'Trying to lay the blame on me; make me look bad when actually you're the bitch.' And then he said, 'It's Adam you really want to see.'

'That's not true,' I replied, quite unconvincingly.

That was when I felt the ground beneath me move. I'm not sure exactly how I fell, but next there was a jolt of pain along my right leg. Sweat was oozing from heat gathering beneath my skin. It pushed wetness on to my upper lip. I was afraid. I couldn't believe he really wanted to hurt me. Not for real. He'd promised me he'd make things good again. I could not give up the dream of what was meant to be. I hoisted myself up on to the couch.

'Please don't do this,' I said. 'How can you hit me if you care for me?'

Khan paced back and forth, clenching his jaw as if he was chewing on my words.

'We have to make things right.'

I thought momentarily that he had understood. He had his back to me and I could see his profile. Then he swung around, backhanding me across the cheek. It stung and burned. I was off the sofa like a penitent upon my knees. A sinner pleading mercy from the Lord. I confess some part of me accepted the things he did to me. At times I felt obliged to offer up my bruised and battered self to him. Pain as penance for my deeds. I don't rightly understand the resignation I felt.

He moved to me. I raised my arms to guard myself against the threat of thrashing arms. But then he moved away.

It was then I saw Nu standing by the fireplace. His fists were clenched, face grimacing. He walked to me and helped me back to the sofa. I couldn't look at him. I took his hands into my lap as he crouched down in front of me, but his arms were taut and he wouldn't release his balled-up fists. I stroked his arms to comfort him. I felt his hands release. He was holding pebbles. Crescent nail marks on his palms. I looked at him and slowly moved my head from left to right. 'No,' I mouthed. He stood and backed away against the wall, lined brow, eyes focused on the floor.

I felt wetness on my cheek. Blood. A trickle charted the same old jagged pathway down my face.

A thought I hadn't fully formed entered my head. And though I could not explain it at the time, I smiled.

It stoked Khan's fury, the rising of my lips, and he struck at me once more. For a while I could not quite recall my name, or where I was.

He left the house, slamming the door behind him.

Chapter Forty-eight

You: bus route 23 to Trafalgar Square

19 January

My dear,

Where were you? We were to meet at Trafalgar Square on the number 23 and I was going to tell you more about my life. I stood up as the bus pulled in but you weren't there. I pressed my face against the glass. My nose was squashed and it was so cold my breath made misty wings on the pane. I could see a queue of people getting on wearing woolly hats, backpacks, jeans and waterproofs. I watched them climbing the steps but couldn't see you. I went down to find you, and then I ran to the window at the rear to look out. I thought perhaps you'd missed the bus and I'd see you running to the stop. Nothing.

I told myself you must have been delayed. There must have been a reason why you couldn't come. I felt it then, on the bus, rising slowly just as I knew it would. The crushing sadness that I cannot name. The feeling when someone you love with all your heart has gone away. I huddled down to muffle my sobs. Don't you see? If you leave me, I may exhale but no part of me will find the strength to breathe back in again. Every time we plan to meet, I feel such urgency. Like the chequered way we live through night and day, my life is mapped by times with you and times when you're away.

I jump off the bus at the next stop. I walk back to Trafalgar Square. Part of me still hopes I'll find you there, waiting patiently for me. As I approach, I see his silhouette. A man in the distance. I wish it was you. Only he is perched on a column, reaching for the skies. Closer in, I look up. Nelson high on his column is like you today, my love, so far away from me.

I go to the fountain on my left. The pool is flat. I know the water's sad like me, waiting to be stirred the way that loving you stirs me. The rush of life, the throbbing in my chest.

My sadness brings back memories and the bruises on my arm seem to throb afresh. I think of *him* and the things he's done. Then I think of the people who have left, the people I love. How every good thing seems to ebb away. I dip my head. Tears are blurring my sight. I blink them out, breathe in deep, then tap the water with my fingertips.

It's no good. It ridges up, and even the water ripples away from me.

I'm about to leave when I hear the fountain to my right splashing out my name. *Mexx*, it says, then *Mexx* again. I go to it, and as I do, I feel its icy spray. It's so cold I burrow my face into my clothes. At the edge, I see her. A girl pinching a rust-coloured coin between her forefinger and thumb. She holds it up as she mouths a wish, and then she throws it in.

I catch my breath and it won't release. I'm thrusting back and forth inside the pocket of my coat, searching for a coin to wish upon. It's a shiny silver ten-pence piece that gives itself to me. With the fountain at my back, I hold it up towards the sky and make my wish. 'Free me from this life . . .' I say. And then, without a moment's thought, I throw it in. Over my shoulder as Tuppence Girl just did.

And that's the moment it hits. I'm panicking. I hoist up my skirt and step right in. Cold water to my waist. My skirt rises in a spin. I gasp. It's so icy I cannot breathe. But still I carry on. I search for my coin amid a thousand others scattered at my feet. They ripple, bend and blur. It's no good. I cannot find my ten-pence piece, the one that's carrying my wish. I delve in and scoop up as many coins as I can. When I straighten, standing in the fountain at Trafalgar Square, I complete my wish. Hands raised and cupped, I plead, unconcerned about the crowd that's gathering.

'Dear Lord . . . please also bring my love to me – my lover on the bus.' You.

After I am done, I throw the coins up high. They shower down like gold and silver rain. I lunge back down and grab some more. I'm so cold, my fingers hardly bend. Through the slightest opening between my palms, a million coins slip out. A celestial waterfall returning to its source.

When I get out, dripping wet and shivering, all eyes

are on me. A tall blond man on my right is cheering, whooping as he jumps and punches at the air, and a cluster of girls over to my left are clapping. I smile back at the crowd of watching faces, water snaking down my back. Someone throws a blanket on me as I rush to catch the number 23 for home, shuddering and shaking as I go.

Do you see, my love? You have made a fool of me. But the best part is that I simply do not care.

Is that not proof enough of love?

Forever yours,

Mexx

Chapter Forty-nine

Pebbles: eleven weeks married

I took out a tub of Wall's ice cream in the afternoon. Nu and I were going to have a treat. The ice cream was so hard that when we tried to spoon it out, a great wodge of it flicked up and landed on the tiles. Instead of picking it up, we catapulted more out of the tub, laughing as the creamy lumps melted to a milky mess, dripping down the walls and spreading on the floor. A chunk of it landed on the living room carpet, by the tomato stain. That was when I put the tub away.

I dabbed the ice cream up and tried once more to clean away the stain on the carpet. It never seemed to disappear.

There was a jangling of keys. Khan was home. He dropped his briefcase on the floor and came to me. His breathing started deepening. I stiffened instinctively. Couldn't tell if his urge was to love or to go at me again. He reached for me and stroked my face gently, his fingers trailing the scratch.

'I'm sorry, Mani,' he said. 'I'm so sorry.' He held me in his arms. 'I need help.'

I nodded in response. 'It's OK.' I always knew he'd be meek and sorry later on. Tortured Khan. 'I'm here for you.' I know it's only me that can help him to be well again.

He kissed me gently on the lips. 'Nothing will ever stop me loving you,' he said, a pained expression on his face. He started stroking the skin on my cheek, my hair and my neck as well. Then he pulled out a little box from his pocket.

'This is for you,' he said. I opened it. Two raindrop pearls hung on silver loops.

'They are beautiful,' I said.

'Anything for you,' he said. 'You must wear them tonight. I'm taking you to a film and then my favourite restaurant.'

So love is real – it really does exist. I knew this as he stroked the bruise on my cheek. As if he had had no hand in it. His agony was heat. I could feel it pulsing in his skin. That's true love, I thought. He loves me even after everything.

As he stepped back, his eyes tearing up, he noticed Nu watching us. Like a ghostly bodyguard he stood against the wall, his arms straight down at his sides. Khan made a breathy noise and left the house, slamming the door behind him.

Nu's silence held a kind of power over Khan, as if he was noting down Khan's sins. Like the angel on our left shoulder that Naboo told us about. Khan never said a word to Nu. I think he feared that surviving death meant Nu could be *majzoob*.* Those rare and special few so proximate to God they lose their mind.

I took Nu's hand in mine and squeezed it gently.

'I'm A-OK, my Nu,' I said as I forced a smile upon my face.

* * *

* A person blessed with such closeness to God that they lose their sanity or some other faculty.

The next day when I awoke alone in bed, a certain strange and deadened thing took up residence in me. I felt a weight inside, like a clutching in the gut. I feared the loss of something. The thing that made me me. This nameless thing was seeping out of me.

After I had taken Nu to school, I placed a prayer mat on the floor and prayed to the Lord as I'd been taught. Then I changed into my favourite red dress, dabbed on a rich and musky Eastern scent, and made hot buttered toast spread with chocolate sauce. But nothing lifted the darkness growing in my chest. Tears filled my eyes and spilled on to my cheeks. I switched on the radio as I had so many times before. It always cheered me up. My favourite show was on and they were speaking of the things we should be grateful for. A new caller came on air.

'Thomas. You're calling to say you're in love with someone you've just met.'

'You could say that, although it's her words that swept my heart away.'

'Want to tell her something live on air?'

'I've written her a letter in reply.'

'Go on then, Thomas, tell her how you feel.'

'I just want to say I love her too – and that she's so special to me.' Thomas cleared his throat and started reading out his words. 'You mean so much to me. Ever since you've come into my life, things have changed. I feel happy now. It's as if you've taken the bad away. Please stay safe and . . . I love you.'

'Thank you, Thomas, that was beautiful. I'm sure you'll hear from her after what you said on air.'

I smiled at Thomas's words, thinking of the way his lover made him feel. But my joy began to fade and I switched off the radio.

Every day felt different from the next. Sometimes Khan was kind, especially after he'd been bad. I'd think of his hugs, his smiles, the sorry face he wore as Tortured Khan, and I would let it go. He deserved at least that much from me, for the way he'd taken us on; saved us from our tragedy.

But there must be a limit, a line I should draw to say that's enough. But I couldn't see where that line should be. It backed away from me. The hurt carried on and on. And I didn't know how to make it stop. I tried my best to be good, to do everything right, but it was never enough.

I finished off the chocolate toast, then opened the kitchen drawer. I took out the scissors hidden at the back. A small pair with sharp and pointy blades. I ran upstairs and wedged them underneath the mattress, beside the hairpin already hiding there. The tightness in my chest eased a little bit as I thought of cold metallic things hidden but in reach.

Chapter Fifty

Circles: three months married

*C*hop chop chop. I was cutting up onions for our meal tonight, even though it was still early in the day. The radio was on. Raw onion fumes were watering my eyes. The little knife was glinting in angled sunlight from the living room. It made me think of how I'd thrashed about for metallic things last night. I couldn't reach them before he locked me down. I shook my head to muddle up the memories a bit.

Nu was back from school, staring out of the window on to Essex Street. That was when the drumming began. Thudding beats, loud and crisp, like the ones I'd heard back in Lahore. Nu beckoned me to him with waving arms.

Out on the street there was dancing going on. Nu pulled at me to come with him. I shook my head, drawing back and saying no. But he was so eager that I gave in and we ran on to the street. Men were dressed in colourful *shalwar kameez* with turbans on their heads. A muscular white horse draped in pink with mirrors sewn within pulled a carriage decked in flowers, pink and white and cream. Inside, just visible, were a bride and groom. Drummers were beating out a swinging rhythm with their sticks, and *bhangra** dancers leapt in unison,

---

* Lively Indian dancing to the beat of drums.

shoulders jolting with every beat.

The dancers dragged people from the crowd to join them. I was drowning in a whirling pool of multicoloured noise, drumbeats vibrating through my chest. We danced around the street, stepping on the flowers that had fallen from the horse. Shoulders jerking, fingers pointing up. The scent of roses and crocuses everywhere. The procession moved along, and we watched and lingered till the sound became a distant din.

As we were walking home, a bearded drunk approached us. He had on a long grey coat smeared with mud and dirt, and as he moved, he cast about the stench of urine mixed with alcohol. He fell to one knee and held up pink-petalled blossoms that he'd picked off the floor.

'For my princess from your prince,' he said. I curtseyed, lifting imaginary skirts, then carried on home.

Dancing in the street had chinked my armour and let a sliver of a dream seep in: the hope of happiness, the way that life could be. It unsettled me. I tried to shake it off, but the uneasiness wouldn't go away.

On the floor of the kitchen was the little knife. It was pointing to the stairs. I picked it up and wiped it down and chopped more onions for the evening meal. When I was done, I ran up to our bedroom and slid the knife under the mattress, making sure to hide the glints of steel beneath the sheets.

Later on that day, I went upstairs to Nu. He was sitting in his room on a prayer mat. I decided I would write him a note. I didn't really have anything to say, but writing would comfort me and help me know what I thought of things. And I missed

Nu even as he sat before me every day, missed the part of him that had gone away.

I ran my fingers through his hair and tapped his nose. Then, sitting by his side, I took up a pen and placed some paper on a hardback book to write.

Dear Nu,
I dream of many things. Especially now that some months of married life have passed. Last night I dreamed of an intense and real love, and in my dream our ma was here with us. I wish that were true. In my dream I could see into the future, only all I saw was darkness. Do you know what that could mean, my Nu? At times I wonder if you understand my words. But I don't mind. You must know that wherever you are, you are my greatest comfort.

I was thinking of the way you used to speak to me. I so wish that you would speak, my Nu. And that you were more part of my life rather than a watcher at the side.

I love you, Nu. Always.
Love,
Mani

He looked at the page, then looked away. He didn't write a reply. Instead he started drawing circles side by side with stars inside.

I picked up a pencil and beside his stars I drew some trailing plants growing round and round. Snaking, suffocating vines with pretty heart-shaped leaves. Nu was staring at the rain-drenched window pane, watching raindrops find their zigzag trail down to the ledge.

I picked up the pen again, meaning to write another note to Nu, and as I did, I swept the sleeve of my fleece up. Nu saw the bruises on the dark skin of my wrists. The colour aubergine. He touched them with his fingertips. I pulled away. A jolt of fury. The impudence of pointing out my shameful inabilities; my willingness to let Khan have his way with me. In that moment it was Nu I hated. Not Khan. I didn't cry when I thought of what Khan did to me, but when I saw Nu's tears I began to cry. I threw the pen on the floor and left.

After dinner that day, Nu and I went to the park. Khan had not come home. The sky was darkening although the air was bright with a glow that seemed to emanate from nowhere. It was chilly and fresh. I remembered this feeling from the mountainous terrain of northern Pakistan, where we went one year after one of Papa's cousins died.

The green was punctured with a thousand tiny blooms. A football that someone must have left. Daisies clustered in small groups. The sight relieved the throbbing in my head. I wondered then: is it possible to be happy and deeply miserable at once? Is that the way of things? After every hit, like clockwork comes his apologetic love. Perhaps that is the way it goes. The good meshed in with the bad in each moment that we live.

The football turned into the moon, the daisies the Milky Way. Nu pulled me by my arm and took me to a corner of the park beside a grand old oak tree, boughs bent as if fatigued. A pair of squirrels chased up and down the trunk then bolted out of sight. He led me to a hidden spot and pointed to a bright red tulip on its own, its petals raised and cupped.

Nu knelt upon the grass. He stroked the petals gently from the base right to the tip. In my mind I saw him praying to the Lord for the praying mantis in Lahore. He curved the flower towards me so I could see its yellow powder sticks and perfect symmetry. I had to step away, was winded by its beauty.

As we walked home, I looked back at the tree. It seemed to me that its arching branches weren't fatigued; they bowed themselves to something hidden that I couldn't see.

Chapter Fifty-one

Mrs Lane: four months married

Four months had passed when there was a knock on the door. It was old Mrs Lane, who often came to see us when I lived at Abdul's house.

'Hello, love.'

'Hello. How are you, Mrs Lane?'

'Fine,' she said.

She looked older than before. She wore her hair in softer curls that day, although the powder on her face still showed, defining the grooves and lines on her pasty skin.

'Just out of sugar – can you lend a cup?' Her lisp more pronounced than I recalled. And then she said, 'How are you, chick?'

She's come all this way for sugar was the first thought I had.

'I'm fine,' I lied.

'You know I'm always here to help . . . if you need anything.' She looked at me with intensity, a frown upon her brow making a V. It reminded me of birds in flight that Nu and I would draw.

'Thank you, Mrs Lane,' I said, not knowing what else to say. I wondered what Khan would do if he saw that she was here. I walked to the sugar bowl and put some in a bag for her.

'Are you sure you're OK?' she asked again. We both danced around the truth even as each knew what the other meant. 'Don't want to talk to me about anything . . . you know? Men can be a pain.' She spoke more to the sugar now than to me.

'No, Mrs Lane, I'm A-OK,' I said.

I was sure she could see the tomato stain on the floor. I picked up an occasional table and placed it over the mark.

Then she said something strange. 'I always think that love is a big-eared bird of paradise and you can crush it with a single word. It doesn't die by striking it. But words . . . They can kill it dead so quick. Just like a bullet from a gun.' She paused. 'My mother always used to say that if you throw your heart around, the cuts and bruises thicken it. Scar tissue.' She smiled. 'What use is a heart that cannot love? That's the only job it has to do.'

She turned to look me squarely in the eyes as she got up to leave. I was shuffling from side to side. The lie was clear. She nodded once and left, to my relief.

After a minute or two, something in my stomach started shuddering. Panic gripped me at once. I picked up the bag of sugar that she'd left behind and ran out of the door.

'Mrs Lane!' I screamed desperately. 'Help me!'

There was no one, just a bus turning the corner. My heart knew something that my head would not accept. I wept, sitting on the pavement. Childlike bawling on the kerb. I threw the sugar far away and headed home.

I found Nu waiting by the door. I looked at him, still sobbing like a child.

'Do something!' I screamed.

Then I ran upstairs and fell on my bed, weeping rhythmically, face buried in the quilt.

After I had cried myself to calm, I sat up and let my fingertips caress the sharp metal things hidden beneath the mattress. Maybe, I thought, only sad and bad things take us to the truth we need to see. And that might be the reason those things kept happening to me.

Chapter Fifty-two

Running: five months married

I took Nu to Exmouth Market today. He loved to see the stalls and so many people wandering about. It was cold. But the sun was casting an orange light and everything seemed to glow. I raised the collar of my jacket to hide the bluish bruising at my jaw. The make-up never seemed to work; it only made it worse.

A trader gave Nu an apple 'on the house'. Nu smiled and nodded. I said thank you on his behalf. Despite the sun, the *raunak* and the freshness of the air, I couldn't feel the beauty of the afternoon. My mind was buckled up on a thought that wouldn't go.

The words Khan had spoken so casually two days before had taken me to the edge.

'You should be grateful that I married you.' He huffed and looked away. 'Let's face it, your family is ugly . . . and dark-skinned too.'

This much I could still take. But then he carried on.

'Funny, Mani, I wonder sometimes . . .' He paused to meet my eyes. 'How is it you weren't even scratched, and yet . . .' he sucked in air, holding it within his loosened jaw, 'Nu got beaten up and your ma is dead?'

That was when I decided I had to run away. I planned my escape. I would go the very next day, after Khan left for work. I wrote a note for Nu and placed it in my bedside drawer so he wouldn't find it too soon. I knew that he would be OK. Khan wouldn't hurt him, and there was always Abdul and Dalal. I dragged a bag from under my bed and started loading it.

I felt the sweat break first. My cold breath upon the rising dampness of my upper lip. It stung under my arms. My breathing deepened and I hadn't even started to run. My fisted hands pressed so hard on the tough fake leather of my bag that my nails began to hurt. I'd packed a couple of pairs of jeans, two blue T-shirts, my lip balm, two scarves and a bar of soap. Hardly worth taking, but at least it was for real. I opened the front door just a little. There was no one around so I slowed my breath – hush hush. As if my baby breaths would make me fade away. I crept out of the house. One foot forward into freedom. Then it pulsated red and raw within me, the truth of what I was about to do, and it made me run.

I ran as if I had been spotted doing wrong. Like cops and robbers in a chase. I ran and ran. I ran so hard I couldn't breathe, but I didn't stop. I felt my chest would split apart, a stabbing pain tearing through my heart. A woman with a shopping bag stopped in the middle of the street. She held up her arms, unsure if she should move left or right as I raced past. I could feel her eyes on me. But I didn't look back.

I had got to know the neighbourhood in the months I'd been with Khan: Mrs Berner's dog, the whistle of the Pearsons' kettle from the next-door house, the smell of spices deep-frying at the Patels' place. I even knew the trees, their shapes, their leaves, the swirls on their bark. They too were trapped. Unmoving, still and yet alive.

I reached the bus stop and sat panting like a dog. Adrenalin electrified me as I realised where I was; what I was about to do.

The noticeboard showed in an orange digital haze the time of the next coach out of London. I had picked it randomly. One of many going far away. Any road to freedom suited me. Two minutes to wait. Two minutes to change my life. Two minutes was all it would take. The racing in me calmed. My sweat cooled, my breathing steadied.

The coach pulled into its slot. A steamy rush of air broke the silence as the door swung out. A small crowd had gathered and now formed an orderly queue. I had noticed the bald man with a pack upon his back. The others were a blur. I stood behind them, my own bag hanging loosely at my side. And then I thought of Nu and knew he wouldn't be OK.

Everyone else had boarded. The doors began to close. Inches from my face. The driver opened them again and asked if I was getting on. I jerked my head to tell him no. He looked at me with sideways eyes, his head slowly swinging side to side. He'd seen it all before. It was tiring for him to see another coward at his doors.

I walked back along the escape route that I'd mapped.

If I was trapped, I thought, it was only me that built the walls. I had nearly changed my life, but I couldn't follow through. It was Nu that held me back. I knew exactly what I wanted, but I couldn't choose it for myself. My head was wise. My heart weak. Pathetic.

Back past the familiar smells and sounds. Passing by the trees, the acer watching me. I pulled the door behind me. Its reassuring click. I turned the key to lock myself inside. I dropped my bag and sat on the floor leaning up against the wall. Nu came and sat beside me. Placed his arms around me as I cried into his collarbone. I pounded his chest even as I accepted his embrace. Angry at his stony nothingness. More angry still that he was the only steady comfort in my life. My brother, maimed and brutalised by my own cowardice. I couldn't make sense of anything.

He put something in my hand. It was a pebble from his special box, a pearl-like thing, barely visible, trapped inside a stone. I stroked it with my fingertips, its cold and silky feel, its glow. I squeezed it in my palm until I couldn't feel my fingers any more.

Jasmine came around unexpectedly. Her face deflated when she saw the way I looked. She whispered something under her breath.

She confessed she had fancied Adam all along. That she'd lied to me and kept him for herself. I placed my arms around her, told her it was OK. Historic stuff that didn't matter any more. I liked her very much for many reasons but mostly because of what she did next.

Nothing.

She knew I couldn't talk of what was happening to me.

'Shall we go shopping?' she said enthusiastically. All I really wanted was to curl up and melt away. But I picked myself up and went.

Jasmine turned to me inside our favourite shop. She

whispered gently, 'Why are you putting up with this? It's nuts.'

'Jas. Sometimes he's good to me,' I said.

I smiled. Had nothing else to say.

Nuts I guess it was.

Chapter Fifty-three

Calls

Every other night Khan would be on the phone. He took great trouble to say it was an aunt or some other relative. Or sometimes he would say it was a friend and tell me too much about the man. I knew it wasn't true. His attentiveness gave him away. But still I searched for beauty in the dirt, hunted out the truth inside his lies.

My bruised and tender heart was trained to keep its place, not ask too much. I feared his sudden wrath. Feared the morphing of the man, the circling from Kind Khan to monster then to Tortured Khan again.

Chapter Fifty-four

You: bus route 23 to Charing Cross

29 January

My dear,
Something has changed and I have to see you straight away. We hadn't planned to meet yesterday but still I left the house in the hope of bumping into you.

And where were you last time? Why didn't you meet me at Trafalgar Square the way we'd planned? No matter how I tried to hide it, everyone could see my grief. As I left, my friend called to me: 'Chin up, lovely.'

There's something I need to talk to you about. Something serious that changes everything. I could have written to you. By pressing words upon a page, my pain so often drains a little through my fingertips. But I went to look for you instead. I took the number 23, stepped off at Charing Cross and waited for you there. I stood by the roadside, staring at the buses as they passed. I know I should have given up. Accepted that there was no way for you to know to meet me there, but I couldn't move. I thought you might be on your way somewhere and would spot me standing here alone. Crazy, I know.

Hours passed, but you didn't come. I tried to mask my disappointment from passers-by, though I'm sure it showed.

The owner of the coffee shop across the road was watching me. Whenever his eyes met mine, I looked away. But then I saw him approaching. The lines on his stripy apron bending as he walked. I pretended I was busy and started fiddling with my nails. I didn't want him to think I'd been waiting emptily for you. I felt ashamed.

'Are you all right, love?' he said. 'You've been waiting here a while.'

'I'm fine,' I lied. 'I'd best be getting home.'

I started walking away.

'Want a coffee, love?' he shouted after me.

I made out that I couldn't hear his words.

I walked through Embankment station and crossed the road to the bank of the Thames. It was overcast, and the river was an oily mass sliding slowly to my left. A gull flew up and landed on Cleopatra's Needle. It perched on top of the obelisk, where the needle tapers to a point. The sphinxes sat serene and still on either side. I had an urge to bury my letters beneath this weighty ancient rock. My testament of love preserved in the earth. And how upon the obelisk I'd carve the words *Love you for ever, and after that as well.*

Don't think you have to prove your love to me. You see, I decided long ago that there are many kinds of love and we must respect them equally. Even unrequited. Is that not the purest of them all? Asking nothing back.

Is it any less for being unreturned? It's an expression in itself. It isn't that I'm satisfied with less. I want it all. It's just there's so much more to love, my dear.

That day while staring at the obelisk I made a choice, and now my mind's made up. I will tell you what I must next time.

Your Mexx

Chapter Fifty-five

Unravelling: six months married

I was losing my mind.

It was evening, and I was on the floor with a bowl of soapy water, scrubbing the tomato stain with a wire brush. But the stain just became more prominent. I had to keep my mind off Khan. Stay busy in my daily chores.

Khan had bewitched me; taken me over in some unholy way. I needed him; couldn't live without him. I had to make things right. Was going to make this marriage work however much it hurt.

I felt his fingers on my shoulders. I turned, still kneeling on the floor, then stood. His hands crept up my body, swept my curves so tenderly, ending with his thumbs on my throat, his fingers round the back. I breathed in deep and juddered as my body readied for a kiss. His thumbs were moving up and down, gently stroking me. The movement sent a ripple over my skin. He said quite calmly, a watery voice, 'You are the worst mistake of my life.'

I doubled up in pain inside, although outside I stood quite straight. *He's probably right*, a whisper in my head told me.

As I straightened up inside, that was when you first appeared before me like a ghost. I couldn't help but smile at your darling face. That was just before the squeeze. Khan's thumbs turned in and he was pressing at my throat. I screamed.

'No, please don't hurt me,' I said as I gagged and coughed. He released me and I fell to the floor. He threw the wire brush at me. I felt it sting as it grazed my arm and rebounded off the wall.

As I sat back up, you appeared to me again. Your arms outstretched, anger and love at once upon your face. I reached to you and said, 'I love you,' before I realised no one else could see you. Still I smiled at you. You took me by the hand and helped me to my feet. I was dazzled by the beauty of your deep blue eyes, your dark hair. I must have seemed so pleased. Joyous. Dare I say, in love?

Khan must have thought I was mocking him. Smiling calmly at the hurt he pressed on me. He raised his arm up high, and that was when Nu appeared. He ran to me and held me behind him. He mouthed something at Khan, pushing hard to voice the words he wished to say, his face red and strained, but only hissing came out.

Khan smiled and moved Nu to one side.

First I heard the ringing in my ear as the slap landed on my face. Then the searing pain. It sent me to a different place. I felt a little bit insane; a looseness in my mind. Surreal. I wondered if I liked it in some twisted way. Or was it that I deserved it anyway? Atonement for my sins. But because of you, my love, nothing really mattered.

When my focus came back, it was as if you were much clearer than before. Your arms about me, your whisper in my ear. More real than the world I occupied. Later on that night,

I crawled into my bed and thought of how you came to save me from the monster inside Khan.

Sweet dreams despite the odds.

When I woke the next day, I heard your voice. You were laughing at my messy hair. The sunshine on my skin was you stroking my face. You warmed my skin and shone so bright you made me squint.

The other Khan was also here. Tortured Khan. The gentle man who didn't know the wicked one, except as a stranger he hated.

He pleaded with me. 'I love you, forgive me, you made me do it . . .' Blah blah blah. He tried to stroke my hair and tell me once again how much he cared. His words were like the rustling of a paper bag, drowning out the music of your voice inside my head. I nodded to stop the noise. And then I listened hard to hear your voice again, but I think you'd gone away.

I got out of bed and ran to Nu. I held him tightly in my arms. He didn't make a noise. Then I felt the lurching of his sobs.

There were steps I had to take. Secrets forming in my head. I had to plan it carefully.

The next day Jas came to visit early, unannounced. Khan was still about. Her eyes met with mine then slid to my cheekbone. The bruising by my eye. I held up my hand to cover it, then let my hair fall over to one side. If looks could kill, hers would have done the job. She trailed Khan with poisoned eyes. Khan took his briefcase and rose to leave for work. He slapped his neck. Perhaps he felt her thoughts.

She spoke to me. I couldn't really hear her words, but I heard yours in the pauses she left. She was a distraction, masking you from me. She tried to get me and Nu to leave with her, for good. I thought of Nu walking away. Perhaps he should take his chance, walk away and leave me here alone. I couldn't go. My legs didn't know how to walk away, or where to go at that.

Besides, I told her, I'd already tried.

I knew the only place my legs could take me to was you. I saw you in the movement of the trees, felt the stroke of your hand in the fabric of my sleeve.

I had to meet with you, my love. Find you wherever you were. Nothing else mattered to me more than that. You were the only real thing to me, and after that I thought of you again and again. Heard your voice in the splash and patter of rain. Felt your touch within the breeze that stroked my hair so gently off my face. Do you see now what you mean to me? Despite the misery and the hurt. How can I explain? You are my jar of joy, contained so deep and safe within. Nothing Khan can do will break that jar and let the joy you give me trickle out.

A group of children in the park were huddled in their winter coats against the chill.

'Sticks and stones,' they sang, 'may break my bones . . .' A pause to breathe. 'But words will never harm me . . . so piss off, get lost, back to where you've come from.'

The park was glistening with a bright white sun. The night of Khan's attack had left me hollow. Nu saw it, but there was nothing he could do.

We threw some conkers at the kids, knowing they'd not reach. They laughed and ran away. I pulled at Nu for us to go back home. He would not move. He sat on a bench as if he had a rendezvous. Now, looking back, I see that he did. It started with the strangest pink, which coloured everything: the trees, the grass, the air. I felt my shoulders drop and my frown release as my eyes took in the view. Pink clouds bleeding into orange skies. My breath became the breeze. My eyes the dying sun. I was no longer me but part of the magnificent scenery. Then orange overtook. The colour of serenity. The sun was a waning stain. Like all that was left of me. Slowly it surrendered to the distant trees. I felt a shard of pain. Beauty of this magnitude seemed rude. And as it died away, it left a yearning deep in me. Everything must pass.

Nu and I walked away and back to our home.

It was that time of day when you could still see the faint stain of tomato sauce on the living room carpet. I took a sponge and carpet cleaning fluid and rubbed at it until a frothy mound had formed. The stain just wouldn't budge.

'Abdul and Dalal have invited us for tea,' Khan said. It was a Saturday.

I didn't want to go. I knew Abdul would see through to the shame of my reality. But I could hardly refuse. They had called so many times before. A gathering to celebrate the newly-weds. Khan's excuses had worked every time. No more. Now Nu and I got dressed and ready to go.

I was warned as clearly as if I had been told. Kind Khan was not about tonight. Something wasn't right and I knew I'd see it soon. Something about the way he held my elbow as we entered Abdul's home. He led me like an animal, gripping me too tight.

With one look at my face, Abdul's mouth opened. I let my hair fall to veil a bruise I'd matted over with a cover stick. He asked if I was unwell. I said I had a cold and was tired out that day. Dalal had made samosas and a ginger *chai*. All evening Abdul stared and kept asking how I was. I stood and gathered up some used plates to take them to the sink. Abdul followed me. He stopped me in the corridor.

'*Beti*, you know you can speak to me. Is he treating you OK?'

There was nothing I could say. My throat closed and I started to cry. Khan walked up to us with urgency. Took me by the arm and led me back into the living room to get our things and leave.

In moments we were home. I was terrified.

'I didn't mean to cry,' I said. 'I don't know why I did. It's just I haven't seen them in so many months.'

Khan walked around the living room, his hand upon his chin, staring at the red mark on the carpet, now surrounded by a water stain. He was calm. I thought perhaps I had misread the signs.

He said, 'You need to be punished for what you did. Making me look bad after everything I've done for the two of you.'

Panic took my breath away. I felt a raw and heated sting after his slap. It was the first.

'I beg you, please don't . . . I'm sorry for . . . Please stop.'

He didn't. He carried on. And on. He didn't listen to my

pleading or my sobs. When he was done, my tears mingled with the blood pooling in my hands. My lip was cut and one eye was closing up. I looked for you, my love, but you didn't come for me. I couldn't soothe myself with thoughts of you inside my head.

As I lay on the floor, I felt a stabbing pain at my waist. I rolled into a ball. I wouldn't believe that Khan had kicked me.

'Where are you?' I cried. Why did you leave me then, my love, when I needed you most?

Khan heard me pleading to the empty space. I must have looked insane, speaking to an apparition in the air. His face began to drop. Just as it always did when he realised what he'd done to me. Nu appeared. I saw him with the eye that wasn't closed. Desperation on his face. He was almost as tall as Khan now. He ran to me and helped me to the wall. I could see Khan watching us, his brow warped and ridged. Tortured Khan was back. Tortured by the person he was.

Everything went black.

I don't remember anything after that.

Chapter Fifty-six

Broken: seven months married

The next day when I woke, something in me broke.

In my mind I was nine again, playing the *bansari* with Naboo. When I was nine, I thought I would meet a prince. He'd be so impressed at how well I played the *bansari* that he would marry me.

And that was it. So I practised hard.

I didn't know then of other things that attracted men: a woman's skin and flesh and the thing they call love. Or that attraction could hold within its folds a kind of hatred too. A hate that clawed away the little joy a life had known.

I tried to tell myself that shadows were not real. They were just the masking of the great Lord's light.

It didn't work.

I had tumbled into an abyss

and I knew that

all my

troubles

were

because

of Nu.

If it wasn't for his djinn-white skin, perhaps my life would be OK. Perhaps right now I would be with my prince. Gentle loving strokes and kisses that didn't need to follow hurt. I felt so confused. Perhaps Nu was born of evil deeds, as I had heard back in Lahore. A part of me still longed for him, but I refused to feel that way. How could I, now that I knew he was the cause of my misery; the cause of my shame? And anyway, Nu had withdrawn into a shell for many weeks. Far away from me.

I went to his room. Pushed open the door. He lay quite still in his bed with his eyes ajar.

'You are my curse,' I said.

He looked at me in disbelief.

I went to the corner of his room and gathered up his paper, pencils and pens. In front of him I screwed the paper into a ball and broke the pens and pencils in half.

Then I found his box of stones and threw them out of the window. As they clattered on to the patio below, Nu's eyes began to well. I brushed my hands on my shirt and left.

Later on that evening, I found Nu huddled in a ball behind the door in his bedroom. He was rocking back and forth. I stifled the urge to comfort him. Instead I walked away to cook. Khan would be home soon.

A week or so went by. I didn't write or speak to Nu. I knew that soon I'd make him pay for what my life had become.

After two more nights, I went to him again. He was sitting on his bed with a piece of paper on his lap.

'Why can't you even speak to me?' I said. There was no reply, as I knew there wouldn't be. And then I said, 'You. Are. Useless,' shouting out the words with pauses in between as if to make out he was dim.

I lifted my fist, about to hit him in the back. That was when I saw. The paper on his lap was a letter written in my hand. And there was a look on his face I'd never seen before; shock about his eyes and a mixture of grief and injury distorting the fine features of his face. I looked at the letter.

Dear Nu,

I've wanted for so long to speak to you about that day, but I never knew the way. I don't even know if you remember it. Do you remember it, dear Nu? I don't want you to hurt, but do you recall the things you saw, the things that happened? And do you remember who was there?

Panic rippled through my skin. How could Nu have that letter in his hand, the letter I'd hidden inside a crack between the window and the sill? My arm was frozen high and ready for a strike. Nu lurched off the bed and jumped to the corner of the room, curling into a ball with arms raised to guard against my threatened blow. He dropped the letter as he moved. And then it was as if the air inside the room became too thick. I could hardly breathe. I lowered my arm; my fist unfurled as my fury morphed quickly into fear.

What was happening to me? Why was I treating Nu the way that Khan treated me?

There before me on the floor, creases hatched in squares across it, lay the confession of my guilt, the truth about the thing I did.

Nu dropped his hands and turned his face towards me.

And despite his fear, in his eyes was love. Only love.

I picked up the letter, crushing it into a ball while struggling to steady the tremble in my jaw. Nu placed his hand on my arm. And that was when I began to cry. Even as I did, I felt Khan's presence at my back. He was standing in the hall, watching us. He said nothing. Only nodded infinitesimally, approval in his eyes, his lips pulled into a line. He moved aside to let me run past, hands raised on either side as if to say, 'This one is not my fault.'

I ran into the bedroom, closing the door behind me. Falling to the floor with pen and paper in my hand, tears streaming from my eyes, I wrote a prayer to the Lord.

Dear Lord,
I am Mani.
   I believe in hidden things.
   I believe in you.
   I believe in your angels.
   I believe in your books.
   I believe in your messengers.
   So please, Lord, help me believe in your people too.

I paused. And then I wrote: *And please, please, please forgive me for what I did to Nu.*

I knew I had been wrong. I loved my Nu so much.

I cried silently, muffling the sobs and moans so Nu would never know, clutching the pain inside my stomach as I retched the sadness out. Everything was wrong and I was no good. I reached under the mattress to the sharp and shiny things. As I felt around for them, something cut a gash in my skin. Blood trickled down my arm. I held the hairpin, scissors and knife and in one move threw them out of the window. Then I lay down on the bed, motionless with disbelief.

How could I hurt my darling Nu, knowing what I knew? He was my charge. The only thing that mattered to me.

Chapter Fifty-seven

Nu: eight months married

I jolt. I'm shot out of a blurry dream and realise I must have
fallen asleep. It's dark outside, and it takes me a moment
to recall why I'm on top of the covers, still fully clothed. I sit
on the edge of the bed and see Khan asleep under the quilt.
Then I think of Nu and at once it comes to me. Remorse like
shards of glass inside my gut. I swallow back the nausea and
fear. The guilt of knowing what I nearly did. I want to go to
Nu. Tell him I love him. That I'm sorry for being a fool. But
it's the middle of the night, so I decide that tomorrow I will
put things right. I lie back down still fully clothed and sleep.

Night. It's late, although I don't know the time. Something
has stirred me into wakefulness and I open my eyes. The
curtains are ajar and a finger of moonlight cuts across the
room and points at me. I turn on to my side and see it lying
on the floor. The letter I balled into my fist. I must have
dropped it as I slept. I creep out of bed, pick it up and read.

It's just that since that day, I've never had the heart to ask
these things of you. First you were unwell, and then . . . well,
then my stomach felt so sick every time I even thought of it.

I screw it up again, clutch my stomach with the pain of

knowing what comes next. I gently flatten out the paper once more and carry on.

But Nu . . . It's hard for me to hold the secret privately, and harder still for you and I to never speak of it.

I skip ahead to phrases leaping off the page.

So here it is. It was Pa. Pa was there, do you remember that? And it was Pa who took away our ma and injured you. Will you forgive me? Because, my darling Nu, what I've never said to you is . . .

I see it then, the secret shame I never shared.

I was there too.

I can hardly write the words, tell you of the shameful choice I made. My Nu, I hid myself away when Papa did the thing he did. Forgive me that I didn't try to save you from his hate. Believe me, it's hard to live with it, my cowardice. But I made my choice and every day I am ashamed of who I am. A girl who saved herself and let her loved ones suffer and die.

The next words I see are: *I lied.*

I think of how Nu must have felt to read these words. My eyes blur with tears. But I carry on.

Nu, I know I stole the truth from you and Ma. But what was I to do? We must be loyal to our own, protect the remnants of our family . . . And so I covered it up: that Pa . . . our own flesh and blood, did that thing he did. And you mustn't ever tell on him. It would be wrong to splinter what's left of who we are. No matter what, he is still our pa.

We never need to speak of it again . . .

Do you forgive me?

My hands are shaking and my tears make the paper transparent where they fall. I realise then that I didn't write it for him; it was for me, so that my hurt and guilt could leave my body through my fingertips. I decide right then to rip it into a thousand pieces, but I know that will not work. The guilt I've trapped within the words would only be let out. Freed so it can enter me again.

I fold the letter neat and small. In a single move I'm in the corner of the room. I pinch the carpet where it curls and lift it to place the folded letter underneath. I rest my hand on the carpet momentarily. And as I do, I yearn to write to Nu. To share my thoughts and fears with him again.

I tiptoe back to bed. But my sleep is fitful and disturbed. When I stir into a foggy wakefulness, my only thought is that I must make things right with Nu. I get up several times at night and walk towards the bedroom door. Every time, hand upon the knob, I stop. Nu is asleep, and it's still dark. Even when night starts paling into day, I reach the bedroom door then pull away.

That is the decision I make. How can I know the consequences and where exactly they will lead?

Downstairs, I wait for Nu to wake so I can tell him what a fool I've been. That I love him. Apologise and make amends. I will speak to him about the letter, and how much I wish the things I did could be undone. I will speak of my regrets and how I meant to come to him last night.

I'm sitting in the living room, staring out into the street, wondering if the Labrador will appear today. I think of Khan. No one else can see behind the veil to who he really is. They only see the person he plays. Even Abdul and Dalal; they may suspect, but still they hope the fantasy is real.

I cannot hear Nu getting up. There are no creaking floorboards or footsteps in the hall. The silence from upstairs is far too loud. As I stand, an uneasy feeling rises in me. I'm taken back to that airing cupboard with the slats. Panic starts to spin inside my chest and I know something I shouldn't rightly know. I make a dash towards his room. At the door, I hesitate. My hand upon the handle.

'What have I done?' I whisper. I know that what I really mean is *What have I become?*

My heart is pounding in my ears and tears are wet upon my heated flesh. I scream. You see, I know, I know that something horrible awaits me on the other side. I hate myself so much. I see my father's ugliness splattered with Nu and Mama's blood. I see the rising of his lips and the blood on his teeth. Red and white and black. I take a deep breath and open the door. No one is inside and Nu's bed is untouched.

I look behind the door, then I rush back out into the hall and check the living room, the kitchen and our bedroom too. I whoop a jagged cry and fall to my knees. My ugly life is repeating itself.

Then I recall that the window in Nu's room is open wide. I run back up the stairs and take small steps towards the open window. Something inside me dies. I feel its final breath and now my tears run silently upon my flesh. I close my eyes, stretch out my arms, stepping like the blind. I am approaching the window ledge, but my eyes disobey. They won't open at my say. I cannot look. I'd rather be blind than see the evil of my deeds come back to haunt me.

I'm at the window now and I can feel a cooling breeze upon my skin. I press my damp hands to the window pane.

They fit into the squares of the raised sash. I allow myself a single breath and then I open my eyes. Condensation forms on the glass around my fingers. Fan-like fingers spread wide.

I look down.

A sharp intake of breath.

I don't think I have ever known a joy like this. My Nu isn't sprawled across the ground. There is no mess of death and blood and ruined love on the patio beneath.

I'm panting with relief. A smile that hurts my cheeks. And in that moment, the world around me has a certain clarity. I see myself, the person I've become and I know it's him.

Khan has bent my soul into an ugly shape.

How could I have treated Nu this way? I think of the first note he ever wrote to me: *Love Mani.* I've always loved my Nu, and I'm failing him terribly. Looking out of the window I know exactly what I must do when I find him.

I tell myself he can't be dead. He's run away from me, that's all. It comes to me almost immediately. The front door isn't bolted from inside. It's raining, grey angled threads pounding down. I run outside, no coat, no bag, no key, and chase away into the rain like death is hunting me.

I go to Angel underground, slip past the barriers and search. I come back out again and smack away the papers on the vagabonds who lie around. I cannot find my Nu.

I'm sodden to the skin and feeling faint. I run out into the road. My head begins to spin but I tense myself and refuse to give in.

A sense, a knowing, hits me like the lurch that happens just before a fall. My skin turns prickly. And then I see, right there ahead of me, a red double-decker. The number 57 bus.

Invisibly I slip past the people getting on. I don't even look around. I run up the steps, on to the upper deck.

In the corner in a ball, Nu is leaning up against the wall. All sodden and small. The window above his head shines his hair a luminous, unearthly red.

I lean down to him and place firm arms around him. He looks at me, red eyes wet, and sobs.

A few days go by. Nu has a fever, but the doctor says he'll be fine. I give him soup and sit with him all day and night.

Khan calls to me. I ignore him. I no longer fear bruises or cuts. I want to be with Nu, no matter what Khan may do.

I try so hard to speak to Nu. He averts his eyes; a sign that his ears refuse to hear. He doesn't listen or pay attention to anything I do. And so I take a pen and paper and I write.

My darling Nu,
Do you remember back to a time in Lahore? The time you brought out a roughened, rounded stone, much like the other stones you hid inside your box, except this one was so much bigger than the rest. You examined that stone as if you saw something no one else could see.

I was angry with you that day for some reason I cannot now recall. I took the stone and threw it to the ground. It hit a brick and split apart, nearly half and half. Inside there was a crystal mountain range. It sparkled purple, pink and blue as the sunlight played upon it for the first time.

You looked at me with childlike wonder in your eyes,

your jaw hanging loose. You weren't angry at me. You said, 'Why are these crystals hidden deep inside where they can't be seen?'

I thought a while. I remember that.

Then I said, 'It's because true beauty hides away. It must be shy. It's a gift for human eyes but mostly goes unseen, like a sunset in a distant galaxy.'

'So why can we see its beauty now?' you said as you stroked the geometric glassy shards.

'Because,' I said, 'we hit it hard, split it right apart.'

I should also have said: my darling Nu, we broke its heart.

I love you so much, my Nu.

Will you forgive me?

Mani

Nu reads the page and smiles his special smile. I find that I am smiling too.

Later, as I lie in bed, I think about Nu and the letter I wrote to him. He has read the confession of my guilt. And he knows my lies. Now the lies are ours, mine and his to share. The relief I feel is real; the burden easier for me to bear. These are the thoughts inside my mind as I lie down that night to sleep.

Chapter Fifty-eight

My dear: eight months married (I think)

Something is new. When life is difficult, I carry on, struggle to make things good again. Dreams of you, my love, also help me through. Like those times you come to me when I least expect you to. But there is a change. A snap. The force that gets me up to try again is gone. Vanished right away.

It is October, I think, or is it November? It's cold outside. There are bruises on my skin and deeper hurts within. At night I think of stories from the Lord that Naboo used to tell. He'd say, 'And when they have no skin or flesh, it forms anew so hellfire can burn it up again. And then they feel the hurt again.'

I know I am in hell. My personal apocalypse is here. I'm eating fruits of the Zaquum tree.* Khan strikes me down, then loves me up; then he strikes me down again.

The structure of my hope, like scaffolding that's broken, is tumbling down and clattering to the ground. My life around me falling, falling down. I am locked inside a blackened box, and someone not only stole the key, but took with them the urge that yearns to see the light again.

---

* A tree in Hell which bears fruits shaped like the heads of devils.

★ ★ ★

I wake in the night. Moonlight is playing up and down the quilt with the movement of the branches of the acer outside. I sit up, my motions slow so as not to wake the stranger at my side, the man who mostly I despise. Tomorrow he could be the other man, Kind Khan, the gentle, loving one. I will never know.

Something isn't right. A kind of double vision in my head. Everything is flat and my thoughts are spliced, as if another person sits with me inside my mind. Confusion, fear and darkness everywhere.

I so badly want to feel you near again, my love. The room is small, and on the wall above the bed there hangs a picture of a perfect tulip bud. A tired wooden dining chair and little dressing table are the only other things in the room. On the dressing table is a pen. Gold and black and angled so the moonlight shines it brighter than it really is.

Quietly I leave the bed and sit at the little table. It's just a pace away, but I feel as if I've stepped upon the shores of a different land. My stomach turns itself in thrill. I look back at the bed. See the tulip, and underneath, Khan's head. Perfect symmetry, so different from the angled asymmetric man sprawling in the bed. The man who smiles and smacks with equal ease.

I reach for the pen with my right arm, the good arm; the other lying limp, with bruises smarting, joints sore. From the measure of shade and light upon the windowsill, I guess I have some sixty minutes before daylight fills the room and Khan wakes. I watch the dawn light slowly enter the room.

My joy is masked by some hardened cataract in me.

I fear a day when all colour fades away – joys and tastes and textures just a memory. I slip back into bed and close my eyes again.

Sunken deep into a death-like sleep, all still and silent, for the briefest, sweetest moment I recollect a fabricated truth, remember everything as being well and good. The dream of Khan before the truth spawned and let its ugliness be known. As I begin to wake, I rush around inside my mind to catch and hold my made-up memory. My dream about another life and a man inside the skin and face of Khan. You. As darkness dissolves and brightness fills the room, I see Khan's skin peel and melt away. Like burning flesh in a budget horror film. And I am standing wrapped tight inside the arms of someone else. My dreamy perfect love. I cannot clearly see his face, but I think I know his scent, musky and warm, his raven hair, his shy blue eyes. It must be you, my love.

As I wake, I feel the tulip's silky petals stroke my face. I can smell the scent of flowers in my hair, and when I open my eyes, I see a shower of blooms falling down on me. Thoughts of Khan fill me up and squeeze my dream away. My perfect love fades as daylight fills the room. The low, resonating sound of discontent begins, its endless droning playing in my ears.

Shortly afterwards, Khan wakes.

I am in the living room. It's dark. It's the middle of the night and everyone is asleep. The time has come. I must remove this stain from the carpet. I've tried everything, and nothing's done the job. I take a pair of scissors from the drawer. It's hard, but I persevere. *Snip snip snip*. I cut the stain away.

Now there is a hole where once the evidence of pain used to reside.

I see the cracked tile to my left. The spidery shape: hole in the centre, eight legs radiating out. As I watch, the spider heaves itself away, no longer trapped within the stony tile. It runs to me with lightning speed. I leap, a sting of panic. I scan the floor frantically, searching. Where did it go?

Then I see that it didn't move. The crack remains, unspidery, just a broken tile upon the floor. I calm my pounding heart, slow my breathing, adrenalin still coursing through my veins.

I go back up the stairs and lie on my bed. It's late, but I don't sleep. Instead I think about the banging on the door some days ago.

'Mani, Mani, Nu, open the door.'

Abdul had come to see me, to save me in some way. Khan was home. He placed his hand over my mouth and told us to pretend that we were out. We did exactly as he said. Abdul went away.

When I sleep, more dreams and visions come.

Just before the break of dawn, I look up towards the window by the dressing table. Khan is asleep. My fear and daring makes shivers on my skin. A skirt of curvy light is forming underneath the curtains. They are not fully drawn, and I can see the trees beyond. I hear the shudder of their leaves. I get up and lean on the table. A cold autumnal wind sends a quiver through the branches of the acer tree. And then a whooshing gust spins the leaves in a random circle round the tree.

Perhaps it is a dream, but I swear an instant count reveals

exactly twenty-three leaves. Twenty-three perfect works of art and beauty circling upon the breeze. In a Rumi spin, they funnel round, a fountain reaching up and out. Then they pause, as if time takes a break, and momentarily I see. Dark veins across each golden leaf spell out the words *my dear*. On each a story of its own. A violent gust explodes from down below. It thrusts the leaves out and about so that they tumble everywhere; some near, others out of sight.

It is a message. I have to cast my yearning up into the air. I have to send it out. Give the love I feel to someone worthier than Khan.

It is then that the moment comes to me. The moment when I know that I have to find you, see you, meet with you. For real. Not just as a dream inside my mind. It seems to me that everything I've suffered at Khan's hands has been to prepare me for this day. Like a person drowning, gasping for breath, I begin to write frantically, my madness spilling on to the page. I'm writing for my life.

Do you want me? No. Need is a better word to use. I need you just as I am sure that you need me. Or more: perhaps you want to own me in some strange, possessive way.

As I write, a little of that thing I recognise as life makes a flutter in my chest. I like it. The defiance, the wrongness and the rightness. A sweetness in the bitterness. The ink a vibrant blue, carving out a groove to mark for ever the love I feel for you. A lover's scar.

I'll believe you love me, truly and for real, when you possess me totally. Possession is part of love. It is. If someone loves you so much that they must own you, body and soul, I'd say it is pure love at its best. Do you understand?

You'd think there was nothing more to say. But that's not true. My love for you has given me a way to survive. To breathe and carry on, despite the torment thrust on me. Something in me grows. A warmth, a love, a sense of destiny, as if magic has been spun. And nothing that Khan may do will get me down. More garbled thoughts, a rush of words and letters.

Let me tell you something. Living life is not the way to be alive. Mere food and drink and cleansing rituals. Life is something else. To marvel. To feel. And the best of any marvelling is love. It is the answer to both life and death. What can we do to make sure it is the real thing? Death is preferable to losing what you feel.

The next days pass by fast, and every moment I am occupied with thoughts of you. I cannot wait to go to bed. I kiss Nu on the head and rush away. Pretend I am asleep when Khan walks in. At first I lie awake, thinking only of my pen and you. When I finally sleep, I know I'll wake just as half-light begins to show.

More words pour out, messed up, confused, not making any sense.

I mean to say that love does not need to be reasonable to pass the lover's test. That's why the man who is a fool for me will be the one I choose. That's why I choose you. That's why I love you, want to be with you. You were meant for me.

Each morning when I write I feel a change. I feel it die and fall away, my monotone of grey, my shame. Words of colour, love and awe begin to fill the darkened void before my eyes, and it starts to morph. The pale turns to the richness of my midnight skin, the cold is warmed and reddened like the smarting of my swollen flesh. I disguise my broken life, imagine my reality away. And focus on you lying secretly with me, beneath the tulip, underneath the quilt.

I see you now, my love. I don't know if I am asleep, or whether it is day and I'm awake. You're stretching out your arm and leading me to you. You take me by the waist and swing me round. I hear a piano playing in the dark. I don't know where the music's coming from. It's making me limp as you hold me in your arms, and your eyes hypnotise me. We're spinning now, spinning round so fast. The world behind you blurs into curved horizontal lines. Binding us together for all time. And when I wake, I still feel your embrace, reaching for me from my dreams. There's dim light at the windowsill. I stumble to the dressing table and write.

Another night.

My head still isn't right. Dreams break into my waking mind. The separation is weak. Sometimes I think I am awake when I'm asleep. But no matter what, when I open my eyes, when night is becoming day, I write.

My dear,
Come to me come to me come to me come come to me come to me come to me come to me come to me come to me come come to me come to me come to me come to me come to me come come to me come to me come to me come to me come to me come to me come to me come to me come come to me come come to me come to me come to me come to me come to me come to me come come to me come to me come to me come to me come

come to me come to me come to me come to me come
to me come to me.

My love, I love you totally.

I hold it up towards the growing light, then screw it up and
throw it in the bin.

I start again.

My dear,

I was thinking about you lots today. Your deep blue
eyes and the way the lines around them smile deeper
than your lips. I'm thinking of you reading this, your
fingers stroking ink. Writing to you makes me feel I've
lived. It's like a need, a gnawing deep inside that this
alone can satisfy. And I will see to it that you get this
letter, whatever it may take. I'll follow you. Make sure
the moment's right. Make sure I'm not seen . . .

I press down the nib to sign my name, but the pen won't
move. It's speaking to me but I cannot work it out. And then
it comes. I must sign the name of who I plan to be instead of
who I am.

That's the moment. The moment that Mani is no more
and Mexx is born. With the signing of that name, I feel a
change. I become a different person. Something rises inside
me. It's bold and strong and full of mystery, and it takes
control. Nothing will stop Mexx doing what she has to do. No
one will stop her writing to you so you know the feelings she
has for you. And she will search the streets of London to find
you. Love will live and tonight's the night that hurt will die.

I step outside. I walk around our small square garden in the dark.

And smile.

I feel the ache of healing in my chest. Something deep inside me begins to mend with every thought and hurt I groove and ink upon the sheet.

A short wait and the morning's here. I step out of the house, banging the door too hard. I'm on my way to you. And I am happy. The first time since my wedding day. Firm stride, wide steps, arms swinging in a march. I love the feeling I have now. It swells so big, it's everywhere. The rust-scabbed iron gate wolf-whistles as it swings me out, and my letter to you is flapping and bending as I walk.

Soon, so soon, I will be with you, my love. My heart is palpitating and I can hardly wait.

Part Four

Chapter Fifty-nine

Spots: eleven months married

Nu and I are frying onions, peeling garlic. Nu loves to help me cook, and we have fun. He knows the basics now, which is no surprise; he's growing up. There's a wildlife show playing on the TV, though no one's watching it. A leopard is walking on a grand and sunny plain. I think about its skin, pale and dark and spotted, and I think about the saying that a leopard's spots will never change. It's wrong, thought up by someone who has never seen the change I see in Khan.

It's early February, and next month is our anniversary. For many weeks life has been good. In three short months things have completely changed. Every time he angers, you, my love, appear before my eyes. I write to you, and for some reason I cannot explain, his anger dissipates. Meeting you, writing to you has changed my reality. Shifted something in me and also, although I don't know how, in Khan. And so these weeks have passed without a single cut or bruise. No purpling of skin.

At first I wasn't sure it would carry on. But it did. And more. Two weeks ago, Khan took me to the cinema, and afterwards we walked for hours in the dark, chatting about life and hopes and plans. Khan spoke of the children we would have. He wanted two; I argued that three is far better company. And afterwards, like a happy couple married many years, Khan made Ovaltine and brought us both a mug to drink in bed. I leaned on his chest as we sipped the milky broth. Khan joked about the measurement of milk to powdered formula to maximise the taste.

Nu stirs the onions as I peel and chop potatoes. With the hiss and spit of the pan, I don't hear the jangle of Khan's keys. He takes my hand and leads me to the sofa facing the TV. I have a tea towel in my hand, and on the screen a leopard crouches down. I think it's about to leap. Khan leans towards me.

'I missed you so much today, my Plum.'

I smile.

'Can you believe how different things are now?' he says.

'I know,' I say. 'I feel it too. It's wonderful.'

'It will always be this way now, I promise you, Mani.'

I hear a clattering. Nu has dropped something on the floor. That's not the reason I get up and run to him. I can smell onions caramelising into brown. So often Nu leaves the onions frying for too long and so their sweetness turns bitter. I remove the pan from the heat and pour a little water in. The whoosh is loud.

'Nu, you must watch onions as they fry.' His eyes meet mine, so I know he's hearing words today. I'm pleased. 'Onions burn so suddenly, and if they do, we have to throw them away.'

I run back to Khan and take my seat beside him, hoping for his arm. He pulls me close.

'You seem so happy now, my Plum,' he says. 'I wonder why that is.' There is mischief in the half-smile on his face.

'I *am* happy, Khan. I can't explain. Things have been great.' As I speak, I cannot help but think of you, my love; of our rendezvous and letters in my head.

'Well, my Plum,' Khan says. 'I've decided we should mark our anniversary.'

'But it's not been a year yet.'

'You're right, but it's a year since we first met.'

My mind is on the cooking again. 'One moment, Khan,' I say. I run to Nu and see he's stirred the chopped garlic into the onions. It smells divine. Just like the scent and beauty of my life. As I breathe in, water wells inside my mouth. I motion Nu to chop tomatoes into chunks, and I take out the *masala* pot, thinking of the mix of spices shortly to go in. The brightness of the yellow turmeric catches my eye and makes me smile. I move it to the side, then pace quickly back to the living room.

Khan sits me on his lap, then stretches underneath the sofa for a tiny box. It has a blue bow on the top, fixed in the middle with a pearl. My mouth opens.

'What is this?' I slide off his lap and sit beside him once again.

'Do you remember Cambridge?'

I laugh a little as I say, 'How could I forget?'

Khan lifts out a necklace with silver daisies tumbling off a chain inserted through a hole in each stem. I cannot help but breathe in sharply at the sight.

'Wow . . . it's beautiful, a silver daisy chain,' I say as I caress it with my fingertips.

'You'll see I didn't make this one,' Khan says.

I laugh softly as he kisses me on my lips, long and soft and deep. I feel a little dizzy as he pulls away. He fastens the necklace around my neck. I see Nu, and notice tension in the setting of his jaw.

Khan rises to go upstairs and change.

'Khan,' I say, holding him close to kiss him on the cheek. 'I just wanted to say . . .' I look down at the floor to hide the wetness forming in my eyes. I always knew everything would be OK one day. 'This will look great with that white dress you bought me.'

'For you, my Plum, anything.' He smiles, and hugs me tight, then runs upstairs to change.

And that's how I know the world got it wrong, the thing about a leopard and its spots. Of course a leopard cannot change its spots, but its attitude is another thing, and I am certain it can change that. On the TV now a leap of leopards, bloody-faced, are ripping at the flesh of baby deer. I look away.

I lie in bed that night and think about my life. It's true, Khan needed me to mend his ugliness. And now it's done. I know the reason why. It's you, my love, and the letters we share. How wonderful to think that loving you has sent its magic everywhere. And all this while, Nu's been happy too and doing better at his special school.

I think about two nights ago. When Khan came home, I was folding clothes. He grabbed me from behind and squeezed me tight. He kissed me on the cheek and wrapped his arms about me firm and strong. His palms, warm and large, cradled my waist. I knew right then that he was back.

The amazing man I knew before we wed. And now I can hardly recall the troubled times between.

'Mani,' he said, sniffing at the pan bubbling away in the kitchen, 'that smells divine.' And then he handed me pink roses that he'd bought for me. He seems to bring me flowers nearly every day. 'I think I'll have to send you back to school, my Plum,' he said. 'Your food's too good and my waist is growing big.'

I chuckled lightly as he ran his fingers through my hair.

I turn to him in bed and see his face half hidden by the sheets. I smile at him even though he's fast asleep.

It's late afternoon and I spread butter on toast. It's a snack I have before Khan and Nu return. I like it crispy and hot so the butter melts on top. I'm staring at the acer tree outside. It keeps me company when I'm alone at home. I've already written to you, my love, the way I do almost every day, ready for the next time we meet. The letter's folded in an envelope in the centre pocket of my bag.

I think of the beauty of a normal life; how wonderful it can be. Dishes to wash, food to cook and eat, a smiling man and hoovering. Perhaps the cup that holds our happiness is chiselled from the hurt and suffering we've felt. So my delight is deep. I feel it more. I am conscious of the magnitude of joy now in my life.

It's as if my love for you, my dear, is like a river overflowing its banks. It's like my loving you has changed the universe. Is this what love can do; can it really change your world?

Nu enters, and shortly afterwards, Khan is home. He approaches me in the living room and takes me in his arms.

'You know I've changed, my Plum.' He pauses, with a clenched, excited smile. 'Do you believe that things are different now, can you see it's true?' His head is down and he is raising his eyes. 'I've understood. I've finally learned.'

'I know, Khan.' I'm so happy that I have to look away. I'm overcome.

'Mani, I've never said this to you before.' He runs his fingers gently down my cheek and holds my neck, his thumbs caressing it. 'I'm so sorry for everything I've done to you.' There is resignation in his face. 'I want to make things right. Apologise. I will never hurt you again.' He breathes in deep. 'You do believe me, don't you?'

I look at him despite the welling of my eyes.

'I have been so terrible to you,' he says. 'I know that.' He looks away, and I see Tortured Khan flash across his face. 'You must be an angel to stay with me through all the things I did to you.' I think of Nu and how he used to call me 'and-gel' so many years ago. 'I know it's no excuse, but things have been difficult for me, you know, at work and everything.'

I can hardly believe his words. The confession of his guilt. I always knew the good in him would win.

'Something else I've never said to you, though I know you'll understand. My problem . . .' He hesitates. 'The way I've been with you. It's because of my father and the things he used to do. But I . . . I . . .'

'I know,' I say, placing my hands on either side of his face. 'I understand. You don't have to speak of it.'

'My angel,' he murmurs. Tortured Khan is fading as he smiles. 'Let's go away,' he says. 'Let's start our new life with a holiday. And Nu must come with us too.'

He falls to his knees and hugs me round the waist, pressing his face against the skin exposed between my waistband and my top.

'This will be our honeymoon. Just a year too late.' He pauses. 'Forgive me, Mani. I've learnt and I have changed.' And with that he takes my left hand, kisses my fingertips, then slides a gold and diamond band on to my middle finger.

'Let's go away,' he says.

All I can do is smile and say, 'OK.' I'm feeling shy again.

Isn't that the way of life: when things are too bad to even contemplate, a ray of light appears and obliterates the darkness. I feel deep relief. As if a curse is finally released. My stomach lurches and jitters rush about my skin. But don't think that you aren't in my mind, my love. I hope you will understand. I love you too, so very much, but if the man I've joined with in a holy way intends to make things right, I must give it a try. I can see that he has changed. His eyes are soft again, the way they used to be. Kind Khan is here to stay.

I am behaving like a child, a bashful little girl. I'm unfamiliar with myself again, just like I used to be.

A holiday is going to set my whole world straight. But first there is one thing I must do.

I run upstairs. Nu is sitting on his bed, paging through a hardback picture book. He doesn't look at me. I run into my room, and with pen in hand I write to you, my love.

My dear
This is the hardest letter I've ever written, and it may
be quite a shock. I've made a choice. I tried to tell you

of it face to face, but I didn't get the chance. Before I tell you what I must, please know that I love you. I always will.

Please remember that.

Loving you has given me the strength to carry on.

But things have changed and I've decided I must stay with him.

He isn't the way he used to be. He loves me once again.

It's a miracle.

I know this will be hard for you, but it's only fair I tell it straight. You see, he hasn't hurt me for some while. In fact he is kind and loving. And though I love you totally, I must give him a chance. He is my husband, after all.

There is something else I must say, though it may sound strange. I know that it's the love we share that made him good again. It has infused my world. Somehow my love for you has mended his brokenness.

I must now say goodbye. For good. I wish you the best of everything. Always. And I will pray for you. Please know that though I am with him, my heart is always yours and that's the way it will remain.

Eternally, with love,

Mexx

I put the letter in an envelope and place it in my bag. As I do, I take the other letter out, the letter I wrote earlier, and put it in the bin.

Next I run to Nu. When I speak to him, he refuses to look

at me, so I know he will not hear the words I speak today. I pick up the pen beside him on the floor, and a piece of paper, and write:

My darling Nu,
Khan has changed. He wants things to be good again. And he is taking us on holiday. How wonderful this is. Nu, he is sorry for the things he did to me. I think he's understood.
    And we've never been away. He's going to take us somewhere far. I'm so excited, Nu, I can't wait!
    Love you always, my Nu.

He takes the pen from my hand. He draws a line gently, diagonally across the page. Then with sudden force he scribbles across my words. He grooves the page so hard, the paper splits in two. There's nothing left to see, just shreds of paper, ink upon the book I leaned upon to write.

I grab his arm and take the pen away. I cup his balled-up fists inside my hands and urge his eyes to meet mine. I say with forceful calm, 'Nu, everything will be all right. I promise you. Khan's really changed. We have been blessed and I think I know why this is happening. Things are going to be OK – you'll see.'

Nu looks away, his eyes defiant, fixed upon the wall.

'And look,' I say, showing him my hand. 'He's even given me a ring to mark our anniversary.'

Chapter Sixty

Honeymoon: twelve months married

I am so excited. We're queuing at Heathrow after checking in. Khan strokes my lower back. It sends a wave of tremors down my legs. And when the queue goes still, he claims me with his arms. Wraps them around me and I go limp. His power over me is so complete that I cannot move without careful focusing. He seems to know. He's playing with me like a kitten with a ball. He runs his fingers through my hair, his thumb trailing my cheek from the bone right to the earlobe. He tarries there a while as he strokes and circles it. I am mesmerised.

Nu is behind us with a rucksack hanging from one shoulder. He looks at people walking, talking, children hanging on the railings upside down. Khan points to a small child with curly hair. 'Do you think ours will look like that?' he says.

I smile.

'Better, by some way I'd say, if they take after you,' he says as he squeezes my hand.

We're on the escalators now. The board emerging as we rise confirms we're heading for Islamabad in Pakistan. Khan says that from there we'll get a taxi to a place called Bhurban, where his family villa is. He's been there once before. It's further north than Murree, where most honeymooners go. I've heard about the beauty of this place, all mountains and blue sky, and I cannot wait. I cannot wait to start my proper life with Khan and to see Pakistan again. It's a shame we cannot also go to Lahore to see Naboo. But everything's arranged. It's been set.

As we wait at the gate, my thoughts slip to you, my love. Although I'm sitting beside Khan now, I cannot help but marvel at our secret love and how it changed our lives, both yours and mine. I think about the letters I wrote you, and as I do, Khan says, 'A rupee for your thoughts.'

I laugh.

'It's nothing,' I reply. It's as if he read my mind. I push the notion aside. 'I'm just so happy now.' I reach to him and kiss him lightly on the cheek. He rolls his eyes and plays out a dizzy head, then winks.

I've been on a plane before, but this feels like my first ever flight. I love the big seats and the mini windows with their fitted blinds; the stewards and the packaged food; the howl of the engines. I watch strangers thrust their bags up overhead before they settle down. One man smiles and nods at me. I smile back. Khan notices. A deep beep comes from the tannoy as a hostess begins to speak. I take the window seat and Nu the one behind. Khan sits beside me. He crosses his legs so his body arches over mine. He makes out he's looking through the window, but I know he's watching me carefully, absorbing every part of me. Enjoying the sight. He sweeps his gaze across my body, focusing on flesh. As if I am a dismembered entity. His eyes don't seek to meet with mine.

* * *

I fall asleep, and when I wake, Khan looks away with a frown on his brow, and swiftly folds a piece of paper in his lap. He slips it into his bag. His frown won't go away and he smiles awkwardly. I wonder if he's hidden something I'm not meant to see. Could it be a gift he plans to give me? I feign ignorance. I'll be patient; wait and see. I smile at the thought of how much he loves me now. How much I mean to him and how I helped to save him from the anger he couldn't control. He needs me and I need him as well.

But there's something in his eyes I can't identify. And a difference in the way he behaves. As if he's hiding something he doesn't want to share. Perhaps he doesn't like flying. The crazy fear of death keeps coming to my mind. Death in a crashing plane or by falling off a cliff. I must banish these thoughts. I mustn't taint the turn my life has taken for the good.

I see that Nu is asleep with his head against a pillow on the window pane. He's holding something in his hand that I can't quite see. I think about waking him, but drowsiness wins out. I yawn and close my eyes again.

I wake with the tannoy telling us that it's time for breakfast. I'm feeling uneasy. I think it must be the altitude, or perhaps the excitement of my new beginning with Khan. The hostess brings some tepid tea and a dry bread roll with jam. I cannot eat, although deep hunger growls in me. I drink the tea and toss the breakfast in the rubbish when the trolley comes around.

Adrenalin is running in my blood. I wonder if my body

senses things my mind won't comprehend. I tell myself it is
nerves from my first flight since I left my homeland. Or
perhaps I'm thinking of what Papa did to Ma. I cannot say. I
read a magazine called *Duty Free*. I stare at a bracelet on page
68. It's silver, with charms that spin around the chain. One
charm is a leaf, another a tree, and there are roses in between,
the flowers of my wedding bouquet. It makes me think about
my life: my letters to my love, my wedding day, the promise
Khan made me on Jesus Green. *I will care for you.* And now I
know it's true.

I get up to go to the bathroom, squeezing past Khan
snoozing in his seat. When I return, I nearly cry as he puts
the very bracelet from page 68 upon my wrist.

'I saw you admiring this,' he says.

'I love it,' I say, bemused, amazed.

He holds me close and says, 'For you, my Mani, anything.'

I can't believe how much he's changed. Maybe, I think, he
was possessed before by some kind of djinn.

When we arrive, it's mid-afternoon. It's taken many hours in
the plane, and from Islamabad we have to travel in a taxi, a
beaten-up old thing, its boot held down by string. I watch the
mountainous terrain from the window. It feels too far away,
like something I'm watching on TV. After an hour on the
road, Khan requests a stop to make a call. We pull up beside
three hut-like shops propped together side by side. Sitting in
the car, I hear him speaking in a dialect I don't understand.
Panjabi, perhaps, I think. The taxi man keeps looking back at
me through a rear-view mirror hanging loosely from the roof.
It must have fallen off and now it's been reattached with wire

and two rusty nails. His eyes flick between me and Khan. Men here tend to stare, and so I dismiss his wandering eyes. I think he understands the dialect Khan speaks, and it could be that he's listening. For the smallest moment I think I hear my papa's voice muffled in the person Khan is speaking to on the phone. A current rises from my stomach to my brain and flames the skin upon my cheeks. I must be hearing things. A *tanga* overtakes the taxi, an old cart pulled by a donkey. The driver turns to glance into the cab. His face is grooved and sunken beneath his embroidered cap.

Nu is dozing, so I step out of the car to stretch my legs. I walk to the edge of the road and marvel at the scale and beauty of the place. Below, the mountainous terrain collapses; giant boulders, trees and crevasses tumbling beyond the cliff. All this right beneath my feet. The sight weakens my knees and so I step away. The sky domes mightily above. It's taller and broader than any sky I've ever seen before. In the distance, a thousand mountain peaks pierce a blur of mist and cloud. The vastness somehow calms my jangled nerves.

As I walk back towards the taxi, a trader in one of the huts waves me over to him.

'*Arey, deko, deko*'. . . Hey, look,' he says, half English, half Urdu. There are a dozen scarves, patterned and plain, folded neatly on the table of his stall. He looks left and right, then leans out to check the street. He reaches to a hidden shelf and pulls out a brown paper bag. '*Shahtoosh*,'** he says. 'You like . . .' He hands me a large camel-coloured shawl. It's so

---

* Hey you, look, look.
** A shawl made from the neck hair of a Himalayan ibex.

soft and weightless I can hardly feel it on my skin. He takes it back and prises off a ring from the little finger of his left hand. He feeds a corner of the shawl into the ring, then, like a magician, pulls it through in one swift and easy move. I am amazed. I don't notice that Khan has finished his call and is standing behind me.

'It's a shawl made from the king of wools, the softest on earth,' he says. 'From a little deer. But it's illegal, so he must hide it from the police.'

Khan ushers me back into the taxi, the anxious trader bartering prices behind us as we walk away. We pull on to the road as a small lorry with a giant load of hay appears. It's loaded up so high, I'm sure that it will topple at the turn. The taxi man waits until it's disappeared, and then moves on. The steep raw landscape unsettles me. I think about the road; just a narrow gravel track upon a precipice. At every bend I fear the taxi man will swerve and we will tumble to our deaths.

After a while, the taxi man points to a villa on its own, high up on a hill. The sun is going down, and further back, a kaleidoscope of coloured roofs rises from the canopy of green. Like man-made treetops reaching for the sun. Lights are dotted on the hills, and look as though the stars above have fallen to the ground.

We arrive. The villa is big. A single-storey residence. Its worn gabled roof is so low, it looks like it is reaching for the earth. It lies deep within a dense, wild forest. It's comfortable, though. Three large bedrooms with en suites, a kitchen at the rear behind a living room that faces south. Plate-glass walls spill on to a bare wooden deck. The house becomes a toy against the distant mountain range. There are no stairs, and the ceilings vault up high. The floors are white stone, and there is modern artwork on the walls.

Khan's aunt Bibi and uncle Younis greet us in the living room. The taxi man also follows us inside. It is customary for hospitality to be offered to everyone, and Younis tells the taxi man to eat and rest before he leaves. There's a *charpai** bed on the veranda where he can be at ease.

Bibi wears a frown and a smile at once. She is a heavy lady with a fleshy face. She embraces me so long, I wonder if she'll ever let me go. She is happy to see us, and runs to fetch us *garam elachi chai*** and samosas that she's already prepared. But something hiding in her eyes is filling me with fear. And I notice agitation in both Younis and Khan. They don't sit down on the sofas in the living room. They walk about, not quite knowing what to do. Are they waiting for someone else to arrive? I wonder as I watch them pace. Khan keeps running his fingers through his hair. He glances momentarily at me, then quickly looks away.

I am so tired I can hardly walk. Nu doesn't want to eat and so he goes to his room. I check on him as he settles for a nap. I run my hand over his head and tell him to rest well. As I leave, he pulls me back, takes paper from his bag and writes: *I am worried. Something isn't right.* I tell him not to worry. That everything is fine. It's a different place and he is tired from the flight. He stares down at the floor as he motions out a 'no' with the swinging of his head. I feel it too, but I keep it

---

* A traditional woven bed.
** Hot cardamom tea.

to myself. I leave him to rest and return to the living room.

I tell Khan I need some air and to stretch my legs. I walk out on to the gravel driveway of the house, which is built in a clearing cut into the dense forest pines. The lights of the villa are now barely visible. The air is light and fresh with the smell of damp and green. The night is cool and makes goose bumps rise on my skin. I stare at the stars scattered messily about the giant canopy.

Khan calls me back into the villa. Another man has arrived and is pacing in the living room. He is tall and thin and stares at me as if I'm something tasty to eat. Khan doesn't introduce him. He hovers at the corner of the room. I drink my tea and watch the man and Younis carefully. Moments pass, and yet another man arrives. This one smiles too widely as he greets the others. His teeth are big and white. The four men huddle in a group, speaking in low voices as they look quite openly at me. I cannot hear what they say. They keep staring at me, measuring, assessing. I feel exposed. I close my shawl around me, cross my legs and squeeze my body small.

One of the unknown men goes to the front door and locks it, then returns to the group at the far end of the room. Their glances gain a certain weight. I call to Khan, asking him to come over so I can speak to him. He hesitates. When he comes, he does so slowly, his hands behind his back, his nose in the air. A crack of fear rushes through my chest. It's something I can see in his face, his gait, the angle of his brow. My hands begin to shake, so I place them underneath my legs on the seat.

'What do you want?' he says, still standing some distance from me. His voice is firm and loud, his face stern, and there is hate in his eyes. I lose my confidence.

'I want to go to bed now, if that's OK.'

I search his face for any sign of my loving husband. There's nothing there. I don't know this man, this person going by the name of Khan that I'm speaking to right now. Except I do. I know him very well. He is the man who hits me fiercely. Bruises me and makes me feel a fool.

'Then go to bed,' he says. 'I'm not stopping you.'

I know now that something is very wrong. I wish desperately that Nu and I were somewhere far away. My stomach clenches and tears well up. The lump in my throat makes it hard for me to breathe. I am a fool, a stupid girl to be here when I know what Khan is capable of. I realise now that he's not in love with me. I begin to see the trick he's played. I fooled myself. Let the dream I had of him become more real that the man he really is. And now I know there is a price to pay. A price I can't afford.

My breath deepens as I stand. All four pairs of eyes flick to me at once. For some reason I cannot explain, I don't go to the bedroom, but walk to the kitchen to find Bibi. She's sitting on a prayer mat with a chain of *tasbee*[*] beads in hand, weeping as she chants the almighty names of God. When she sees me, her tears turn into sobs, and for some reason I am weeping too. I run to her and she embraces me. We sit together on the floor. Two women in a house full of men.

'*Bachi*,[**] what did you do?' she says in Urdu.

'Nothing, Aunty,' I say. I am crying now, knowing that

[*] Prayer beads threaded like a rosary.
[**] Child.

something bad is happening. She looks at me with pity, horror, sympathy all at once. 'Please tell me what you know,' I ask. 'What's going on? What are they going to do to me?'

She releases a guttural sob, then catches hold of it. She contains her grief, her *dupatta* pressed against her mouth. She cannot look at me; she ducks and shakes her head and averts her eyes repeatedly like an apology.

'*Ahyah khair*,' she says, and then again, '*Ahyah khair*.' God protect you. She strokes me from the top of my head to the tip of my chin, gently grasping it. I feel as though I'm facing the precipice outside. And I'm going to have to jump. I see it now: she's mourning me. She's looking at me like I'm wrapped up in a *kafan** at my own funeral. She sees my youth; the dreams and hopes I harbour in my heart. They're pouring out of me, leaving me just like the teardrops that I weep.

'Help me,' I say.

'*Bachi*, I am *majboor*,** a helpless woman trapped here with you.' She weeps and wipes her face with the *dupatta*. 'And I am old. What do you think I can do?'

'He's your nephew, surely you can do something,' I say. She clicks her tongue; surrenders her hands in a gesture of resignation; shakes her head and lowers it in shame. She is a prisoner as well. To her, the deed's as good as done. I am a dead girl walking.

I see the gleam of something bright beside the kitchen sink as I stand to walk away. Silver, sharp and pointing right

---

* White death shroud.
** Helpless.

at me. I take it as I leave. I wedge the blade inside my left armpit, the handle sticking out, although it's buried deep beneath my shawl.

I walk slowly back into the living room and over to the bedroom that is to be mine and Khan's. As I reach the door, Bibi calls out to me. 'Wait half an hour, have more tea before you sleep.' I turn towards the sofa and take a seat.

The men look up as another man enters the room. They place their right hands upon their hearts and bow their heads to greet him. It is the *sadar*,* the village chief. He looks at me, a long, slow stare. The taxi man walks in and glances at me as if he wants to speak to me but dares not say a word.

Bibi brings in tea. As I take a sip, I see Khan's bag beside me on the floor. It looks like a black beast: gaping mouth with paper like a tongue lolling to the left.

My eyes focus on the words upon the page.

My dear, I love you very much . . .

They are my words. It's a letter I wrote, the one I threw away before we left.

I get up without saying a word and leave. I walk briskly past the men, straight into the bedroom. I hold in my sobs until I've closed the door. And then I fall. My legs give way and my mind resigns; I cannot think things through. I look up at the door. There is no lock. I pull my suitcase up against it, but even as I do, I know that it won't work. There's nothing I can do. I stare out of the window and search for hope, a sign, a route away. The woods are totally black, but the moon is shining out. Its glow reminds me of Nu's face.

---

* Village chief.

It dimly lights the trail the taxi drove upon. I think I might run and chance it anyway. But what about Nu? I get up to make my way to his room. And that's when there's a knock on the door.

'Dear Lord,' I pray, whispering the words, and in my mind I'm writing them as well, my fingers moving back and forth.

I love you; you know that from the letters I have written
you. I think of you so much, you're always on my mind.
Lord, you know I've tried so hard to be good. It hasn't
always worked. And though I know I don't deserve
much of anything from you, I ask, I plead, please please,
Lord, save me and Nu from this place and the evil that
I feel.
   With all my heart,
   ~~Mexx~~ Mani

Khan pushes open the door with ease. The suitcase slides across the floor. He picks it up and sets it to one side. And then in the most natural way, he walks to me and strikes me. My cheek is stinging and I'm on the ground. My breath is short and tears are welling up in my eyes.

There is no shock, no remorse upon Khan's face. No sense of hating what he has done; he's only hating me. His chest expands a little at the sides as if he's breathing in. His eyes lift, his lips pull back. There is an expression on his face that he directs at me. Pride, dominance, superiority.

He smiles.

Not a smile that shows affection or connection. But one that lords its power over me. He has me then. He has me totally. And I know that I am doomed.

I see that something is different from before. He now accepts the evil part of him. The devil in him wins; the angel flies away. There is no struggle in his soul. And that's what seals my knowledge of my fate.

'Why did you sit so shamelessly before those men?' he says. 'You didn't move away. You *besharam** oloo ki pati,*** you shameless bitch.'

Why am I such a fool? I think. I'm filled with hate. Not for the man who's cursing me, but for myself for believing Khan was a changed man. Something in me always knew it wasn't true, but I believed the lie. It was a choice I made. I see that clearly now. As clear as the shameless sparkle of the stars in this godforsaken wilderness.

The other men enter my room: Younis and the two strangers as well. I run towards the bed. They form a line before me as I crouch behind the frame. Younis clears his throat to speak.

'You violated Khan. You transgressed and took another man. You have dishonoured us; brought disrespect upon our family.' He pauses, a stern expression on his face. 'There is nothing much that can be done about such things in London. But it's different here. The elders have decided what your fate should be.'

I look at Khan, my eyes pleading.

'I don't understand what you mean,' I say. 'What you do you think I've done?'

---

* Shameless.
** A derogatory term meaning 'daughter of an owl'.

'You lying bitch,' Khan says with fury in his face. 'You meet with Adam frequently, and you've been writing to him too. Did you think I didn't know?'

A dizziness is making me feel sick.

'You're wrong,' I say. 'It's not true. You've misunderstood. I didn't see him, not at all, not even once.'

'What?' he says. 'Shut your mouth. Don't lie to us about the *haram** things you've done.'

'I didn't meet with anyone,' I say. 'I only wrote out dreams and possibilities. And . . .'

They don't hear a word I say. It's as if I didn't speak.

* Immoral or unlawful.

Chapter Sixty-one

Buses

My mind spins back through the months I've been with Khan. I see it like a movie reeling out. Between the hits and slaps, I'm smiling to myself. I'm pouring out my dreams of love in my letters. My pen is grooving loving words; navy ink upon the paper, which I place inside an envelope.

I'm sitting on a double-decker bus, top deck. The number 57. I see a man, a stranger, with greying hair and ragged skin, sitting at the front. He looks down at his hands, despondent. I know exactly how he feels. Today he is the one for me. I walk towards him carefully, making sure he doesn't see. I am so close that I can touch the skin of his neck, breathe in his muskiness. He doesn't know I'm standing at his back; I'm just like any other passenger heading off to work. I wait. I check the seats behind. Someone may be watching me. Then, when it is exactly right, when he looks out of the window, I drop the letter into his lap. He didn't see me, doesn't know I'm still watching him.

At first he thinks it's someone else's and he looks around. (They all do that.) Then he pauses as he reads the front. It says: *This letter is for you, so don't look around. It's not been left behind. It's from Mexx. With all sincerity. And love.*

He opens it (as every man I've handed one will do). He reads it. Then I see it start. Like the charge electrifying air before a storm. He shuffles on his seat. And then he smiles.

The bus has stopped. I rush to the stairway and descend, my feet clapping down the steps. As I jump off the bus, swinging from the vertical steel bar, always, every time, I find that I am smiling too.

Next day it is another passenger on another bus.

And so you see, Khan, I never wrote to Adam, or to any man I know. I wrote to you, I wrote to him, I wrote to every man that ever lived. My love could land on anyone.

I'm jolted back to the now as Younis starts to speak.

'The council of our village gathered yesterday; *sadar*'s order has been made. And what the chief says is always done. The act you have committed with another man is the punishment he has ordered against you.'

'Please, please don't do this, don't touch me. You have it all wrong,' I beg between sobs. But Younis carries on.

'It is you who has it wrong,' he says. 'We are not going to touch you.' Whirling confusion in my brain. 'Nu will be paying for your deeds.'

The tall man says, 'I've always preferred boys anyway, especially pretty ones.' The four men laugh in unison: a quiet, breathy laugh. The one with the big teeth goes to the door.

'I'll get the boy. She needs to see what we're going to do.'

The world about me stills and the present and future seem to merge. My fear is gone, dissipating like a spoken word, a puff of air, and I know with total certainty that no one will hurt my Nu. Not now, not ever. There have been many times when I've wondered at my own capability. This night I know.

I am the daughter of a murderer; I am my father's girl.

I hear the words inside my head that Naboo used to say so many times a day. I think that Bibi may be saying them outside the room I'm sitting in. I find myself speaking those words out loud. They comfort me. They tell me that these men cannot do a thing. The words I say – *la hawla wala quwwata illa billah* – remind me that there is no might or power except with God. The Lord of all the sticks and stones, of the evil men and me.

Nu walks in. He hasn't got a clue what's going on. He stops abruptly when he sees my face. He looks around the room, at the men huddled in a group. He knows; he senses with great clarity the terror starting to unfurl.

The men move towards Nu. I pull him close and whisper, 'Nu, God himself entrusted you to me. I was placed on earth to care for you. I won't let anyone hurt you. I am the daughter of a murderer and I will kill to see you safe. Do you hear me?'

I turn to the men. 'Take me, not Nu,' I say.

And then something in me breaks. A feeling only those facing death could ever know. I think it may be bravery, but most likely I am slipping to insanity. Visions of a mess of death sprawled across the floor are merging with my papa's smile, the blood on his teeth and the cuts on Nu's glowing skin. I feel the months of healed bruises hurting me all at once, the sex, the hate, the sight of Nu balled up inside the bus. And then I see the smile. The smile on Papa's face morphing into Khan's.

I laugh. It swings about the room, my loud melodic howl.

I'm looking directly into their eyes, and they look away. My shawl is sliding off my shoulders with each rhythmic judder of my lungs. I feel cold steel upon my skin. The knife gripped under my arm and pressed against my chest has cut into my dress. A current pulls at me; bionic forces rise in me. I feel no fear. My tiredness has disappeared and I'm filled with the love the letters gave me. I hear my raucous wail as if it is someone else. Things are clear and I know everything there is to know, all mysteries and complications gone. My being dissipates around the room like spoken words. Time has stopped. Future, past and present stacking up.

'Or better still, why don't we take you, you idiots, *kusorey*, *haramzaday*?' I hear the words as though I'm hovering above. I've called them transvestites, bastards, and still I feel no fear. My vision is blurring at the outer edges. I'm in a bubble. I'm not me at all.

The men know that something is wrong. They are confused. I'm not supposed to act this way. I see their fear. It's visible to me, like a purple mist. Finally one of them says, 'She's gone mad, the *shaitan*'s entered her.'

'That's right,' I say. 'I am the devil's daughter, though you know that anyway. I curse you, curse you, curse you. To die a painful death, to lick dirt from the streets, to drool like dogs.' I feel an ocean rising in me. 'Come on, then, you *madre choords** what are you waiting for?' I challenge them. 'But be warned. If you touch me or Nu, you'll not live another day. You'll die an agonising death, wishing the bitch that birthed you had never let you out. And I'll haunt you when I am dead, *kassem sey*,*** of that you can be sure.'

---

* Extremely rude and abrasive swear word.
** I swear.

I am a theatre show, a heroine prepared to die. My eyes are spears, I speak with deranged confidence; I'm loud and brash, inviting attack. The rise of something strange begins. It's an urgency, the need to feel steel sinking into flesh. With a swoop, a crazy lunge, I grab the knife from under my arm and wave it in the air, serpentine and smooth, dancing from left to right. I take a step towards the group, then shock myself as I find I've thrown the weapon at the men instead. Moonlight glints off the blade as it spins and flies.

I scream the scream of insane folk, a terrifying wail, and recite more of Naboo's words: 'Everything on earth will perish. But forever will abide the face of God.'

They look at me now utterly confused, just as the knife lands near someone's collarbone. I see a man go down. Two others swoop to his aid. And while they're focused on the pandemonium, Nu and I hold hands and run towards the door.

The last man standing grabs my sleeve. Nu turns to him.

And speaks.

'Let go of her,' he says. There's gravitas and danger in his voice. And then he shouts, a deep and resonating 'NOW!'

The man obeys. Wailing fills the room; men are crying out for help.

We run out of the house, and when I look up, another man is standing right in front of us. It is the taxi man who drove us here in his beaten-up old car.

'Help us,' I say.

He pauses, then runs towards his car with Nu and me trailing desperately behind. He unties the string that holds the lid of the boot down and tells us to climb in.

'*Khamoosh*,'* he says. 'We must be quiet, we mustn't say a thing. I overheard them speaking,' he continues. 'I know what they will do to you.' And then he says more slowly, 'Don't give me away or I'll have no choice but to say I didn't know a thing. Had no idea you'd climbed into my car. I can't protect you if they know I've helped.'

We nod. He ties the lid back down.

I am rolled up in a ball and Nu is pressing at my legs. I will not breathe; I'll die right here rather than let Khan and those men notice us. I smell damp and petrol on the metal walls. There is a blanket underneath us and I am sure I feel an insect crawling on me. The metal on my shoulder is cold. The string that holds the boot shut lets a sliver of the outside world seep in. Through the gap of half an inch, I can just make out what is happening outside.

I hear the driver's crunchy steps upon the gravel track. He's walking slowly back towards the house.

Moments pass before there is a mess of noise coming towards the car. The men are now standing by the vehicle.

'Where are they, did you see where they went?' a voice beside us says.

'Who, *sahib*?** What are you talking of?' our taxi driver says respectfully.

'They must have run away,' says a different voice.

* Be quiet.
** Term of respect for a man.

'The girl and boy, no *janab*,'* he offers. 'Are they not inside the house?' Now he is saying too much. I will him to shut up.

'They'll perish in the cold, in this brutal wilderness. There's no one else around for miles. They'll get lost in the forest and the hills.' It's Khan speaking now. 'Anyway, he's cut deep. We need to get him to a doctor.'

Someone climbs into the cab. 'Take us to the hospital,' a voice says.

The taxi begins to drive, swerving round the verges and the precipice. As it bumps along the uneven surface of the road, the boot lid's biting up and down, restrained from opening by the smallest piece of string. Fresh air rushes in. The ring and bracelet that Khan gave me glitters in the moonlight. I pull off the ring, break the bracelet and press them through the gap. They fall on to the road. I see the ring bounce once before it drops out of sight.

After some time, the taxi stops. I hear voices and feel the car begin to rock. It rises as the men step out. Just as the taxi man is about to leave, someone says, 'Is that a chain on the bumper of the car?' The taxi man lifts something up that momentarily catches the light and says, no, it's some kid's plaything. One of the men walks towards the boot. I can see the fabric of his clothing. Then he walks away.

The taxi man gets back into the car. Says he'll park it round the back. He doesn't. When we stop again, he tells us we're at the British High Commission in Islamabad. He helps

---

* A term of respect, like sir.

us out of the boot and takes us to the door. It's early, and hardly anyone is there. He explains things to someone inside that he seems to know. I listen, say nothing. I'm holding someone's arm too tight and with the other holding Nu. I feel so safe.

Nu and I are draped in deep blue blankets and sit on grey plastic chairs, sipping steaming tea. I don't know who put the blankets around us. I turn to thank the taxi man for saving us from certain death, but he has gone. I never asked his name or where he was from. A woman with kind round eyes, dark brown and densely lashed, leads us to a private room. She wears a scarf on her head, but loosely draped. I see the grey swirl of roses on it, and though I try, I cannot focus on anything but that. There is a man with us as well. He has thin lips and a gentle smile. He looks at us as if he knows us from before. It occurs to me that he does. Other girls and boys like me and Nu have passed before his eyes. We're not the first, and I know we will not be the last.

There are questions asked, but I find it hard to concentrate; details of events that brought us here, passports, tickets and why Nu doesn't speak. There is a soft quality to the things I see. As if they are not real, but images on a spongy screen. And my hearing isn't right. I feel as if I'm sitting in a bubble and everyone else is outside.

'Do you have any relatives in Pakistan?' Scarf Lady asks.

I say, 'Only Naboo, but he lives in Lahore,' knowing it's a lie. I think of Ma and what Pa did to her.

'You said you were with your husband's relatives, but explain to us again exactly why you came,' the man says.

'It was a sort of honeymoon . . .' I say. It hurts inside to even think of speaking of the things we've seen. Then the world goes dark, spooling in front of my eyes until the blackness is complete.

'Here, darling, have a sip.' Grey roses come into focus before my eyes. It's the lady in the scarf. I'm lying on a cold tiled floor. 'You fainted, Mani dear. Please take a sip of this.' She's tipping drops of water from a plastic cup into my mouth. 'Let's find you something to eat, and you can rest as well.' She strokes my hair. 'Then you can tell us where you live, so we can get you home.'

Nu and I sit at plastic tables, picking at bread rolls. Scarf Lady comes to us again.

'Do you feel up to telling me some more?'

'Yes, OK,' I say. But when I start, I find I cannot voice the horrors we've endured. And so I give only a partial account. She nods lightly at my words. I think she knows.

There is a hotel stay. But before we know it, we're on the plane heading home to the UK. Home. I mull over the thought. How in a few short years my home is now a different place, the place I want to be, not the place where I was born. Both Nu and I sleep on the flight. Nu's sleep is peaceful, but mine is fitful and disturbed. I'm gripping a ridge over a cliff, and when I let it go, I wake with a jolt. A sting of heat rushing through my skin and the sense that I'm falling through the air. The first thing I do is reach for Nu. My hand on his arm and I am calmed. I whisper to myself that I'm OK.

As we leave the plane, I stop when I see him: a tall man with chocolate-coloured hair who's overtaking us. I know it can't be him, but still I breathe in sharp and cannot let it out.

Nu and I walk out of customs under a green sign that reads *NOTHING TO DECLARE*. We have no baggage to collect. Nothing looks or feels quite right, as if I'm walking in a dream. Glass doors open automatically, and my knees go weak. There before me, standing together in a group, are Abdul and Dalal and Naboo too. Naboo ducks awkwardly under the metal bar and makes the motions of a run, although with his old limbs, it's no faster than his walk. Joy and relief curl and turn inside and morph into deep sobs. I'm a little child, burying my face in Naboo's flesh, breathing in the scent of Surf and cardamoms on his white *kameez*. The three of us – me, Nu and Naboo – grip each other tight as we cry and smile in disbelief. Abdul and Dalal embrace us one by one as they lead us to a taxi that will take us home to Clerkenwell.

I see the balding brown sofa in the living room and sparks of joy erupt inside my chest. I'm home and safe and even the swirly orange carpet pleases me. I jump on to the sofa, lean back and close my eyes. There's only the sound of quiet voices on TV. When I open my eyes, I see a woman on the BBC. She's reading something out and dabbing at her eyes. It's a preview of some show. Just then Abdul enters the room, hesitant and slow. He takes a seat. It looks as though he's going to lecture me. He lays his right hand on his heart and bows his head.

'Mani,' he says, '*inshallah*, one day soon, will you teach me? Teach me of courage and of strength.' He lifts his head. 'And forgive me, Mani. Forgive me if I have let you down.'

He gets up to leave.

'Abdul, *khaloo*,'* I say, but then I hesitate, scrambling inside my mind to find the words I want to speak. 'Writing is the key,' I say eventually. 'It saved my life.'

Abdul frowns as he runs his fingers through his beard. I carry on.

'With words I recreated life, and sliced the badness out.'

The ridges deepen on his brow.

'Perhaps . . .' I pause to gather my thoughts, 'like you always said, the pen *is* mightier than the sword.'

Weak sunlight streams in through the lacy nets hanging at the window at my back. It makes patterns on the wall.

'Mani, you must rest,' Abdul says. He nods as he walks into the hall.

'You're a good man, Abdul,' I whisper when he's gone, 'and you've never let me down,' I add, even though I know he cannot hear me any more.

I look at the TV. Something catches my eye, and reaching for the remote, I turn the volume up.

---

* Respectful term for an uncle or male elder.

Chapter Sixty-two

BBC

They're reading out my letters on the news. The BBC. They say they're from the secret lover on routes 23, 78, 12 and many others besides. They're interviewing men, so many different men, who hold my letters in their hands. They're sending me a message through the screen. They say that my letters have helped heal and get people through the troubles they face. They say that I'll be fine. And that if I need help, I can come to them. And then they smile, gently, lovingly into the camera.

A reporter makes a plea. She is blond and thin, her nose red and swollen from the cold. She clutches the fabric at her neck as she holds a microphone.

'Mexx,' she says, 'you need to know that we all love you very much. The things you wrote have helped so many troubled souls. We have stories from people like Harry and Jonathan who read your letters out. Harry was at the end of the line. After he got a Mexx letter, he felt loved. He marvels at the love you gave, despite the things you had to face. He felt he had a reason to go on. You heard him say what it did for him. You've helped so many men, Mexx, and we don't even know who you are.'

She pauses to blow her nose. I'm sure I see tears in her eyes, although it could just be the cold. And then she says, 'You're amazing, Mexx. And to think of everything you've endured. We'd love to meet you some day. To check that you are safe. Away from the abuse you've had to face. If you're listening, please identify yourself.' The camera zooms right in.

'And if we meet one day,' she says, 'one thing I'd love to ask is: what made you do this thing? Why did you write love letters to so many unknown men?'

They say they'll place an advert in a local rag. They'll ask those who got a Mexx letter to bring it to the BBC. They want to publish them, and maybe one day put them together in a book. My letters full of love.

I am thinking back as I watch the lady speak to me on the TV. We must have looked strange, Nu and I; me a dark and golden brown, Nu so tall and fair and strong for his age, his stunning ethereal face. The two of us, like ghostly djinns, floating up the moving stairs at Oxford Circus. Boarding buses at Chancery Lane and Clerkenwell, our destination: anywhere. Searching for lost and lonely people, people that I understood. The ones who hurt inside, who'd lost their way, the sad ones hiding their grief and pain within. I was like Nu's shadow, he the sun as I led him around the streets of London with my letters for no one. My letters for everyone.

At first, when the hurt was bad, it seemed to me that love from a distance was far more real. Love that doesn't do the ironing. Love that hopes and dreams more than it ever actually receives. At that time I wondered: is it true – does all love sour in close proximity? I don't believe that now. Slowly, slowly I began to see.

As I wrote my letters to the world, that was when I understood the greatest love of all. And that true love might be foolish, unreturned; but if it is, that doesn't mean it's less. It may even mean it's more.

Chapter Sixty-three

Dear you

Dear you,

I saw you on TV, the BBC, and in answer to the questions you ask, I write this love letter to you; my last. To you, the lady on the screen, the men who read my letters and the passengers on the number 23, 78, 12 and all the others buses too.

You need to know that you are worthy of so much love. I know we've never met, and never will. I know that you don't know me and I don't know you, but please don't think that matters even a bit. Love doesn't need an answer to exist.

There was a question asked by the reporter on the BBC. There are many reasons why I started writing letters full of love.

I was very sad. There was death and hurt and loss about me everywhere. When I tried to put things right, they just got worse and worse. And then one day something in me broke, split apart. And out of dust and ashes and hurt, Mexx rose up. You may know this if you've seen the letters I wrote. The man I married hurt me very much. Not just my skin and flesh, but worse than that, he nearly killed the hopes and dreams hidden deep within. My love was landing on such barren land. You won't know this, but my papa was the same. He hurt my mama too.

Then one night I dreamed there was another woman in bed beside my husband as he slept. And when I woke, I knew the man I had married wasn't really mine. No part of him belonged to me. He was a stranger. I only loved the dream. The dream I wanted to believe. The man I hoped he could be.

When I realised this, I thought my love was dead. And so I lifted up that dream and cast it far away from him. It landed on and in between so many different men. Not a single one, but all of them. I realised then that my dream of love hadn't died. It didn't need to land upon a single man to grow. Love never dies. It survives. It can live on in paper and ink and in visions in my head. In the little time we have, why should we not express the love we feel inside, no matter how real or imaginary our target is?

And when I wandered round watching strangers on the street and on the buses, they were no longer strangers to me. I not only looked but I saw. Their faces spoke to me. The look in their eyes would tell me of the love they felt; the lines upon their skin, the way they held themselves would give away the love they'd lost and all the happiness and hurt they held inside. I felt their hearts, saw the colours in their souls. And a sort of love began to form.

I rose early one day and saw an autumn tree with

browning leaves. The branches bent and shuddered in the breeze. And then a gust of wind blasted through the branches from below. It thrust leaves out and about so that they tumbled everywhere, some near, others out of sight. On each leaf that parted from the tree, I saw a story written down, the veins forming the letters and the words. They all started: *my dear*. They rose from the tree, travelled up and far away.

That was when I knew what I had to do.

Abdul always told us that the pen has more power than the sword and that secrets hide inside the written word. But I never understood. Then slowly it started making sense. Things fell into place and I found a way out of my misery. That was when I started writing to him. My imaginary lover. My perfect man. The only thing to overcome was that I had made him up – there was no real flesh or blood. The men I gave the letters to were all a part of him. Together they formed the lover of my dreams.

So to answer you, the love within me was invisible, unseen, like an asteroid or star shooting out its beauty in a distant galaxy. And the hurt was making me turn hard. I was afraid that my heart would ossify. I feared the loss of my ability to feel the love within me. I wanted a witness for my love so that others felt it too. Like an artist painting a vision of the world for another to enjoy.

What I didn't know back then was that words can shift the universe. Slowly, slowly, the lies I scribed began to feel like truth. In writing to my imaginary love, a real love within began to form. So real that the man who hurt me mattered less and less. The holes in me began to mend and my reality started to bend. The letters gave me strength, made me believe that I was a woman worthy of the greatest things.

That is the story of those letters and those words. And why I sent them out into the world.

And nothing has changed, so remember: I love you too, I love you all, as I always have and always will.

With all my heart.

I doodle on the paper on the coffee table where I sit. Then I add: *I'll say it now. It's time to come clean. Things are never as they seem. My name isn't really Mexx.*

I never wanted fame or notoriety. I only ever said that those letters were from me. The real me, the person that I really am. I write down the words: *From Me*, then add two kisses – *xx* – so that it reads *Mexx*.

Part Five

Chapter Sixty-four

Trophy

At Abdul's flat in Clerkenwell, where we live now, I get up to answer a knock on the door. I'm drinking tea with Jas, chatting away.

'Hey, M,' she says, 'just a moment. What do you say, pink or red?'

She holds a lipstick in each hand and raises first one then the other towards her lips. We're going to the cinema and Jas is dressing up.

'The pink,' I say. 'It matches your eyes.'

'Ha, very funny,' she says. 'Careful now.' She tilts her mug over papers scattered on the table where we sit. 'Or I'll spill tea on your timetable.'

As she speaks, she smirks. I feel thrilled that I'll be going back to school.

'Wait, Jas,' I say. 'I'll just get the door.'

I think it might be Mrs Lane coming round for something the way she does most days. There's no one there. Perhaps local kids are playing pranks, or a leaflet has been dropped. I step outside and look around. Something draws my eyes over to the left. It's Khan, walking down St John Street. Panic rushes me to the kitchen drawer. Sharp knife in hand, I run back to the door. Like a sniper lining up, I peek out at the street. A woman appears. She's running across the road, running to him. She loops her arms around his neck. They embrace, her coffee-coloured hair, long and silky, draping on his arms.

You might think I'd want to cut him, draw blood, but I don't. I don't want to lay my hate upon him with a blade. Don't want to strike a knife into his flesh the way Papa did to Ma. I know this is a dare, a challenge. To show me that he still matters in some way. I refuse him the control he seeks. And best of all, I don't even feel. My shoulders drop; my frown lines straighten out. He's nothing to me now, and perhaps he never was.

I choose freedom. I choose love. I clutch it like a trophy I have won.

I place the knife back in the drawer and watch from the window in the hall. They're walking arm in arm. Khan stops and stares directly at Abdul's flat. I see his face. I'm sure he cannot see me, but still I jolt and step aside. He looks a little bit afraid.

'It doesn't matter,' I whisper to myself.

I go back to join Jas.

'Definitely the pink,' I say, 'and your eyes look great.'

Jas sweeps the colour on her upper lip, then stops.

'M,' she says, 'are you all right now, honestly . . . after everything?'

I smile, more to myself than her.

'You know,' I say, 'I think everything was always going to be OK. If my life had worked out in a different way, that would have been fine. The fact that I survived that terrible ordeal with Khan was also meant to be. But Jas, I feel such relief that I don't need him any more. The things I thought only he could give I realise have always been inside me.'

'Hmm,' Jas says, half-smile, half-frown on her face. I know she's thinking of my ma. I carry on.

'Of all the things I've seen and suffered; the terrible things I've done, almost everything remains a mystery, except for love. Now I know for sure that when you give it out, it multiplies and fills the emptiness you feel inside; it sets you free.'

I write one last letter to my imaginary man.

My dear,
Thank you for everything. I marvel at the beauty hidden everywhere in life. And how in seeing things, shadows and darkness, the angry, bitter ugliness all disappear.

Some things matter more than life and death. Like love. You showed me that. And when wickedness or hurt attempt to draw my joy away, they fail and I know that I can smile and walk away.

Love,
Mani

I fold it up into a paper aeroplane. Step outside and throw it high into the sky. I close my eyes and see my imaginary man standing in a meadow by some trees. He fades into the scenery. What's left of him takes flight. He draws my eyes up high like the movement of a bird or butterfly. Up into a pale blue sky.

I know my love is real and that he heard every word I said. And as I open my eyes, I have a vision of Mama smiling back at me. I feel her love, her strength, her suffering. A woman who will see her children safe no matter what it takes. I feel the terror that she felt the day Papa took her from this world. It was my terror too; the fear I felt as I escaped with Nu and survived the very fate that took my ma away.

I think back to that day. The day that everything changed. The day I finally knew that I would walk away. Not with anger or revenge, but with knowledge of who I am. Who I became.

Nu calls to me from the garden.

'Come. Over. Here,' he says, each word staccato and separate.

He takes me to where a spider's web reclines between two roses in full bloom. It's as if the flowers speak. Their curled-up beauty looking back at me. They are the darkest burgundy, red veiled in black. And on the silken threads are three drops of dew suspended in mid-air; perfect motionless spheres. Like silver tears of joy above the fresh and fertile soil.

Nu marvels at the beauty he is showing me.

He smiles.

A smile that showers affection and connection. One that pours its love all over you. A smile that says, *I have you*. And he does. He had me then. He has me now.

He has me still.

Glossary

ahya khair	colloquial expression; may God bring good
Allah	God
aloo	potato
anarkali	a large marketplace in central Lahore
arey deko deko	hey you, look look
ata	flour
azaan	call to prayer
bachay	children
bachi	child
bahadar	brave
baji	respectful term for a woman (literally: big sister)
bansari	flute
bechow	save us
bersaat	monsoon season
besharam	shameless
beta	son; this term is also traditionally used for daughters as a term of endearment
beti	daughter
bhangra	lively Indian dancing to the beat of drums
bismillah	in the name of God
chadar	blanket or shawl
chai	tea

challo	go
chapal	sandal
chapati	flat bread
charpai	a traditional woven bed
choori dar	a traditional dress worn with tight ruched leggings
daal	a lentil meal
dupatta	scarf women wear around their neck and upon their head
garam elachi chai	hot cardamom tea
haram	immoral or unlawful
haramzada(y)	bastard(s)
Hira Mundi	red-light district in Lahore (literally: diamond market)
houris	virginal companions in Heaven
insaan	human being
inshallah	by the will of God
isaat	respect
ither ow	come here
janab	a term of respect, like sir
jaroo	broom
jhingur	chirping night insects
kafan	white death shroud
kameez	shirt
kassem sey	I swear
khaloo	respectful term for an uncle or male elder
khamoosh	be quiet
Khidr	a mystical figure widely known as the spiritual guide of Moses (literally: the Green Man)

kusorey	transvestites
la hawla wala quwwata illa billah	all power and ability is with God alone
ludo	a sticky round golf-ball sized sweet made from lentils, milk and sugar
maafi	forgiveness
madre choord	extremely rude and abusive swear word
majboor	helpless
majnun	madman
majzoob	a person blessed with such closeness to God that they lose their sanity or some other faculty
masala	a generic name for Indian and Pakistani spices
masoom	innocent
mitai	Asian sweets
namaz	a term for prayers
nana abu	grandfather on the mother's side
nasr	the evil eye
oloo ki pata/pati	a derogatory term meaning 'son/daughter of an owl'
pir	a spiritual guide or saint
pook	transmitting the blessing of a prayer onto another by blowing on them after recitation of the prayer
poother	term of endearment for a son
raunak	vibrant busy environment
Rumi	Famous Turkish Islamic scholar and poet behind the whirling dervish
sadar	village chief

sahib	term of respect for a man
salamu alaykum	peace be upon you
sammili	mid-brown of skin
sat sri akal	a Sikh greeting meaning 'God is the ultimate truth'
sau jow	go to sleep
shahtoosh	a shawl made from the neck hair of a Himalayan ibex
shahtoot	mulberry tree
shaitan	Satan, devil
shalwar	loose leggings worn in Pakistan
soosth	lethargic
sujood	prostration, where you kneel and place your forehead on the ground
tanga	horse and carriage
tasbee	prayer beads threaded like a rosary
tava	hotplate for cooking *chapatis*
taweez	amulet
vay-va	wow
Zaqqum tree	a tree in Hell which bears fruits shaped like the heads of devils

Acknowledgements

A big thank you to my agent Jon Elek and his colleagues at United Agents for all their support and for finding me the perfect home with the amazing Mari Evans of Headline. Jon, your belief in me and SET ME FREE has always been unflinching. In a business built around words, I never needed any from you. The way you looked at me when we first met said it all. Choosing you was easy. Mari, your deep insights were priceless. You felt my emotional truths in the manuscript and telling me SET ME FREE made you cry was an unforgettable moment in my life. Thank you both for choosing me.

I am doubly grateful to Sarah Savitt, as both my brilliant editor at Headline and my teacher at the Faber Academy. Your piercing intellect and vision always left me feeling you could do the editorial equivalent of piecing together a jigsaw in a blindfold. I have no doubt SET ME FREE is a far better book because of you. Much thanks to Celine Kelly, Jane Selley, Sara Adams, Katie Brown and the whole excellent team at Headline. I owe a lot to everyone at the Faber Academy, especially tutors Gillian Slovo and Shelly Weiner and my classmates Liz, Dave and Rebecca. I must also thank my school teacher who started the ball rolling – thank you, Mrs McCusker, wherever you may be.

Stephen Kelman, thank you for being there during my journey to publication. Sharing my success with you made the whole experience so much sweeter.

To my young sons Zak and Haris, you are an unending source of inspiration, awe and joy, and my wonderful husband Kam. Without your support and encouragement, I couldn't have written this book. To my uncle Shahid, thanks for your tips, and to my brother and sister Asim and Mona. After our eight weeks together ending on 19th March 2016, I have no doubt our eternal bond will be stronger than ever.

Lastly and most of all, I thank my mother and father, Kaniza and Aziz. I owe everything to my beautiful, feisty, big-hearted mother who kept giving even when she had nothing left to give. Your love is boundless and your encouragement never-ending. You were more excited than anyone about this book and so proud of me. I am heartbroken that God, in His infinite wisdom, took you back to Himself so close to its publication. I love you, Mum, and miss you so much. In every way, this book is for you.

Q & A with Hina Belitz

1. SET ME FREE is a novel with big themes at its heart: so-called 'honour killing', domestic violence, immigration, arranged marriage, teenage love, to name a few. Did you begin the novel knowing you wanted to write about these issues, or did the characters come first – or did something else entirely spark the story?

SET ME FREE started in an organic way without a clear sense of where I was going. I did have a few core ideas and the main characters came to me from the outset. Mani and Nu were immediately real. I knew how they would react to the situations they would face. I knew their fears, their weaknesses and I also felt their wonderful, gentle, sibling relationship.

There were three underlying elements I knew would feature in Mani and Nu's life. Firstly, I was fascinated by the surprising and unexpected behaviour of a woman in an abusive relationship choosing to stay even though there doesn't seem to be anything stopping her from leaving. I wondered why some women do that. And why often the worst acts of violence take place between those supposedly in a loving relationship. It seems akin to an addiction; knowing something is harming you, but not being able to let it go. If someone were to launch an attack of that sort against a woman on the street, I have no doubt she would run! Secondly, I was intrigued by the hidden aspects of people. That an apparently good person may be concealing a darker side only ever witnessed by one or two other people. And thirdly, I knew I wanted to explore the power to recreate our lives by the stories we tell ourselves. It was interesting to ponder the popular modern philosophy that imagining you have what you desire can make it come about in reality. Could that work for love, I wondered?

Since writing SET ME FREE, I am a real believer in the mysterious connection between the conscious and subconscious mind because, although I always knew I would be moving towards these themes, much of the story actually revealed itself during the writing process.

2. Mani tells us early in the novel: 'From the day Nu was born, I knew that Mama loved him more. I became a thought her mind had room for only after she was sure that Nu was safe and fed and warm.' Why does Mani's mother favour Nu?

There are a couple of reasons why Mani's mother favours Nu. Certain cultures around the world such as the Indian Sub-continent and China tend to favour boys over girls. As a UK employment and discrimination lawyer, I can confidently say the same still applies, although to a lesser degree, in Western cultures, hence laws to protect against sexual discrimination. Even when girls are much loved and supported, this underlying preference seems to kick in under pressure. I have always been intrigued by this almost universal tendency to prefer boys.

So Mani's mother's preference for Nu is in part due to that, but it is also because of Nu's skin colour. Nu is born with white skin whereas the rest of the family have dark skin.

As a British-Asian woman, I straddle two cultures, so I have had the advantage of being able to personally observe the tendency to prefer pale skin in certain cultures (and tanned skin in other cultures). Such attitudes are sometimes so deeply ingrained people may not be consciously aware of them. It is fascinating to explore the impact of the different sexes and skin colours of Mani and Nu on how they are treated by their mother and the world in general as they move from Pakistan to the UK.

3. At the time of putting this book to press, much of the country was gripped by the domestic violence storyline on The Archers, *and* SET ME FREE *explores this topic with incredible emotional intelligence from a teenage girl's perspective. How did you go about researching this subject?*

Part of my research was based on people I knew who had gone through such an experience, and it became clear that such relationships are highly complex and therefore incredibly interesting. Love appears to become confused with harsh and hateful behaviour to such an extent that the woman struggles to extract herself from the situation. And interestingly, even though Mani is a teenager when she is subjected to this treatment, from the research I did, it doesn't make any difference if the woman is older and/or highly educated. I watched a TED talk by Leslie Morgan Steiner which explained the twisted justifications and confused outlook that victims of domestic violence develop. The book, *Women Who Love Too Much* by Robin Norwood includes multiple accounts of women explaining why it was so hard for them to leave violent relationships. It seems that such women believe they are helping their partner become normal, that only they can fix whatever is making their partner so aggressive and violent. Often women subjected to such violence also believe they deserve the treatment they are getting. Finally, I was also intrigued by the controlling behaviour and hurtful language which accompany the physical violence. My goal was to depict life from the perspective of such a person by exploring Mani's dilemmas and confusions in her marriage to Khan.

I met with Diana Nammi of the Iranian and Kurdish Woman's Rights Organisation and spoke to her about the work she did to bring the murderers of Banaz Mahmod (her father and uncle in a so-called 'honour killing') to justice. This inspired another aspect of SET ME FREE which is the difficulty the authorities have in establishing how seriously to treat such acts of violence.

4. In a busy city like London, people so rarely communicate with each other on public transport. In the novel, it is revealed that Mexx's letters are written to strangers on London buses, giving them hope. Why was it important for Mexx to write her letters to strangers?

In an increasingly digital world, I was attracted to the idea of handwritten letters. I had purchased a copy of *Letters of Note* by Shaun Usher and loved the personal feel and character of pen and ink on paper. Given the nature of Mani's relationship with Khan, and Nu becoming mute, Mani becomes very lonely. She addresses her loneliness by reaching out to strangers with whom she perceives she has an inexplicable connection. But she is also ashamed of her predicament and so cannot actually reveal herself to them. She is thrilled to see the strangers react positively to her letters and seeing them smile becomes a sort of self-healing. I felt too that Mani's anonymity would free her to write from the heart.

5. The women in the novel have suffered greatly, and they are also brave, loving, and inspiring. Who inspires you?

My mother inspires me, as do women who survive the extremes of adversity and don't pity themselves or allow it to define them.

My mother was a strong, determined matriarch with a big heart who never let me or my siblings to develop a victim mentality. I think the ability to remain grateful for the gift of being alive despite the challenges life throws at us is truly inspirational.

7. Is there a particular scene or chapter in the book that was the hardest to write and why?

The hardest parts to write were the chapters on violence and wickedness. I knew they were necessary for the development of Mani but it was moving to see her suffer and observe how she strains to find justification for Khan's violence. Denial is a key feature of this aspect of Mani as she was more in touch with the idea of who Khan should be as opposed to who he really was. Describing a rape, in particular, was a big challenge.

8. What's one thing you want your readers to take away from having read SET ME FREE?

I think the key message is the power of the human spirit to not only survive, but flourish in adversity; that we don't need to be damaged by the difficult experiences in our lives if we put them into context. Telling the right story to ourselves about the things we suffer can transform such adversity into valuable life-enhancing lessons that make us who we are. I was captivated by a talk I saw on post-traumatic growth and I'm very much in favour of advocating this over the alternative of falling on your sword.

The first letter in SET ME FREE includes the following, which I believe sums up the key message of the book quite well:

'People hate bad things happening to them but they really shouldn't. I don't. We mustn't judge the forces that make us. And when I tell you all, you will know how I became the person that I am and why I love you so.'

9. What is your writing process like? Do you have a favourite place or a preferred time that you like to do your writing?

I write every day and at varying times and places but I do find the early hours wonderful. I love silence when I write as it aids deep focus. I have a dusty attic in my house which is great for creativity. When I have to edit and revise, I enjoy going to the Cambridge University Library and the London Guildhall Library.